HOMELAND INSECURITY

BOOKS BY J.L. ABRAMO

Jake Diamond Mysteries
Catching Water in a Net
Clutching at Straws
Counting to Infinity
Circling the Runway
Crossing the Chicken

Chasing Charlie Chan
A Jimmy Pigeon Novel
(featuring Jake Diamond)

Nick Ventura Mysteries
Brooklyn Justice

Sixty-First Precinct Novels
Gravesend
Coney Island Avenue

Stand Alone Novels
American History

Non-Fiction
Homeland Insecurity

J.L. ABRAMO

HOMELAND INSECURITY

Down & Out Books
3959 Van Dyke Road, Suite 265
Lutz, FL 33558
DownAndOutBooks.com

Cover design by J.L. Abramo

ISBN: 1-64396-202-7
ISBN-13: 978-1-64396-202-3

For Isis Alexandra

If there must be trouble let it be in my day,
that my child may have peace.
—Thomas Paine

Disney Girls (1957)

Clearing skies and drying eyes, now I see your smile.
Darkness goes and softness shows, a changing style.
Just in time, words that rhyme, well bless your soul.
Now I'll fill your hands with kisses and a tootsie roll.

Oh, reality, it's not for me and it makes me laugh.
Oh, fantasy world and Disney girls I'm coming back.

Patti Page and summer days on old Cape Cod.
Happy times making wine in my garage.
Country shade and lemonade, guess I'm slowing down.
It's a turned back world with a local girl in a smaller town.
Open cars and clearer stars, that's what I've lacked.
But fantasy world and Disney girls, I'm coming back.

Hi Rick and Dave. Hi Pop, good morning, Mom.
Love, get up guess what, I'm in love with a girl I found.
She's really swell because she likes church,
bingo chances, and old-time dances.

All my life I spent the night with dreams of you.
And the warmth I missed and for the things I wished,
they're all coming true.

I've got my love to give and a place to live, guess I'm going to stay.
It would be a peaceful life with a forever wife and a kid someday.

Well, it's earlier nights and pillow fights and your soft laugh.
Fantasy world and Disney girls, I'm coming back.

—Bruce Johnston,
from *Surf's Up,* The Beach Boys, 1971

Americans celebrate the allied victory in Europe with a scale model of the Statue of Liberty in New York City's Times Square in May, 1945.

A Troubled Peace
July 1947 to February 1957

*You can get much farther with a kind word and a gun
than you can with a kind word alone.*
—Al Capone

Whether you believe you can do a thing or not, you are right.
—Henry Ford

There is no Democratic or Republican way to clean the streets.
—Fiorello LaGuardia

Fear Itself

In his first inaugural address, in the midst of the Great Depression, Franklin Roosevelt said *the only thing we have to fear is fear itself.*

And, in time, a nation took those words to heart.

After all, Americans had prevailed in a heroic struggle for independence, repelled an English invasion in 1812, sent the Mexicans packing, preserved the Union, and been victorious in their efforts to help rescue the peoples of Europe in the Great War.

America was slowly moving away from isolationism, and the attack on Pearl Harbor would change our role in the world.

The Monroe Doctrine had spelled out America's intention to protect its hemisphere.

The Truman Doctrine and the Marshall Plan would greatly expand the boundaries of our commitment to freedom and democracy abroad.

After surviving the *Great Depression*, and once again being on the winning side of a world war, Roosevelt's words resonated.

American's had nothing to fear and moved toward the second half of the twentieth century with confidence and determination.

Their children would be prosperous.

And safe.

But then things began to get a little too disquieting to ignore.

And *fear itself* became a genuine concern.

The Hook

On January 30, 2003, an article in a daily newspaper caught my eye. The piece reported the arrest of a 69-year-old man at his home just miles from where I lived at the time in Columbia, South Carolina.

Ten years earlier, in a box of used books purchased at a yard sale, I came across a book by a prison inmate—written while he awaited execution.

Those two discoveries stimulated my interest and my imagination, and subsequent investigations have led me here.

This, on one hand, is the story of two men accused of taking the lives of three fellow human beings and changing the lives of many.

Two men born 8 days apart in 1934.

Two men who died 57 days apart in 2017.

Crimes committed 140 days apart in 1957.

At a time when Americans were beginning to feel less and less confident about the safety of their families.

One convicted murderer spent nearly fifteen years on death row at New Jersey State Prison in Trenton—one-time home of Lindbergh baby kidnapper Bruno Hauptmann and Rubin 'Hurricane' Carter—continually professing his innocence.

The other perpetrator escaped arrest and conviction for more than 45 years.

At the same time, this is an account of the hits and misses of the law enforcement agencies and legal institutions which—over the course of nearly five decades—eventually stumbled upon justice.

Finally, it is a look at the post-World War II American experience leading up to the murders in 1957, and the profound changes to come after.

When *Rock & Roll*, rebels without a cause, and catchers in the rye burst upon the American scene.

When the fear of nuclear annihilation and real-life scary monsters crept into the national consciousness.

And when those three murders in 1957, and a growing sense of national insecurity, may have had mutual effect.

Exits and Entrances

I was born in the summer of 1947.

I came to appreciate the advantages of the timing.

I was never required to be in school on my birthday.

For the first ten years of my life, I knew little about the world outside the borders of a predominantly Italian-American neighborhood called Gravesend—nestled between Bensonhurst and Sheepshead Bay in Brooklyn, several miles from Coney Island.

At the beginning of 1945, the four most powerful men in the world were Franklin Roosevelt, Winston Churchill, Josef Stalin, and Adolph Hitler.

On April 12 of that year, President Roosevelt passed away at the *Little White House* in Warm Springs, Georgia.

Harry S. Truman took office.

On April 30, Hitler ended his own life in Berlin.

On July 26, Churchill resigned as Prime Minister of the United Kingdom following a landslide Labor Party victory in the general election.

Clement Attlee took the reins.

Stalin remained in power.

And Joe had plans.

The *big question,* as 1947 dawned, was whether Truman and Attlee could stand up to Stalin's bullying as forcefully as had their predecessors.

I learned, over time, that 1947 had been a particularly eventful year—apart from my appearance on the scene.

President Truman was never a strong proponent of what his successor would later call the *Domino Theory*.

But the red scare was real in Congress and among the American people, and Harry Truman needed to demonstrate his strength.

He had big shoes to fill.

On March 12, 1947, the President announced the *Truman Doctrine*.

"I believe it must be the policy of the United States," Truman said to the Congress, "to support free peoples who are resisting attempted subjugation by armed minorities or by outside pressures. I believe we must assist free peoples to work out their own destinies in their own way. I believe our help should be primarily through economic and financial aid which is essential to economic stability and orderly political processes."

The *Truman Doctrine* called for financial aid to countries in political turmoil. A policy further developed in the *Marshall Plan*.

The doctrine was triggered by the interest in keeping the Turkish Straits, connecting the Black and Mediterranean Seas, from Soviet control.

At the same time, Greece was in the throes of a civil war that threatened to put communists in power.

There was no disguising Truman's message.

The United States was moving from a policy of *détente* to a policy of *containment* with respect to the Soviet Union.

On March 21, again due to pressure from doomsayers, Truman signed Executive Order 9835—also known as the *Federal Employee Loyalty Program*—established to root out communist sympathizers within the government.

And in July, as ground was broken for the new headquarters of the United Nations in New York, Truman signed the *National Security Act* creating the Department of Defense, the Central

11

Intelligence Agency, the Joint Chiefs of Staff, and the National Security Council.

The *Cold War,* a term coined by Bernard Baruch, was in full swing.

Meanwhile, notwithstanding the emphatic objections from former prime minister Churchill, the United Kingdom was greatly reducing the extent of what remained of the British Empire.

In August, the British left the Indian subcontinent after a two-hundred-year rule and, soon after, left Palestine. But not before the partitioning which would create a separate India and Pakistan, and a divided Jerusalem.

The exit of the British meant freedom of self-government for millions, while at the same time activating conflicts between Hindus and Muslims and between Israelis and Arabs that proved devastating.

Al Capone, Henry Ford, Bugsy Siegel, and Fiorello LaGuardia all gave up the ghost in 1947.

As well as a twenty-two-year-old aspiring actress who would come to be known as the *Black Dahlia*—and whose brutal murder would never be solved.

Hillary Rodham, Arnold Schwarzenegger, Stephen King, O.J. Simpson, and David Letterman checked in.

In 1947, Edwin Herbert Land demonstrated the first instant camera—later known as the Polaroid—and Earl Tupper patented a plastic food storage container.

Actor Ronald Reagan and his wife, Jane Wyman, named names at the hearings of the House Un-American Activities Committee.

Jackie Robinson took the field in Brooklyn—breaking the Major League Baseball color barrier.

Thor Heyerdahl and a crew of five set sail from Peru in a raft, the *Kon-Tiki*, that would travel 4,320 miles in 101 days.

Pan Am became the first worldwide passenger airline.

Test pilot Charles Elwood 'Chuck' Yeager broke the sound barrier—flying a Bell X-1 rocket-engine aircraft he nicknamed

Glamourous Glennis.

The Taft-Hartley Act, limiting the power of trade unions, was passed by the congress despite President Truman's veto.

A White House presidential address and the World Series were televised for the first time.

Meet the Press, created by journalist Martha Rountree, premiered on NBC. Rountree was the first, and only, female moderator.

An unidentified object crashed near Roswell, New Mexico. Reported by the United States Army as merely a weather balloon, it was believed by many Americans then—and to this day—to be a flying saucer carrying alien beings.

The film *Miracle on 34th Street,* featuring nine-year-old actress Natalie Wood, was released by Twentieth Century Fox in May.

Het Achterhuis (The Secret Annex) was first published in Dutch. It would later be translated into English and released as *The Diary of a Young Girl* by Anne Frank.

A play by Tennessee Williams, *A Streetcar Named Desire,* directed by Elia Kazan and starring Jessica Tandy and Marlon Brando, premiered at the Ethel Barrymore Theatre in New York and ran for 855 performances.

What came to be called *The Great Blizzard of 1947* began on December twenty-fifth, crippling the northeast. When snowfall finally ended the following day, it was measured at 26.4 inches in Manhattan's Central Park.

It would be many years before I learned of these events in the year of my birth, or of their impact.

But that December of 1947, a six-year-old girl in Ramsey, New Jersey would experience the whitest Christmas in more than a half-century.

Roswell, Rockwell, Rock & Roll

On Tuesday, November 6, 1956, Dwight David Eisenhower was re-elected thirty-fourth President of the United States.

Ike—and vice-presidential candidate Richard Nixon—carried 41 of 48 states (Alaska and Hawaii were not granted statehood until 1959), 457 of 530 electoral votes, and 57.4 percent of 61,607,280 popular votes.

Two weeks before the election, on October 23, Soviet tanks had entered Budapest in response to the revolutionary uprising. In early November, the Soviets staged a full-scale invasion to retake control of Hungary.

Eight days before the election, on October 29, Israel had invaded Egypt—stage-one of the *Protocol of Sèvres*, a joint agreement with England and France to end Egyptian control of the Suez Canal—an act threatening intervention by the Soviet Union.

As Eisenhower contemplated another four years in the White House, the *cold war* was becoming increasingly frigid.

Although the *Domino Theory* (suggested by Eisenhower in 1954) was not crystal clear to the majority of Americans—following Hiroshima and Nagasaki, the communist takeover in China, and the development of the atomic bomb in Soviet Russia—the threat of nuclear war was palpable.

Air raid drills were sending school children ducking under their desks.

Government committees including the Senate Committee on Government Operations, headed by Senator Joseph McCarthy of Wisconsin, and the House Un-American Activities Committee (which former president Harry S. Truman would later call *the most un-American thing in the country*) were investigating the armed services, Hollywood, and private citizens in an attempt to identify and prosecute or blacklist suspected communists and Marxist sympathizers.

Julius and Ethel Rosenberg had been accused of passing atomic secrets to the Soviet Union, tried and convicted of treason in 1951, and executed in 1953.

Leaving behind two young sons.

Regardless of the unusual and frightening Rosenberg death sentences, there remained strong support along the *Main Streets* of America for all efforts to stop the enemy—the Russians, the commies, the Reds—from overtaking the world.

And the cold war became a subject for novelists, demonstrated by Ian Flemings' *Casino Royale,* published in 1953, and Mickey Spillane's later Mike Hammer novels.

Mike Hammer was a straight, honest private eye who had soured on a real world of corrupt cops, crooked D.A.s, and judges who had sold out. He was the avenger, the man who took justice into his own hands, a man who shot first and asked questions later. However, Hammer's focus seemed to shift drastically by the time *The Girl Hunters, The Snake,* and *Survival—Zero* came along.

America's obsession with the *Cold War* was so great it convinced Mike Hammer to stop chasing the garden variety of gangsters and to concentrate instead on stopping domestic Communist subversion.

Kenneth Davis went so far as to refer to Mike Hammer as a reflection of the McCarthyite soul of the country, "the ultimate cold warrior, a super-hero for frightened Americans who had heard tales of baby-eating Stalinists. Mike Hammer's methods went beyond loyalty oaths, smears, and blacklisting. The evil of the Communists was battled by the only weapons Hammer possessed—a blast from his forty-five, a bone-shattering kick, strangulation by Hammer's meaty hands."

As much as Ian Fleming had, Mickey Spillane brought attention to a new kind of adversary, whose evil was universal.

And Spillane's protagonist was a lot more recognizable to the American working-class reader than the suave, cultured, and world-wise James Bond.

However, for some Americans, the paranoia and persecution became a call to protest government practices—marking the infancy of a counter-culture that would reach maturity in the following decade.

By election night, 1956, long-time icons were beginning to be replaced by a new crop of individualists—in music, film, and writing.

The Billboard charts in the early fifties were dominated by number one hits by the likes of Patti Page, Doris Day, Nat King Cole, Perry Como, Frank Sinatra, Tony Bennett, and Eddie Fisher.

On July 9, 1955, *(We're Gonna) Rock Around the Clock* by Bill Haley and the Comets climbed to the top of the charts and held the spot for eight weeks.

Rock & Roll had broken into the mainstream—and would go on to break all records.

On March 23, 1956, a self-titled album by a twenty-one-year-old kid from Tupelo, Mississippi produced four number one hits and earned a total of twenty-five weeks at the top of the charts.

The RCA Victor record was simply called *Elvis Presley*.

By 1957, Elvis, Buddy Holly, and The Everly Brothers monopolized the charts. By 1958 it was *all* Rock & Roll.

With the release of *Love Me Tender* in November, 1956, and *Jailhouse Rock* in 1957, it looked as if Bud Anderson (*Father*

Knows Best) had seen his last days as a teen idol, and that the new *star* of *The Adventures of Ozzie and Harriet* would soon be their *rock-and-roll* singing son, Ricky.

The fifties began with two memorable films, *High Noon* and *The African Queen*. In retrospect, those films could be considered *swan songs* for their legendary lead actors.

The Wild One and *Rebel Without a Cause,* both appearing soon after, introduced a new sort of anti-establishment protagonist.

And a new brand of movie star.

The aura possessed by the matinee idols of the forties and the early fifties—James Cagney, Cary Grant, Gary Cooper, Jimmy Stewart, Humphrey Bogart—was fading.

Elvis Presley, Marlon Brando, and James Dean were shining.

And, of course, there were J.D. Salinger's Holden Caulfield (*Catcher in the Rye)* and Jack Kerouac.

Role models more dangerous and exciting. More rebellious.

When American servicemen and women returned from the second great war in 1945, they set their minds and their energies to raising and supporting families. There was peace and increasing prosperity in the homeland.

Little attention was paid to the conflicts and atrocities that continued overseas.

The end of British Empire rule of the Indian sub-continent in 1947, and the partition that resulted, led to bloody conflict between the Hindus of India and the Muslims of Pakistan.

At the same time, the withdrawal of the British from the Middle East and the partition of Palestine incited decades of armed conflicts between the new state of Israel and the Arab world surrounding it.

However, in small towns, as well as in the ethnic urban areas that were much like small towns, Americans were more interested in caring for their *own* families and those of their neighbors.

Had aliens actually set down in Roswell, New Mexico, they would have learned little about the turmoil beyond our shores.

Instead, they may have seen Earth as a tranquil, idyllic planet populated by the offspring of Norman Rockwell and Ozzie Nelson.

Americans were feeling happy and secure in their private little world.

Then, in his speech at the Philadelphia Convention Hall five days prior to the general election, Eisenhower reminded Americans there was *us* and there was *them*—and we would defend not only the freedoms of Americans, but also those of mankind.

"We know, as our forefathers knew," Eisenhower professed, "the firm ground upon which our beliefs must stand. Freedom is rooted in the certainty that the brotherhood of all men arises from the Fatherhood of God. And thus, even as every man is his brother's keeper, no man is another's master."

The line was drawn.

The *red scare* was pervading American life—but we were the *good guys* and we would prevail against the evil empire.

However, be aware.

Parents who had been sending their children unaccompanied to school, and watching them play safely in the center of city streets, now became more vigilant.

At the same time, the image of the domestically blissful American family of 1950s television was being challenged in syndicated newspaper columns by identical twin sisters from Iowa—Ester and Pauline Friedman—who became known as Ann Landers and Abigail van Buren. *Ask Ann Landers,* 1955, and *Dear Abby,* 1956, were hinting that at times there was trouble in paradise.

At the start of 1957, Americans were introduced to a plastic flying disk called *The Frisbee.*

At the end of the year they were introduced to mass-murderer Ed Gein, called *The Butcher of Plainfield.*

Young Americans were trapped under their school desks—

longing to break away from their black and white television world.

And for some—including a teenaged girl from Ramsey, New Jersey, and two El Segundo, California police officers in their twenties—1957 would be the beginning of the end.

End of year holidays and celebrations, Christmas and New Year's Eve, tend to turn family focus inward.

To the pleasures of home and hearth, and away from the confusing and often frightening *big bad world*.

That, and a number of newsworthy events in early January, 1957, served to temporarily put darker global concerns aside.

Children returned to school in 1957 were more frightened by the Salk polio vaccination than by the prospect of being crushed by a nuclear bomb.

In the 50s, baseball had a firm hold on the term *America's pastime*—particularly in the east where the Brooklyn Dodgers and New York Yankees had dominated league and world championships, while the West Coast could claim no Major League teams of their own.

Imagine Jackie Robinson and Willie Mays on the same ball club.

It might have been, after the Dodgers traded Robinson to the rival New York Giants in December, 1956.

Jackie wouldn't go—and one of the first major news stories of 1957 was Robinson's announcement, on January 5, that he was retiring from the game.

In workplaces and neighborhood watering holes, the subject of the hour was the possible relocation of the Brooklyn Dodgers and the New York Giants to points west—rampant rumors filling easterners with lament and westerners with hope.

In living rooms, a new television program was capturing the imaginations and fantasies of Americans.

It was called *The Price is Right*.

Teens were gearing up for the appearance of Elvis on the Ed Sullivan Show on January 6.

The first weeks of 1957 provided distractions for every age group of Americans.

But the escape from reality and the renewed sense of safety was short-lived.

Eisenhower's inaugural speech on January 21 rekindled the *red scare*.

And a pair of events reported a few days later were a rude reawakening.

January

Following the Christmas break in December, 1956, I began the second half of fourth grade in Brooklyn.

Granted, by that time, I had learned some about the world.

Arithmetic. Vocabulary. History.

Mostly American history. Revolutionary War. Civil War.

Of course, I knew a lot about Jackie Robinson and the Brooklyn Dodgers.

I was all too aware of the polio vaccine and the *duck and cover* drills.

But I knew little of the news and the politics of the day—beyond the knowledge that Dad *liked Ike.*

Yet, by the end of that first month in 1957 something was noticeable in the air.

Parents began paying much closer attention to where their children were.

Doors began to be locked more conscientiously.

Three events occurring in the fourth week of January seemed to dampen whatever remained of Christmas and New Year cheer.

On January 21, in his second inaugural address, President Eisenhower reminded the American people about the *big bad red wolf.*

21

In our great nation, work and wealth abound. Our population grows. Commerce crowds our rivers and rails, our skies, harbors and highways. Our soil is fertile, our agriculture productive. The air rings with the song of our industry— rolling mills and blast furnaces, dynamos, dams and assembly lines—the chorus of America the bountiful.

Great news.
But the address soon turned from optimism to threat and warning.

Now this is our home—yet this is not the whole of our world. For our world is where our full destiny lies—with men, of all peoples and all nations, who are or would be free. And for them—and so for us—this is no time of ease or of rest.

In too much of the earth there is want, discord, danger.

Across all continents, nearly a billion people seek, sometimes almost in desperation, for the skills and knowledge and assistance by which they may satisfy, from their own resources, the material wants common to all mankind.

No nation, however old or great, escapes this tempest of change and turmoil. Some, impoverished by the recent World War, seek to restore their means of livelihood.

In the heart of Europe, Germany still stands tragically divided.

So is the whole continent divided.

And so, too, all the world.

The divisive force is International Communism

and the power that it controls.

The designs of that power, dark in purpose, are clear in practice. It strives to seal forever the fate of those it has enslaved. It strives to break the ties that unite the free. And it strives to capture—to exploit for its own greater power— all forces of change in the world, especially the needs of the hungry and the hopes of the oppressed.

We look upon this shaken earth, and we declare our firm and fixed purpose—the building of a peace with justice in a world where moral law prevails. The building of such a peace is a bold and solemn purpose.

To proclaim it is easy. To serve it will be hard. And to attain it, we must be aware of its full meaning—and ready to pay its full price.

Splendid as can be the blessings of such a peace, high will be its cost—in toil patiently sustained, in help honorably given, in sacrifice calmly borne.

We are called to meet the price of this peace.

To counter the threat of those who seek to rule by force we must pay the cost of our own needed military strength and help build the security of others.

Eisenhower had painted a crystal-clear picture, in response to the Soviet invasion of Hungary and the on-going Suez crisis.

A picture both hopeful and ominous.

America the bountiful was putting the Soviets on notice.

Mess with the eagle, you get the talons.

A message not conducive to a good night's sleep—even at a time when no more than a handful of Americans had ever heard of a Southeast Asian country called Vietnam.

And even before the paint had dried, there was news of other bumps in the night.

These much closer to home.

Just before midnight on January 21, the day Eisenhower presented his mixed-message to the American public, George Peter Metesky was arrested in Waterbury, Connecticut.

Metesky was suspected of planting bombs in public places throughout New York City over a period of sixteen years—including Grand Central Station, Pennsylvania Station, Radio City Music Hall, the New York Public Library, Port Authority Bus Terminal, in movie theaters and on city subways.

Metesky told arresting officers that in 1931, employed by a subsidiary of Consolidated Edison, he had suffered an injury in a work-related accident.

A boiler backfire had produced a blast of hot gases filling his lungs with fumes.

Because the company had denied him compensation—even after several appeals and hundreds of letters to the newspapers, the Mayor, and the Police Commissioner—Metesky began placing bombs in 1940, targeted specifically at Consolidated Edison buildings.

Going over a police list of thirty-two bomb locations, though never using the word *bomb*, Metesky remembered the exact date where each *unit* had been placed and its size.

He then added to the police list the sizes, locations, and dates of fifteen earlier bombs the police had not known about—all deposited at Con Edison locations and apparently never reported.

The first bomb had been accompanied by a penciled block-letter note.

CON EDISON CROOKS, THIS IS FOR YOU

When the Con Edison bombs were never mentioned in the newspapers, he began planting bombs in public places to gain publicity for what he termed the *injustices* done him.

In 1951, *The New York Herald Tribune* received a note in block letters.

BOMBS WILL CONTINUE UNTIL THE CON-SOLIDATED EDISON COMPANY IS BROUGHT TO JUSTICE FOR THEIR DAS-TARDLY ACTS AGAINST ME. I HAVE EX-HAUSTED ALL OTHER MEANS. I INTEND WITH BOMBS TO CAUSE OTHERS TO CRY OUT FOR JUSTICE FOR ME.

Two days before his arrest, in an open letter to the *New York Journal-American,* Metesky told of *lying unnoticed for hours on cold concrete after his injury without any first aid being rendered*—then *developing pneumonia and later tuberculosis* as a result of inhaling the gaseous fumes.

A Consolidated Edison clerk, Alice Kelly, had for days been searching through old workers' compensation files for employees with a serious health problem.

On January 18, while going through the final batch of *troublesome* case files—those where threats had been made or implied—she discovered a file marked in red with the words *injustice, permanent disability*, and *dastardly acts.*

The same types of words and expressions that had been used in letters to the newspapers.

Police investigators, who later described the trail leading to Metesky, claimed that Consolidated Edison had *impeded* the investigation for several years by repeatedly claiming that all records of employees whose services were terminated prior to 1940, the group Metesky fell into, had been destroyed.

Following his interrogation, Metesky was transferred to Bellevue Hospital in Manhattan for psychiatric evaluation.

At the time of his arrest, most Americans beyond New York had never heard of the man who had come to be known as *The Mad Bomber.*

The frontpage news of George Metesky's apprehension was heartening, but the fact that he had been undetected for sixteen years was troubling.

As was the nagging thought something of the kind could occur again.

And then, on the very same front pages, came scary news of the Grimes sisters.

They were two of seven children.

On December 28, 1956, Barbara Grimes, 15, and Patricia Grimes, 12, traveled together to see a movie in Brighton Park—a neighborhood in south-west Chicago.

The Brighton Theater was one-and-a-half miles—a short bus ride—from their McKinley Park home.

The film was *Love Me Tender* starring Richard Egan, Debra Paget, and first-time movie actor Elvis Presley.

The girls never arrived home that night.

Loretta Grimes, the girls' mother, called in a report to the Chicago Police Department at two in the morning on December 29.

Initiating one of the most intensive missing persons investigations in the city's history.

In the weeks following their disappearance, there had been a number of unconfirmed sightings.

Several people claimed they saw the two girls board a Chicago Transit Authority bus at Western Avenue heading east into the city—halfway between the theater and their home—after the movie screening.

Two teenage boys reported seeing the two girls that night, *giggling and jumping out of doorways at each other*, two blocks from their home.

A security guard offered directions to two girls the following morning, who he thought were the Grimes sisters.

There was a reported sighting on a train in a northern section of the city—as well as sightings in restaurants, department stores, and hotels.

There were theories that the girls had found a way to travel to Nashville, Tennessee—to search for their idol, Elvis Presley.

And on January 19, Elvis sent a message.

If you are good fans, you will go home and ease your family's worries.

On the 22nd of January—while George Metesky was being transferred from Connecticut to Bellevue Hospital—a construction worker spotted what he described as *flesh-colored things* behind a guard rail as he drove along a rural country road in Willow Springs, Illinois, 13 miles from the Brighton Theater.

Initially unsure of what he had seen, and believing they may have been mannequins, he later returned to the site with his wife who fainted when she realized what they had discovered. The nude, frozen bodies of two young girls—revealed by a recent snow thaw.

The couple immediately reported their finding to the Willow Springs Police Department.

The bodies were later positively identified as those of Patricia and Barbara Grimes.

Autopsies, performed by forensic pathologists, concluded both sisters had most likely died within five hours of the time they had last been seen alive at the Brighton Theater.

The official death certificates of both sisters would list their cause of death as murder—the specific means of which, in both cases, was officially listed as *secondary shock* resulting from exposure that had reduced each girl's body temperature *below the critical level compatible with life.*

During the last week of January, several suspects had been picked up and held for questioning and interrogation—including a man who had at first confessed to the abduction and murders and later recanted his confession.

All of the suspects were released due to lack of evidence.

The Grimes sisters murder case—as had the case of Elizabeth

Short, the *Black Dahlia*, ten years earlier—seemed destined to remain unsolved.

In the fifties—before photographs began appearing on milk cartons, and long before cell phones lit up with *Amber Alerts*—children enjoyed a good deal of independence.

Even in the larger cities, where ethnically homogeneous neighborhoods much resembled small towns and villages.

Children, as young as seven and eight years old, traveled to schools and local movie houses accompanied only by classmates and friends their own age.

After school, it was in and out of houses just long enough to drop books and grab bats and mitts, rubber balls and jump ropes.

Then it was off to playgrounds, parks, empty lots, or out onto streets decorated with chalk outlines of slap ball bases and hopscotch courts.

If there was one hard and fast rule, it was that the family sit down together for the evening meal where talk centered around questions like *how was your day* and *what did you learn at school.*

There is a Portuguese expression, *Em uma casa de alguém que foi enforcado, não está inclinado a falar de corda.*

In a house of someone who has been hanged, one is not inclined to speak of rope.

Mad bombers and murdered girls were not fit subjects for family dinner conversation.

But were surely discussed among parents privately, because questions at the dinner table began to subtly change.

Who are you walking with to school tomorrow morning?

What are you plans after school, and with who?

A formerly unfelt cynicism was disturbing the carefree American home.

A lack of confidence in the safety of the children.

Then a story broke at the beginning of February.

An account of good will and heroism that offered a brief respite from pessimism, and a bit of brightness to the recent darker days.

Ironically, the event involved a plane crash.

It was, of course, a tragedy—marking the deaths of twenty passengers.

But what resonated among the public over the following weeks was the courageous rescue of the survivors by the most unlikely heroes.

The Island

By the end of January, 1957, Barbara and Patricia Grimes had been laid to rest at the Holy Sepulchre Cemetery in Worth, Illinois.

The person or the persons responsible for their deaths remained undiscovered.

George Metesky was indicted on 47 counts—which included attempted murder, damage of buildings by explosion, maliciously endangering human life, and violation of New York State's *Sullivan Law* by carrying concealed weapons.

Seven counts of attempted murder were charged, based on the seven persons injured in the prior five years, which was the statute of limitations in the case.

Metesky was brought to a courtroom from Bellevue Hospital, where he had been undergoing psychiatric evaluation, to hear the charges.

At the United Nations, a resolution was being drafted calling for the withdrawal of Israeli troops from Egypt.

The Congress accepted the *Eisenhower Doctrine*—under which a Middle Eastern country could request economic assistance or aid from our military forces in order *to secure and protect the territorial integrity and political independence of nations requesting such aid against overt armed aggression from any nation controlled by international communism.*

The phrase *international communism* made the doctrine much broader than simply responding to the *Soviet* threat.

Aggression linked to communists of *any* nation could conceivably invoke the doctrine.

Cold War temperatures continued to fall—dropping closer to freezing.

And at the same time, bitter cold weather in the northeast had residents planning escapes to the sunny warmth of the south.

Shortly after two in the afternoon of February 1, 1957, Northeast Airlines Flight 823 began boarding passengers at LaGuardia Airport in Queens, New York.

Ninety-five men, women and children—plus a crew of six—went aboard.

Snow had been falling for several hours.

The Douglas DC-6A was scheduled for a 2:45 departure to Miami.

The flight was delayed as ground crews tended to icy runways and, while sitting at the gate, snow and ice had accumulated on the wings of the aircraft.

Because of the continuing snowfall, attempts to clear off the wings out-of-doors were unsuccessful.

Near four that afternoon, the aircraft was taxied into a hangar—with crew and ticketed travelers still on board—for snow and ice removal.

It was later learned that a number of passengers had asked to leave the plane while it was being de-iced but were dissuaded by a stewardess who told them *it could initiate a mass exodus* that would only cause further delay.

At 5:45, the flight crew advised ground control that they were ready to taxi from the hangar to the tarmac for departure.

Flight 823 was then cleared to take-off from Runway 4.

Shortly after six, the DC-6 lifted into the air.

Minutes later, the plane crash landed a few miles from the airport.

It seemed a miracle had prevented all from perishing.

31

J.L. Abramo

Had the aircraft crashed anywhere else in the vicinity it would have dropped into the East River, the Flushing Bay, or in a populated residential area.

Instead, it came down in an open field on Rikers Island—home of one of the country's largest and most secure correctional institutions.

"We were playing cards when we heard the explosion," reported a prisoner. "We all jumped up to the windows. The whole sky, even through the snow, was lit. We saw the people tumbling out of the ship—they were all lighted too, by the flames. We saw their shadows, we saw them stumble. We were locked up then, but we wanted to help. We saw people running and falling in the snow."

Twenty passengers had perished.

The snow was covered in blood.

The wreck of the aircraft was in flames.

Survivors were helping those more critically injured get away from the wreckage—to the relative safety of the prison buildings.

The danger of further explosion and additional fatalities was very real.

Prisoners were throwing blankets down from their cell windows.

Then, the warden made a fateful decision.

Fifty inmates—trustees—were released to assist in the rescue of the survivors and to also collect the bodies of the deceased.

None of the released prisoners attempted to escape.

All of them saved lives.

Witnesses on the island would later describe it as a caravan.

A steady procession of facility personnel and inmates transporting passengers from the burning aircraft to prison buildings.

A six-week-old boy, nearly buried in the snow, was literally stumbled upon by an inmate who carried the child to the prison infirmary and located the boy's family.

The most critically injured were taken to the prison hospital to be cared for by doctors and nurses.

The prison hospital was, at the time, filled to near capacity by inmate patients.

Prisoners gave up their beds in the facility to accommodate crash survivors.

Less seriously injured survivors were tended to by inmates themselves—who supplied blankets, dry clothing, food, drink, applied salves to burns, and cleaned and bandaged wounds.

An injured passenger later recalled being offered a cigarette by one of the inmates. He politely declined, explaining he only smoked cigars. The prisoner rushed off and soon returned with a cigar obtained from a cellmate.

A six-foot-tall, three hundred pound African-American inmate walked slowly around a room rocking a three-year-old boy in the cradle of his arms. The man hummed softly, oblivious to everyone else in the room, never shifting the burden in his arms lest he disturb the sleeping child.

A few hours after the disaster, a first group of ambulatory and stretcher cases were removed by ferry and transported to Bronx hospitals.

By 11:30, the last of the eighty-one survivors had been transferred to hospitals on the mainland.

Families, now aware of the disaster, waited to hear the fate of their loved ones.

For their part in the rescue, thirty inmates who rushed to aid victims were granted release—and sixteen had their sentences reduced by the New York City Parole Board.

New York City Mayor Robert Wagner presented Assistant Deputy Warden James Harrison with the Medal of Honor—the Correction Department's highest award.

The story of Flight 823 broke at a moment in time when a testament to the better parts of human nature was extremely welcome news.

But, the rejuvenation of faith in the goodness of mankind was short lived.

The Boy in the Box

In the following days of February, the world kept turning.

Families buried their dead—the fatalities of Flight 823.

Survivors related details of the harrowing night on Rikers Island to relatives, friends, and newspaper reporters.

In an effort to ease mounting tensions in the Middle East, the United Nations called for Israel to retreat from Egypt.

The question remained whether or not the Israelis would comply.

Andrei Gromyko became Minister of Foreign Affairs of the Union of Soviet Socialist Republics, leaving Eisenhower and his *fellow Americans* to wonder if and how this change would affect the already chilly relations.

There were uncertainties.

There were also distractions.

Grade-school children continued playing out in the streets.

Their older brothers and sisters—with money earned from paper routes and babysitting—pushed Elvis Presley's *Too Much* to the top of the charts.

The Pluto Platter—later to be known as the Frisbee—was gliding through the air above college campus lawns throughout the country.

Children were watching *Captain Kangaroo*, and their parents were watching *Gunsmoke,* on the first portable black-and-white television sets.

I Love Lucy, The $64,000 Question and *The Ed Sullivan*

Show were the most viewed programs.

The Cat in the Hat by Dr. Seuss, and *The Untouchables* by Eliot Ness were released.

Peyton Place remained at the top of the New York Times Best Seller List.

Love Me Tender, Lust for Life, and *Giant* continued drawing movie house audiences months after their initial releases.

It was feeling a little less scary in the homeland.

A man, checking his illegal muskrat traps, first discovered the body.

Afraid that the traps would be confiscated, he failed to report his discovery.

Several days later, a college student stumbled upon the body.

He waited a full day before contacting police.

Police arrived at the scene, in the Fox Chase neighborhood of northeast Philadelphia, on February 26.

The boy was estimated to have been four to five years old.

His naked body was wrapped in a plaid blanket inside a large cardboard box.

The boy's hair had been recently cut, possibly after death.

Clumps of hair clung to the body.

There were signs of severe malnourishment, surgical scars on the ankle and groin, and an L-shaped scar under the chin.

All efforts at identification were unsuccessful.

No one came forward with any helpful information.

The *Philadelphia Enquirer* printed 400,000 flyers with the boy's likeness which flooded the area and were included in every utilities bill in the city.

The crime scene was combed over and over again by nearly 300 police academy recruits who discovered no more than a child's blue corduroy cap, a handkerchief and a scarf.

All clues that led nowhere.

The victim, who came to be known as *The Boy in the Box* and *America's Unknown Child*, was buried in a potter's field.

The boy was not identified and the case remained open.

Once again, parents found tangible reason to keep a closer eye on their children.

There is an old saying, popular in the northeastern United States, *March comes in like a lion.*

March 1957 came in with the battered body of a fifteen-year-old girl discovered in a sandpit in Mahwah, New Jersey.

Winston Churchill, Franklin Roosevelt, and Josef Stalin met at Yalta from February 4-11, 1945 to discuss plans for Europe after an allied victory. FDR died on April 12, and Adolph Hitler committed suicide on April 30. Churchill resigned as Prime Minister on July 26. It would be up to Harry Truman and Clement Atlee to deal with Stalin's grand plans for the USSR.

On March 12, 1947, President Truman introduced the *Truman Doctrine*, "supporting free peoples who are resisting attempted subjugation by armed minorities or outside pressures."

The *Marshall Plan* would soon follow.

On March 21, Truman signed *Executive Order 9865 (Federal Employee Loyalty Program)*, and in July signed into law the *National Security Act*—creating the Department of Defense, the Joint Chiefs of Staff, the Central Intelligence Agency, and the National Security Council.

The Cold War was shifting into high gear.

Senator Joseph McCarthy lecturing on the suspected Communists infiltrating the American public, the Government, and the military. McCarthy hearings led to *blacklisting* and the creation of the *House Un-American Activities Committee.*

First nuclear test by the Soviet Union. Russia and the United States both raced to be first to develop a hydrogen bomb.

Duck and cover drills became routine in schools in the fifties, along with air raid drills, as Americans were made more fearful of nuclear attack by the U.S.S.R.

In July, 1947, an unidentified object crashed near Roswell, New Mexico. Reported by the United States Army as merely a weather balloon, it was believed by many Americans then, and to this day, to be a flying saucer carrying alien beings—an invasion scarier than the Soviet threat.

In the fifties, Rock & Roll took control of the music charts—with rockers like Elvis Presley and Buddy Holly.

These artists—along with a new breed of actors including Marlon Brando and James Dean—and writers Jack Kerouac and J.D. Salinger—introduced young people to a more rebellious and much less predictable picture of American life than the one presented by the icons of the previous generation like Frank Sinatra, Gary Cooper, Lucille Ball, *The Honeymooners*, and Billy Graham.

In his second inaugural address on January 21, 1957, President Eisenhower warned Americans of *the divisive force of International Communism and the power it controls* and put the Soviets on notice—America would counter the threat from those who seek to rule by force.

The day following Eisenhower's address, Americans heard the disturbing stories of the Mad Bomber in New York and the Grimes sisters in Chicago.

Prison inmates come to the rescue and aid of survivors of
Northeast Airlines flight 823 which crash landed on Rikers
Island minutes after taking off from LaGuardia Airport in
Queens, New York on February 1, 1957.

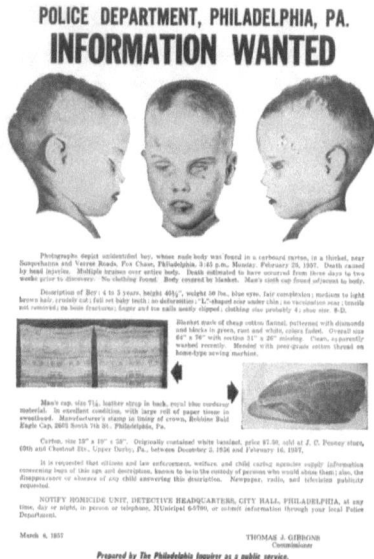

Young Americans were being made aware of the Communist threat and alleged Russian spies like Julius and Ethel Rosenberg—executed in 1953.

Flier inserted with every utilities bill in the Philadelphia metropolitan area in February 1957—in hope of identifying *The Boy in the Box.*

Blood and Sand
March 1957 to April 1957

*Someone has to die in order that
the rest of us value life more.*
—Virginia Wolfe

*There is no tragedy in life like the death of a child.
Things never get back to the way they were.*
—Dwight D. Eisenhower

*No one can confidently say that he will
still be living tomorrow.*
—Euripides

Victoria

Victoria Ann Zielinski celebrated her fifteenth birthday on the sixth of September, 1956.

Six months later she was gone.

Vickie, as her friends and schoolmates called her, was a sophomore at Ramsey High School in Bergen County, New Jersey.

Ramsey, a town of 8,000 inhabitants in 1957, sits three miles from the New York State line and twenty miles from Manhattan.

Victoria was both an honor student and a cheerleader.

Five-foot-two, one-hundred-twenty pounds, brown eyes, shoulder length dark brown hair.

Victoria lived with her parents, two sisters, and a brother in a wood-framed house four hundred feet from the Ramsey-Mahwah town border.

The Zielinski family had relocated to Ramsey in 1950 from northeastern Pennsylvania, where Victoria was born.

On the evening of March 4, 1957, Victoria was preparing to take the half-mile walk to the home of a classmate, Barbara Nixon.

The girls had arranged to meet and to study together for an upcoming school exam.

At seven-thirty, following dinner with her family, Victoria was ready to leave.

The temperature was in the low thirties, the ground covered with patches of snow.

Victoria wore blue jeans, a red cardigan sweater, a blue and gold jacket, a pair of red gloves, and black loafers.

She carried a handbag, containing books and class notes for study.

Her younger sister, Myrna, agreed to walk with her half-way—at which point the younger girl turned back to return to the Zielinski home and Vickie continued on to Barbara Nixon's house.

Before parting ways, the sisters had agreed that Myrna would meet Vickie at the halfway point again, an hour later, for the walk back home.

At eight-thirty, Myrna left her house to meet her sister. Myna walked all the way to the Nixon home and had not crossed paths with Victoria.

She was told Victoria had already left.

Myrna could not understand how they could have missed each other along the route.

Myrna hurried home, arriving just after nine, to report to her parents.

She found her mother in the kitchen.

Her father had already gone to bed.

Mrs. Zielinski did not want to wake her husband, Anthony, with the news.

Instead, she waited—rationalizing reasons for Victoria's delay. When her oldest daughter, Mary, arrived home from a date at 10:45, the seventeen-year-old insisted she and her boyfriend go out to look for Victoria.

They drove through Ramsey and the surrounding towns for more than an hour, stopping at all the spots where teens were known to congregate.

Victoria was nowhere to be found.

When they returned to the house at 12:30, Victoria's mother decided it was time to awaken her husband.

Anthony Zielinski dressed quickly and he joined his daughter, Mary, on another search for Victoria.

They stopped at Robbie's Corral, a popular diner on the town's main street. The owner was turning off the lights when they reached the door.

The owner said he didn't know Victoria.

Mary and her father returned to their car.

Before driving away, Mary spotted a Ramsey police vehicle.

She flashed her headlights, signaling the cruiser to stop.

Father and daughter reported Victoria's disappearance to the two officers and returned home.

Following a sleepless night, and no word from or regarding Victoria, her parents drove to Ramsey Police Headquarters in the morning.

They brought a photograph of their daughter, supplied additional details about what she had been wearing and the route she should have taken to return home.

Then they left the station to search on their own.

They had been driving aimlessly over the back roads of Ramsey and Mahwah for an hour when Anthony Zielinski spotted a black loafer on the roadway.

Twenty feet farther, they spotted Victoria's kerchief.

Mrs. Zielinski rushed on foot to a nearby house to telephone the police, while her husband began searching a small patch of woods across the road.

He eventually came to a dirt road leading to a flat area above a sandpit.

He discovered a pair of red gloves.

His wife called him back to their car, and they remained at the vehicle to wait for the police to arrive.

The first on the scene was Mahwah Police Captain Edmund Wickham.

The investigative report filed by Captain Wickham revealed that he had no prior knowledge of a girl's disappearance in his jurisdiction.

Mahwah had not been notified by the Ramsey police.

It seemed the Ramsey police had not taken the report of the girl's disappearance very seriously eight hours earlier.

"I proceeded to Fardale Avenue and Chapel Road where I met Mr. and Mrs. Zielinski," Wickham stated in his report. "They told me of their missing daughter, Victoria, who had last been seen at approximately eight-forty-five the previous evening."

Wickham asked Victoria's mother to stay with the car. He and Victoria's father walked the dirt road.

Wickham's report described the following:

> After notifying the Ramsey police by radio, Mr. Zielinski and I walked onto a dirt driveway at the end of Fardale Avenue, on the west side of Chapel Road.
>
> The road is at the intersection where the west end of Fardale ends or runs into Chapel, the general direction north and south.
>
> At about 150 feet from the dirt roadway, I saw a pair of red gloves with leather palms lying on the ground. Anthony Zielinski stated his daughter had a pair exactly like them.
>
> The gloves were later identified by his wife.
>
> Near where the gloves were found, I saw tire marks which indicated the driver had driven to the area and backed around heading out to Chapel Road.
>
> I walked around those tire marks.
>
> Zielinski called to me that he had found his daughter's locket and chain.
>
> Then he called that he had found her body.
>
> I saw the body of a girl in a semi-crouched position, with the body facing downward.
>
> Mr. and Mrs. Zielinski identified the body as

their missing daughter, Victoria.

I walked over and I felt the arm of the girl. It was stiff and cold.

The left part of the skull was bashed in.

Wickham radioed his headquarters to report his findings.

Within minutes both radio and telephone alerts went out to the Bergen County Prosecutors Office, the Bergen County Medical Examiner, state and county police, and the Ramsey police. Soon the scene would be crowded with medical and law enforcement personnel. And news reporters.

The Zielinskis were encouraged to return home.

They would have the horrible burden of facing their three other children with the news that their sister was gone.

Forever.

Adolescent defiance of the boundaries set by their parents was not an uncommon occurrence in those small New Jersey townships in 1957.

The discovery of a battered dead body was rare.

What had been casually addressed by the Ramsey police as simply another case of a teenager staying out past curfew, and failing to call her parents, was about to become a spectacular homicide investigation.

Bergen

In New Jersey, the investigation of a major crime is the responsibility of the prosecutor of the county where the offense was committed.

On the morning of May 5, when Victoria's body was discovered, the call from the Mahwah police was received at the Bergen County Prosecutor's office in Hackensack at 9:46.

By 10:35, James Stewart, chief of Bergen County detectives, had arrived at the sandpit with two of his assistants.

Chief Harry Voss of Ramsey, Chief Charles Smith of Mahwah, Captain Alvin Doremus of Ramsey, and patrolmen from both towns were already at the scene.

Detective Stewart took charge—immediately ordering the cordoning off of the area.

A photographer was called in, as were technicians to take plaster impressions of tire tracks and footprints.

Medical personnel arrived.

After a preliminary examination, and many photographs, the corpse was finally removed at 11:45.

The body was taken to the Van Emburgh Funeral Chapel in Ramsey, where an autopsy would be performed.

Police personnel searched the area, looking for anything that could pass as a clue.

Nearly as many additional officers were required to control the growing crowd of spectators.

Other officers were sent to interview the Zielinski family, to obtain a list of Vickie's friends and acquaintances.

William Nixon, the older brother of Victoria's friend Barbara, was the first name on the Zielinski's list—since Victoria had been at the Nixon home before she went missing.

William was brought in for questioning, but it was soon evident he was not a suspect.

The questioning of others on the list provided no help.

Boys Victoria had dated, those she knew casually, friends of her sisters and of Barbara, anyone from whom she might have accepted a ride.

Stories were checked, and all who were questioned were cleared.

Captain Wickham remembered a man who lived in a trailer park a mile from the sandpit who had been seen loitering at a grammar school, and had attempted to lure girls into his car.

Police officers questioned the *suspect* for more than an hour, searched his trailer home, examined his automobile, and came up with nothing. He had an airtight alibi for the entire evening.

Another lead came up when a resident on Fardale mentioned a boy in the neighborhood had spent time in a mental institution.

More questions, more home and auto searches, and again nothing.

Other residents in the area near the scene were questioned.

Not a single person recalled having seen or heard anything unusual. No loud voices or sounds, no sound of automobiles in an isolated area normally so quiet the sound of a car could be heard a half mile away.

All leads seemed to be exhausted by late afternoon.

All that could be done at the scene of the crime had been done.

The body was at the funeral chapel, autopsy completed.

Evidence from the sandpit that included clothing, strands of hair, bloodstained stones, and plaster casts—as well as clothing removed by the autopsy surgeon—had been boxed and had been sent to the Edel Forensic Laboratories in Newark.

It was nearly twenty-four hours since Victoria had last been seen alive and investigators were stuck on square one.

Joe Gilroy had been talking with several friends at Tony's Amoco Station in downtown Ramsey when he spotted police officer John Cozma standing across the avenue.

It was around seven-thirty on the evening of March fifth when Gilroy crossed over to Officer Cozma and told the patrolman about the blood in his car.

The Mercury Convertible

Tony's Amoco Station on Main Street in Ramsey was a regular hangout for a group of locals.

William Anderson, Tommy Doyle, and owner Tony Saveriano were talking about the news of the girl found at the sandpit when Joe Gilroy arrived at the gas station.

Joe led his friends to his car and pointed out a stain on the front seat.

He asked if they thought it was what *he* thought it was. A blood stain.

They all agreed it was possible.

He told them the brownish spot had not been there before.

When they asked *before what,* Gilroy said *before Smitty borrowed the car last night.*

Tony suggested Gilroy go to the police.

If Smitty had anything to do with the body at the sandpit, and it involved the Mercury, if Joe failed to report it he could be seen as an accessory.

If Gilroy did report it, he would be throwing suspicion on one of his best friends—whether or not his friend was actually guilty of anything.

He was struggling with the decision when he noticed Officer John Cozma standing in front of the bank across Main Street.

After hearing what Joe Gilroy had to say, and taking a look at the seat of Gilroy's car, Officer Cozma asked Joe to park the vehicle behind the gas station and lock it.

Cozma radioed the Ramsey Police Station for instructions. He was told what to do.

Cozma escorted Gilroy in his police car to Mahwah Police Headquarters, where assistant prosecutor Fred Galda was ready and waiting to interview the man who might be able to provide the first solid lead in the Zielinski case.

With Galda in the interview room were Detective Gordon Graber and Captain Edmund Wickham.

"All right now, son," Galda began, "what's this about finding blood on your car?"

"It's on the seat cover, not the car. You see, Eddie Smith had the car, and when he didn't have the shoes, and I found the blood and remembered…"

"Hold on," Galda interrupted, "who is Eddie Smith?"

"Eddie's a friend of mine. He borrowed my car last night and now it has blood on it, and Eddie had this pair of shoes, and…"

Galda interrupted again.

"Look, at this rate we'll be here all night. Grab the chair over there, sit, start from the beginning. When did Eddie Smith borrow your car? By the way, where is your car now?"

"It's behind Tony Saveriano's gas station, in Ramsey. The Ramsey cop told me to leave it there. It's locked."

"What kind of car?"

"A Mercury. A 1950 turquoise convertible."

Galda turned to Detective Graber.

"Gordon, you and Wickham take this boy's keys and go check out his car. And don't be all night about it."

And then Galda went back to Gilroy.

"Now take your time and don't leave anything out. But first, give the detective your keys."

Gilroy pulled a chair over to Fred Galda's desk and lit a cigarette. He handed his cars keys to Graber.

Once both Graber and Wickham had left the room, Joseph Gilroy began his story.

. . .

At around three-thirty the previous afternoon, Eddie Smith called Gilroy at home and asked to be picked up at the Paramus Bowling Alleys.

Gilroy arrived at four-thirty, they bowled some games, and then drove to Tony's Amoco in Ramsey.

Smith asked to borrow Gilroy's car. His car was in the shop and he needed kerosene for the heater in his trailer home.

Smith drove Joe home in Gilroy's car, and then took the Mercury.

Later that evening, Eddie called Joe. Smith said the heater in the trailer wasn't working and asked if Gilroy would drive Eddie, Smith's wife, and their baby girl to his mother-in-law's home in Ridgewood.

Gilroy agreed, and Smith picked him up around ten.

Smith told Gilroy that he had thrown up on his pants and had to discard them.

They collected Smith's wife and baby at the trailer, and Gilroy dropped them off in Ridgewood on Monday night.

Just after noon on Tuesday, Gilroy and another friend, Donnie Hommell, drove out to Ridgewood to pick up Smith and his family.

Smith, his wife and baby were in the back seat. His wife found a lipstick on the floor of the car and passed it up to Donnie who threw it out the window.

They stopped at the trailer to drop off Eddie's wife and baby. Smith went into the trailer for a minute and then came out carrying an old pair of shoes.

He got into the car with Gilroy and Hommell and they drove to Tony's Amoco.

Gilroy and Hommell ran a quick errand. When they returned, they saw Eddie coming from across the street, without the shoes he had been carrying.

Donnie and Joe went to play basketball.

When they returned at around five, Joe saw Eddie sitting in Dave Villarosa's car.

That was the last time Gilroy had seen Smith that day.

Joe drove home and he spotted the blood on the seat of the Mercury for the first time. He went back to Tony's to show it to the guys.

Then he had bumped into Officer Cozma who drove him out to Mahwah to speak to Galda.

"Have you told Hommell or Smith about finding the blood?" Galda asked.

"No, they weren't there at Tony's."

"Did Smith know the Zielinski girl?"

"I suppose so. I don't think *he* ever took her out."

"But Hommell did?"

"Yeah, a couple of times."

"Did you?"

"No."

"And how about Smith's pants. Did he mention where he threw them?"

"No, he didn't say."

"Did you ask him about the shoes?"

"I was wondering, but I didn't ask him."

"How is it you didn't notice the blood until tonight? You used the car after Smith brought it back last night, and again all day today, right?"

"Yeah, but I never noticed."

"Do you know where Hommell was last night?"

"I didn't see him. But coming up from Ridgewood today, Donnie told us he'd seen Vickie's kid sister, Myrna, walking last night—and he had honked the horn to her."

. . .

At that point Graber and Wickham returned.

They informed Galda that the stain on the seat of Joe Gilroy's car was positively blood.

Galda asked Wickham to contact the Ramsey police—to find out if Gilroy, Hommell or Smith had police records.

"Find out if the Zielinski's know any of these guys, if any of them dated Victoria, if Gilroy has any personal reasons for fingering Smith, and anything else they can tell you."

Galda was concerned about the time line.

Joe Gilroy could account for Eddie Smith's whereabouts from around ten the previous evening.

Victoria had been last seen at around eight-forty-five.

It was a tight window.

Galda took Detective Graber aside.

"Find Smith and bring him here. And bring back some coffee, it's going to be a long night."

Eddie

Edgar Herbert Smith Jr. was born in 1934—as were Hank Aaron, Sophia Loren, Carl Sagan, Frankie Valli, Leonard Cohen, Roger Maris, Giorgio Armani, a cartoon character named Donald Duck, Charles Manson, and the man who many years later would come to be known as the *Lover's Lane Bandit*.

Smith grew up in Hasbrouck Heights, a borough of Bergen County, New Jersey, near Teterboro Airport.

His parents divorced in 1941.

In 1948, Edgar's mother remarried.

That September, Smith entered ninth grade.

In December, as the family sat at dinner, a police officer came to their door.

They were told a neighborhood girl, several years younger than Edgar, had accused him of trying to molest her ten minutes earlier—several blocks from their home.

Finding Edgar planted in front of a half-eaten meal, the police officer doubted the boy could have been in two places at the same time.

Nonetheless, the fourteen-year-old was locked up in juvenile hall for two weeks before seeing a judge who cleared him of charges.

By 1950, the family had relocated to Ramsey—where Edgar found school unbearable.

President Truman had just deployed troops to Korea.

At sixteen-years-old and nearly six-foot-tall, Edgar tried

unsuccessfully to bluff his way into the Marines.

At eighteen, having quit school and having spent a winter in Fort Pierce, Florida, he returned to New Jersey and enlisted.

Smith's tour of duty in the Marines took him to Florida, Virginia, jump school and training in parachuting and survival equipment maintenance in New Jersey—and later to California, Hawaii, and Korea.

He was discharged in November, 1954, and he returned to his family home in Ramsey.

Within a year he had held and lost jobs as a sewing machine salesman, a truck driver, and a high school football coach.

He then took the federal civil service exam for the Border Patrol of the U.S. Immigration and Naturalization Service.

In the late summer of 1955, Smith was invited to a party. There he met an 18-year-old girl. Five-foot-seven, green eyes, auburn hair.

In early 1956, Smith was offered an appointment with the Border Patrol.

However, the girl he had met—and planned to marry—was against having to relocate to El Paso, Texas.

He declined the job offer.

Edgar found a good position as a car mechanic, and the newly married couple rented a furnished apartment.

Soon his wife Patricia, who was expecting a child, wanted a place of their own.

They purchased a two-bedroom trailer home.

Their daughter, Patricia Ann, named after her mother, was born two days before Christmas, 1956.

Seventy-two days later, Edgar Smith was brought into Mahwah Police Headquarters for questioning.

Famous First Words

On the fifth day of May, 1957—shortly before midnight—Edgar Smith was brought to the Mahwah Municipal Building.

He had turned twenty-three-years old on February 8.

Smith was taken into a small, crowded room.

Present were Assistant Bergen County Prosecutor Fred Galda, Bergen County Prosecutor Guy Calissi, Chief of Detectives James Stewart, Detective Captain Carl DeMarco, police chiefs of Mahwah and of Ramsey, and Captain Edmund Wickham.

The interview was in the public record.

Galda led off the questioning.

> Galda: Before we begin, Mr. Smith, would you like to sit?
>
> Smith: I'll stand.
>
> Galda: Fine, as you wish. We're all friends here. Now, as we understand it, you borrowed Joseph Gilroy's automobile Monday night. Is that correct?
>
> Smith: Correct.
>
> Galda: Why did you borrow the car?
>
> Smith: Mine was having some transmission work done.
>
> Galda: No, I don't think you understand. We want to know why you took the car instead of asking Gilroy to take you wherever you wanted to go.

Smith: Oh, that's no problem. Joe wanted to get home for supper. I had to get some kerosene or heating fuel. I didn't know how long it would take because the heating unit in my house trailer wasn't working.

Galda: Did you get kerosene?

Smith: I didn't. Kerosene is not easy to find these days, so then I went up to Moore's Truck Stop and picked up five gallons of number one diesel fuel, it's the same thing as heating fuel, in a can that I borrowed from Tony's Amoco.

Galda: What did you do then?

Smith: I went home and worked on the heater. I thought the tank was low. The oil man was due the next day.

DeMarco: Where do you live?

Smith: Bogert's Trailer Ranch, on Pulis Avenue, over in Fardale. I have a new house trailer I bought in December.

DeMarco: Is that the place down near the sandpit? About a mile away?

Smith: That's it.

Galda: All right. Go ahead, what happened with the heater. Did you get it working?

Smith: No. The damn thing wouldn't start. It was cold in the trailer, so I told my wife I'd get some more fuel oil. If it didn't work after that, we'd go down to her mother's house for the night. I'd been sick on and off for a day or two. I was in no mood to play with the heater all night.

Galda: You were sick? What was wrong with you?

Smith: I don't know. A virus or something.

Galda: Fine. Did you go for more kerosene?

Smith: Yes. I tried the Fardale Esso station on

Wyckoff Avenue. They didn't have any, but the woman there said that I could find some at Secor's Sunoco on the highway in Ramsey.

Galda: What time did you get to Secor's?

Smith: I got there about eight-twenty, maybe eight-thirty. After getting five gallons of kerosene I headed for home.

Calissi: What time was that?

Smith: Eight-thirty, eight-forty, probably about eight-forty or a few minutes later. I figure a few minutes later because I got home about five to nine.

Galda: How do you know that? Are you certain?

Smith: Pretty close. I fiddled with the heater for ten minutes at the most. Then gave up and decided to ask Gilroy to drive me, my wife, and baby out to Ridgewood. I called Joe at nine-ten. I looked at the electric clock on the range in the kitchen.

Calissi: What happened on the way home from Secor's? Did you stop anywhere or see anyone along the way?

Smith: Well, on the way home I started to get sick. I'd been sick for several days. I didn't want to mess up Gilroy's car so, when I got near St. Paul's Church on Wyckoff, I stopped real quick and threw up at the edge of a wooded area alongside the church. I took the back route after that—Young's Road, Chapel Road—just in case I got sick again. When I got to Chapel, near the sandpit, I began feeling sick again. I turned into the dirt road to the sandpit, went in one car length or two, and threw up again. Then I got back in the car and went home.

Galda: What happened after you got home?

Smith: As I said, the heater still wouldn't work so I called Gilroy. He agreed to drive us to Ridgewood. I picked him up close to nine-thirty. Then we went back to my trailer to pick up my wife and the baby.

Galda: What did you and Gilroy talk about when you picked him up?

Smith: I told Joe that I had messed up my pants when I got sick and had to throw them away.

Galda: Where did you throw them?

Smith: Just past the stone bridge on Pulis Avenue.

Galda: And what did you do with the shoes you were wearing that night?

Smith: I threw them away. The shoemaker said they weren't worth repairing. I threw them in a garbage can.

Galda: What shoemaker? And what garbage can?

Smith: The old guy in town. Nick something or other. Right in the middle of town. After going to the shoemaker, I went over to Robbie's Corral for a cup of coffee. Robbie has a side door going out to an alley. Behind his place there's a row of garbage cans. I walked back there after having coffee and dumped the shoes.

Galda: And how did you happen to get that scrape on the back of your index finger?

Smith: Oh, that's from an automobile tailpipe. It's nothing. I was putting on a new hanger, the thing the pipe hangs on, and the kid helping me shoved the pipe backward too soon. The end of the pipe scraped my finger.

. . .

At this point, Galda and Calissi conferred privately.

Galda spoke to Detective Captain DeMarco, and DeMarco approached Smith.

"Smith, you're going to take a ride," he said. "We want you to show us where you discarded your pants, and where you were sick. Do you mind?"

"Do I have a choice?" Smith asked.

"Nobody gets choices in murder cases," DeMarco said.

The rights to remain silent and to have a lawyer present for questioning would not be constitutionally guaranteed until Earl Warren's Supreme Court ruled on *Miranda v. Arizona* in 1966.

A Night Without Sleep

Three separate trips were taken to the areas where Edgar Smith claimed he had been sick and where he had discarded his pants. Nothing was found.

The shoes were discovered in a garbage can behind Robbie's Corral, with a spot of what appeared to be blood.

Back at the Municipal Building, Prosecutor Guy Calissi asked Smith to describe exactly what he was wearing on the night of the girl's disappearance.

"Well, I had on black shoes, work pants, gray pants, a black and red striped shirt, vertical stripes, and a dark-blue nylon jacket with a white fleece lining."

"Were you wearing gloves?"

"Yes, brown leather."

"Where are those clothes now?"

"You have the shoes, the pants were probably picked up by garbage men, the shirt and jacket are at my mother-in-law's, and the gloves are probably at home."

Calissi asked Detective Graber to go to the mother-in-law's and pick up the shirt and jacket, then go to the trailer to look for the gloves.

Calissi asked Smith if he would be willing to take a lie-detector test.

Smith said he didn't trust the prosecutor or the tests and wouldn't agree until he got advice from a lawyer.

An hour later, Galda ushered Smith into an office.

He pointed to a jacket lying on a desk

"Is that the jacket you wore Monday night?"

"That's it."

"The night Victoria Zielinski was murdered?"

"I don't know when she was murdered."

"You know it was Monday night, don't you?"

"I don't know anything."

"You're a liar. You were there and we know you were there," Galda said. Then he lifted the jacket, revealing a pair of leather gloves. "Are these your gloves?"

"Where did you get them?"

"Don't worry about that. Are they yours?"

"They're mine. You can see where the palms are blackened from the kerosene. So, what?"

"That's all we want to know. Now we want a sample of your hair. Captain DeMarco will pull out a few strands. Do you mind?"

"Do I have any choice?"

"I told you once tonight that you don't get choices," DeMarco said.

"I figured that, but I'll pull them out myself."

"No, you won't," DeMarco said, "I'll do it."

"We're going to Hackensack now," Galda said. "You'll ride with DeMarco. We have done all we can up here, we will all be much more comfortable and relaxed at the prosecutor's office."

When they had all arrived at the Bergen County Courthouse in Hackensack, DeMarco received a phone call.

"Good news, Smith," he said, "they found the pants."

"Where? In the garbage dump?"

"Nope. Along the back road to the sandpit. Right where you tried to hide them."

"You're out of your mind. They couldn't have been. I threw them on Pulis Avenue, and I wasn't trying to hide them."

"We'll see about that later."

DeMarco said he needed to talk to the prosecutor, and left

Smith in the care of Detective Charles DeLisle.

DeMarco told the suspect that when he returned, they would need to talk about the discarded pair of pants found near the sandpit.

Smith insisted they were not his.

DeLisle invited Smith to sit and offered him a cigarette.

The detective noticed Smith looking out of the window at the county jail across the way.

"Not a very pleasant view, is it?" Delisle said.

"Not much."

"Terrible place. I hope you never wind up in there. How long have you been awake?"

"What time is it?"

"Eight-forty."

"I don't know. I guess twenty-four hours or so."

"Well, maybe we can get this over quickly. It's up to you whether you cooperate or not."

"What does cooperate mean?"

"Why don't you begin by telling me your story?"

"Man, I've told you people my story half a dozen times. I'm tired of telling it, and I'm tired of hearing it."

"But I wasn't with you earlier. I haven't heard it. I'd like to help you get this over with, but I can't if I don't know what you told the others."

DeLisle was the *good cop*, gaining the suspect's trust.

Smith went through it again.

DeMarco returned with a photographer. During the overnight interview Smith had been asked to roll up his pant legs, and it was discovered that both his knees were scraped. He explained that he slipped and fell while he poured fuel into the tank at his trailer. Detective DeMarco asked the photographer to take pictures of Smith's knees and his scraped finger.

"What are the pictures for?" Smith asked.

"We merely want a record of your injuries to show that you had them before you came here. It's just a precaution, as much for your protection as ours."

When the photographer was done, DeMarco took Smith to the office of Assistant Prosecutor Galda.

Galda unwrapped a package that sat on his desk.

A pair of khaki trousers.

He spread the trousers on the desk. The right leg, just above the cuff, was heavily stained with blood.

"What about that?" Galda asked.

"What about what?"

"They're yours, aren't they?"

"The pants or the bloodstains?"

"The pants, goddammit. You know goddam well what I mean."

"Never saw them before in my life," Smith said, "they aren't mine."

Galda turned to DeMarco.

"Take him back. If he wants trouble, he came to the right place."

Smith kept insisting he needed to talk to his wife and to a lawyer.

DeMarco kept insisting he didn't need a lawyer.

He was left with DeLisle again.

DeMarco, following Galda's orders, left to pick up Smith's wife, Patricia, at her mother's home in Ridgewood to bring her to Hackensack.

Sometime later, Smith was taken to the prosecutor's office by Detective Walter Spahr. On the way, Smith spotted his wife in the corridor.

"What is my wife doing here?" he asked Spahr.

Spahr didn't answer.

Instead he pointed out a number of jars sitting on the prosecutor's desk.

"Do you know what that is in those jars?" Spahr asked.

"No, what are they?"

"The jars are your ticket to the electric chair if you don't co-operate. They are samples of dirt from various parts of the sandpit, from Chapel Road to the dirt mound. We checked your pants and shoes and recovered bits of sand and dirt that match those samples. Not only can we prove you were in the sandpit, but exactly in what parts you walked."

"What pants are you talking about," Smith said. "I've told you, the pants you people found were not mine."

"You must think we're stupid. Your wife wasn't brought down here for a tour of the courthouse. She has already identified your pants and is giving us a written statement."

Spahr brought Smith over to DeLisle and told him to stand there and not move a muscle.

Detective Walter Spahr was the *bad cop*.

DeLisle offered Smith a seat.

"He's a short-tempered guy, you'd better start cooperating before he really gets angry," DeLisle said, referring to Spahr. "Sit, it's alright."

Spahr reappeared.

"Who said you could sit, wiseguy?" he snapped at Smith.

"I told him he could sit, Walt, he's been up all night."

"Well, don't get too comfortable," Spahr said, and he walked off again.

"Smitty, that's what they call you, isn't it?" DeLisle said.

"Yes."

"Smitty, I don't know what you did or why, but I do know you were at the sandpit with the girl. We can prove it, and you know we can prove it. If you deny it, we will prove it and you will look bad for having lied. And the blood on your pants proves something happened to the girl while you were there. What, I don't know. Maybe just an accident—but something happened."

Smith was about to interrupt, but DeLisle put up his hand.

"No, let me finish, Smitty. Your wife is outside asking to see you. If you cooperate with us, we'll let you see her and she can go home. You have a little baby. Your wife should be home with the baby, not here answering questions *you* should be answering. But she can't leave until we get the answers. All you have to do is cooperate, that's all."

"How?"

"It's very simple. Just give us a statement. If there are some things that you don't want to say, you don't have to. You're a smart boy. You know you can say *I don't want to talk about that* or *I don't remember*."

"You've got to be kidding. You people are not looking for cooperation, you want a confession."

"No, not a confession. We don't want that. Just a statement. You won't even have to sign it. Think it over, I'll give you a few minutes."

"I'll think it over," Smith said.

They sat quietly for several minutes.

"Okay, I'll give you a statement," Smith finally said. "If I don't have to sign it and I can see my wife."

The Night Before

They began at approximately one in the afternoon of March 6, 1957.

In the room were First Assistant Prosecutor Fred Galda; Chief Harry Voss of the Ramsey Police; Chief Charles Smith of the Mahwah Police; Lewis Kalstad, member of the panels of jurors available for that term of the county court—who was there as an impartial observer; Detective Walter Spahr; Arthur Ehrenbeck, an official stenographic reporter for the county court; and Edgar Smith.

The Q&A was transcribed by Ehrenbeck for the record.

First Assistant Prosecutor Galda conducted the entire interrogation.

His superior, Prosecutor Guy Calissi, was not present.

Edgar Smith sat without counsel.

After questions dealing with age, marital status, place of residence, and activities prior to the borrowing of the vehicle, Galda proceeded.

> Galda: What automobile did you have at this time?
>
> Smith: Joseph Gilroy's Mercury. It's a light blue or aqua 1950 convertible.
>
> Galda: Then what happened?
>
> Smith: I went to Reinauer's service station. It's in Mahwah on Route 17. They didn't have

kerosene. I went down the road to Moore's Truck Stop.

Galda: Do you know the approximate time you got there?

Smith: I would say that it was twenty-five to eight, twenty to eight, somewhere around there. I got there and picked up the five gallons of fuel I needed. I went straight home. I went straight to my trailer, put the fuel in the tank, and tried to light the heater. It wouldn't light. I told my wife and mother-in-law I couldn't get it going and needed to get more kerosene. Then I went back to Ramsey, to Secor's, and I got five gallons of kerosene there. On the time on that, I don't know. I would say it was somewhere around twenty after eight, eight-thirty.

Galda: By the way, what clothes were you wearing then?

Smith: Gray khaki pants, black and red striped shirt, blue nylon jacket, white socks, black shoes.

Galda: And after you went to Secor's, what did you do?

Smith: I started back home. In the vicinity of Fardale Avenue, Mahwah, as I was riding along, I saw this girl walking.

Galda: Did you recognize her?

Smith: Yes, I recognized her. I knew her from meeting her in town.

Galda: Who was the girl?

Smith: Vickie Zielinski.

Galda: Vickie Zielinski?

Smith: Yes. I intended to keep on going. I don't recall whether she waved at me or yelled or said something. I pulled into a driveway down the road, turned around, came back, and stopped. She asked for a ride home.

Galda: What time was this approximately?

Smith: About twenty to nine. It was somewhere around that.

Galda: Did she get into the car?

Smith: Yes.

Galda: What happened after that?

Smith: I headed back toward her house on Wyckoff Avenue. Just before we reached her house, she said that her sister was coming to meet her. She didn't want her sister to see her riding in the car. She said she had gotten in trouble with her father for taking rides. She asked me go on and drive around. I turned up Crescent Avenue, went up to what I think is Young's Road, and down to Chapel Road. When I got down to Fardale Avenue, there's a sandpit there. I pulled to the end of the road and I lit a cigarette. Then suddenly, she said she was going to get out and walk home and she was going to tell her father I was just like the rest of the guys—or something like that. I didn't know what she meant. The first thing I thought was I couldn't let her walk home. I had to take her home. Then she started to get out of the car.

Galda: Was this in the sandpit?

Smith: This was in the sandpit. She opened the door and got halfway out. I reached across the seat and grabbed her arm or her jacket or something.

Galda: What clothing did she have on?

Smith: She had a heavy wool jacket of some kind. That's all I remember. I didn't notice her clothing at all.

Galda: Did she have anything over her hair?

Smith: I didn't notice. I really didn't notice at all.

Galda: When you held her arm, did she have gloves on?

Smith: I don't think she had gloves on. I wouldn't say for sure. I don't think so. I think I had hold of her wrist. I wanted to pull her back into the car and take her home. She was almost completely out. I worked my way over to the passenger's side of the front seat and tried to get out. I don't know what she said, but she started swinging at me and slapping at me.

Galda: Did that make you upset?

Smith: All I remember is letting go of her arm and I remember swinging with my right hand.

Galda: Did you hit her?

Smith: I don't know. I imagine she hit me. I'm not sure, but I didn't feel anything.

Galda: Did she get back into the car with you?

Smith: No. Then whatever happened in between is vague to me. I don't know exactly what it is.

Galda: What was the condition of the ground at the time?

Smith: Soft.

Galda: And did you have your shoes on?

Smith: Yes, I had my shoes on. The thing about the shoes is that I didn't lace them because I had hurt my ankle bowling in Paramus earlier.

Galda: Then what did you do?

Smith: Next thing I actually remember is getting back in the car.

Galda: Were you alone in the car?

Smith: Yes. I started to back the car out. I

couldn't see where I was going. I had to keep getting out of the car, looking to see where I was going. I finally backed the car out onto Chapel Road and turned south toward Pulis Avenue.

Galda: And then?

Smith: I went home. I only had one shoe on. I took off a pair of khaki pants and threw them out onto the patio. I asked my wife to bring me another pair.

At this point, Smith went over what had been heard before.

After failing to get the heater going, he called Joe Gilroy to ask for a ride to his mother-in-law's house in Ridgewood.

Smith told his wife he was going to pick up Joe.

Galda: Then what did you do?

Smith: I picked up the khaki pants with the blood on them.

Galda: Where were they at this time?

Smith: Lying outside on the patio.

Galda: Where were your shoes at the time?

Smith: One was in the trailer. I left it there. I got back into the car, went down Chapel Road, left the car parked there, and walked up into the sandpit with a lantern. At the end of the road I found my other shoe and I picked it up. And I saw a glove there, a red glove. I didn't think anything of it. In fact, I kicked the glove over to the side as I walked away.

After Smith once again went over the trip to pick up Joe Gilroy, the ride back to the trailer to pick up his wife and baby, and the drive to his mother-in-law's in Ridgewood, there was a short recess.

The Sandpit

When they resumed, Galda began with questions regarding the events from the time Joseph Gilroy dropped the Smith family off in Ridgewood into the next day.

The only thing investigators had not heard previously was Smith's claim that it wasn't until he first heard of Victoria's death, on Tuesday morning, that he recalled being with her the previous evening.

Then, Galda steered the questioning back to the sandpit.

> Galda: Ed, are these your pants?
>
> Smith: To the best of my knowledge, they are.
>
> Galda: I beg your pardon?
>
> Smith: They are. To the best of my knowledge.
>
> Galda: Look at them please. Are they your pants?
>
> Smith: They are.
>
> Galda: And did you throw these pants away?
>
> Smith: I don't know.
>
> Galda: Ed, did you wear these pants when you were in the sandpit?
>
> Smith: I did.
>
> Galda: Was Vickie bleeding at that time?
>
> Smith: I don't remember. I don't remember if she bled at all.

Galda: Now, you say you had on a blue jacket? Is this it?

Smith: Yes.

Galda: Is this the shirt you wore Monday night when you met Vickie?

Smith: Yes.

Galda: And is it the shirt you washed Tuesday morning?

Smith: Yes, I washed that with the jacket.

Galda: Ed, can you identify this undershirt?

Smith: It's mine.

Galda: Is it the undershirt you wore Monday evening?

Smith: I can't actually recall whether it is. I won't say definitely.

Galda: Now, what kind of socks did you have on that night?

Smith: White cotton.

Galda: Do you know what you did with the socks?

Smith: No.

Galda: No?

Smith: No. Somebody told me they were in the pocket of the pants.

Galda: Now, when Vickie got out of the car in the sandpit, did she leave her books in the car?

Smith: That I will have to guess. I would say yes.

Galda: Now, when you went back to the sandpit to look for your shoe, or whatever you went back for, you say you saw a glove?

Smith: Yes, in the same vicinity as the shoe.

Galda: Can you describe it?

Smith: It was a glove or a mitten. Something,

red wool that looked like a glove.

Galda: This appears to be a pair of gloves. I ask you whether or not these are the gloves you saw near your shoe at the sandpit.

Smith: That I don't know.

Galda: You say Vickie wore a heavy jacket?

Smith: Some type of heavy jacket is all I remember, but I don't recall exactly what it was.

Galda: Would you recognize it if you saw it?

Smith: Well, from association with her, I would recognize whether she owned the jacket but not whether she had it on or not.

Galda: Was it a solid-color jacket, if you know?

Smith: I don't know.

Galda: Isn't this the jacket she had?

Smith: I'm not sure.

Galda: What other clothes did she have on? A dress or pants?

Smith: I don't know. I think she had slacks of some kind.

Galda: Dungarees or jeans?

Smith: I don't recall. It was not a skirt or shorts.

Galda: Did she have anything on her head?

Smith: Not that I can recall.

Galda: When you struck her in the sandpit, did you use your fist?

Smith: As far as I know, the only thing I remember is swinging with my hand. I'm not sure if I hit her or not.

Galda: Did you struggle at all with her?

Smith: Not that I recall, other than struggling to keep her from leaving the car. Once we were out of the car, I just don't know.

Galda: Did you fall to the ground?

Smith: I'm not sure of that. I fell somewhere.

Galda: You fell somewhere. Did she fall?

Smith: I don't know.

Galda: Did you at any point run up the bank in the sandpit?

Smith: I don't recall.

Galda: Did you fall with your hands and knees on the bank?

Smith: I don't think so.

Galda: Is this the kerchief Victoria was wearing when you picked her up and went to the sandpit?

Smith: I don't recall if she was wearing one or not.

Galda: Do you recall what type of shoes she wore?

Smith: No.

Galda: Ed, I show you what appears to be a large rock. Will you examine it very carefully?

Smith: I don't recognize it.

Galda: Did you strike her with or throw any article at her?

Smith: I don't know.

Galda: You don't know?

Smith: I don't know at all. I don't know anything other than swinging with my hand.

Galda: Can you say what Victoria wore under her jacket?

Smith: No.

Galda: When you held her wrist, what did you do?

Smith: I tried to pull her back toward the car.

Galda: Do you recall which hand you held her with?

Smith: I think the left hand.

Galda: Your left hand?

Smith: No. I held her with my right, her left.

Galda: What, if anything, did you do with your hand?

Smith: Tried to get out of the car. I was trying to pull her in. I was off balance across the seat.

Galda: Was she able to get out of the car completely?

Smith: Yes.

Galda: Did you chase her at all?

Smith: No. I don't think I did.

Galda: Did you wear any gloves?

Smith: I have to say, I don't know. I had them in the jacket I wore. They were leather gloves. But whether or not I had the gloves on that night, I just don't remember.

Galda: I show you a left glove and ask can you identify it?

Smith: That's mine.

Galda: This appears to be a right glove. Can you identify it?

Smith: Mine.

Galda: When Vickie said she was going to tell her father—did that make you angry?

Smith: No. I didn't understand. I just thought that I should take her home because if she walked home from there, and said I left her there—or something like that—I wouldn't know what to do.

Galda: Why would she suggest to walk home?

Smith: I don't know.

Galda: Did she say *what* she would tell her father?

Smith: Just something like me being like the

rest of the guys or something like that. I don't
know.

Galda: Did you wash any clothing other than
what you showed us so far?

Smith: Definitely no.

Galda: When you grabbed Vickie by the
wrist, didn't she fight back?

Smith: As I recall, she was pretty well out of
the car.

Galda: Did she grab for your hair?

Smith: That I don't know. She was slapping. I
let go of her wrist then. She didn't make any
attempt to run, I don't think.

Galda: How many times did you swing at
her?

Smith: Once that I know of. I remember
swinging once. I don't remember if I hit her or
not.

Galda: And you don't know if you struck her
more than once?

Smith: No.

Galda: Did she grab your hair at any time?

Smith: I wish I could tell you. I can't.

Galda: When you went back to the sandpit
for a second time, to look for your shoe, didn't
you see Vickie there?

Smith: No, I didn't.

Galda: Did you look for her?

Smith: No. I didn't even think about it. I just
thought about my shoe.

Galda: When you saw the glove, did you
think anything about that?

Smith: No. I just gave the glove a glance and
kicked it as I walked past. All I remember is losing my shoe up there.

Galda: Did you look for anything else?

Smith: No, I didn't.

Galda: Did you go up on the bank?

Smith: No, I didn't. In fact, I didn't go all the way into the sandpit. I went to the edge of the road, where the car was parked the first time.

Galda: Did you leave the car out on the road?

Smith: Yes.

Galda: How long would you say you were in the pit with Vickie?

Smith: I want to think for just a second. I would have to take a guess. With the time in between there, I don't remember. It seems like a minute or two, but it had to be longer.

Galda: Why would it have to be longer? Did you argue any length of time?

Smith: Time doesn't coincide in there. I don't know.

Galda: Were you arguing for any length of time, Ed?

Smith: No. I hardly said anything. I was smoking a cigarette.

Galda: She said she would tell her father you were like the rest of the boys?

Smith: Something like that. She had been raving about school and cutting classes and being in trouble. I can't remember.

Galda: How many times did she hit you?

Smith: Two or three times.

Galda: How many times would you say you hit her?

Smith: I don't know if I actually did hit her. I swung at her, but I don't know.

Galda: Did you lift any heavy object at all while you were in the sandpit during this period?

Smith: I don't know.

Galda: Prior to this swinging, did you kiss her goodnight or anything?

Smith: No. I didn't even touch her.

Galda: Did you put your arms around her inside the car or outside?

Smith: No.

Galda: Didn't you try to kiss her?

Smith: No.

Galda: Did she try to kiss you, perhaps?

Smith: No. Not that I remember.

Galda: Did you feel any parts of her body?

Smith: No.

Galda: How do you account for all of the blood on your pants?

Smith: I can't account for it. It's just there.

Galda: Didn't you realize there was blood all over your pants when you got home?

Smith: I think I knew it was blood, but I don't know.

At this point, Smith was told he would be taken—with those present in the room—to all of the places he had indicated in his testimony.

It was approximately two in the afternoon.

Edgar Smith had been awake for nearly thirty hours and had been continually interrogated for fourteen hours.

They had the suspect retrace all of the ground he had covered—in and out of the vehicle—from the moment Victoria Zielinski first entered the car to the time Smith picked up Gilroy.

Later, at the Municipal Building in Mahwah, representatives of the press were granted the opportunity to take photographs of the suspect.

Then, told that he would be brought before a local magistrate and not a judge—that it was only a formality and he would not require a lawyer—Smith was escorted to a courtroom.

Arraignment and Indictment

Edgar Smith and Frank Young, the magistrate, knew each other.

They were both regulars at a local tavern.

"Hello, Smitty. Got yourself in a jam, didn't you?" Young said.

"Sort of."

"This will be over in a minute. I will read the complaint and ask you to plead. You don't have to answer since a plea of *not guilty* is mandatory and I'm required by law to record that plea and remand you to the county jail—without bail—for action by the grand jury. It's just a formality, to bring the complaint against you. No evidence will be heard or admitted. Do you understand that, Smitty?"

"I'm not pleading to anything, Frank. I'm not taking part in any legal stuff until my lawyer is here."

"Are you represented by counsel?"

"I want to get Judge Dwyer, from Ridgewood. You know him. These people have been telling me all day and all night that I don't need a lawyer. You're the judge, can't you postpone this until I get my lawyer up here?"

"Eddie, the county prosecutor wants to get on with this. He tells me you'll be permitted to speak with your lawyer as soon as it can be arranged. So, we are going to go ahead. A complete record of this proceeding will be available for your lawyer to examine. Now, just stand there, Smitty. You needn't say a word."

Young read the complaint prepared by Detective Spahr and signed by Chief Smith alleging that on or about March fourth, 1957, in the Township of Mahwah, State of New Jersey, Edgar Smith had willfully, feloniously, and with malice aforethought, killed and murdered one Victoria Zielinski.

"That's it Smitty," Young concluded. "I've entered a plea of not guilty for you. Now, the county prosecutor will take you back to Hackensack."

"What about my lawyer?"

"It's out of my jurisdiction, Smitty. It's a county court matter now."

It was five-thirty on the afternoon of March sixth.

At seven-fifteen, Edgar Smith was committed to the Bergen County jail on a charge of murder.

The United States Congress approved the *Eisenhower Doctrine* on March seventh.

On March eighth, Israeli troops withdrew from Egypt and the Suez Canal reopened.

At the same time, there were reports of an *Influenza A* sub-type H2N2 virus which was spreading throughout China and surrounding countries in Asia.

Great Britain was preparing to be the third nation to test detonate a nuclear bomb.

George Metesky was awaiting trial for his *mad bombings* while he was still undergoing psychiatric evaluations.

Suspects continued to be identified and interrogated in the search for the murderer of the Grimes sisters. However, there was never enough evidence to charge anyone with the crime—and parents in the Chicago area were keeping their children on a short leash.

All efforts to identify the *Boy in the Box,* discovered in Philadelphia, had failed.

12 Angry Men, directed by Sidney Lumet and filmed in three weeks, was scheduled for theatrical release.

Tab Hunter's *Young Love* nudged Elvis Presley off the top of the Billboard Charts—but only temporarily.

Meanwhile, Presley had his sights set on a property at 3734 Bellevue Boulevard in Memphis.

Later that year, the twenty-two-year-old superstar would purchase the fourteen-acre Graceland Farms property with its twenty-three-room mansion for $102,500.

Prosecutor Guy Calissi wasted no time setting the legal machinery in motion.

Two days after Edgar Smith was arraigned, Friday, March eighth, Calissi went before the grand jury.

After the testimony of just one witness, Detective Charles DeLisle, Calissi obtained the following indictment.

Indictment No. S-276-56
(Filed March 8, 1957)
Superior Court of New Jersey
Bergen County—Law Division
September Term A.D. 1956
Second Stated Session

The State of New Jersey
v.
Edgar Smith, Defendant

The Grand Jurors of the State of New Jersey, for the County of Bergen, upon their oaths present that EDGAR SMITH on or about the 4th day of March, 1957, in the Township of Mahwah, in the County of Bergen aforesaid, and within the jurisdiction of this court, did willfully, feloniously and of his malice aforethought kill and murder VICTORIA ZIELINSKI, contrary to the provision of N.J.S. 2A:113-1 and N.J.S. 2A:113-2 and against the peace of this State, the government, and dignity of the same.

Guy W. Calissi
County Prosecutor
William S. Davis
Foreman

Three days later, March 11, Smith was brought before Judge Arthur O'Dea of the Bergen County Court for arraignment on the indictment and to enter a formal plea.

Joseph Gaudielle, Smith's lawyer, entered a plea of not guilty.

The prosecutor was not letting up.

Calissi petitioned the court for the *constitutional right* of the defendant, and the *desire* of The People, to proceed without delay.

Guy Calissi would not allow the public emotions, inflamed by virulent publicity, to cool down.

Judge O'Dea scheduled the murder trial to begin in May.

April

In April, 1957, the Bergen County Prosecutor's Office led by Guy Calissi was preparing for the Edgar Smith murder trial.

In Iran, the Carrolls of Issaquah in Washington State were ambushed by desert bandits. Anita Carroll was kidnapped by the attackers, after they had killed her husband. Two weeks later, on the first of April, came the report of her death at the hands of her captors. At the time few Americans knew much about Iran, formerly Persia, beyond what was learned about Alexander the Great in world history class or from the popular film *Omar Khayyam* released that year.

On April fourth, 47-year-old Canadian historian and diplomat Egerton Herbert Norman jumped to his death from the roof of an 8-story building in Cairo. His career and his reputation had been damaged by unsubstantiated accusations of Communist affiliations and Soviet sympathies while he had served as a Canadian envoy in Washington D.C.

Leaders in Ottawa blamed American *red scare* paranoia and McCarthy Era witch-hunting tactics for Norman's suicide—straining diplomatic relations between the United States and Canada.

On Saturday, the thirteenth of April, due to a lack of funds, the United States Postal Service announced the suspension of delivery service across the country until no sooner than the following Monday.

The public was up-in-arms over the suspension—many

Americans had waited until the last minute to prepare their income tax forms and were now scrambling to get the paperwork posted to the Internal Revenue Service before the deadline.

Sidney Lumet's first theatrical movie, *12 Angry Men,* was released that weekend to rave reviews from critics. The movie did fairly well at the box office initially, but not for very long. Theater-goers appeared to be more drawn to epic extravaganzas in Technicolor and Cinerama—like *The Ten Commandments* and *Giant*—and by the end of the year the film had sold fewer tickets than *Peyton Place* and the third Elvis Presley movie, *Jailhouse Rock*. The black-and-white jury room drama did earn Academy Award nominations in the categories of Best Picture, Best Director, and Best Adapted Screenplay.

The Bridge on the River Kwai captured all three of those prizes.

On April 18, George Metesky was brought before Judge Samuel Liebowitz in a New York courtroom. A number of psychiatrists had conducted extensive evaluations. Metesky was designated paranoid schizophrenic. Liebowitz ruled Metesky *hopelessly incurable both mentally and physically*, legally insane and incompetent to stand trial. Metesky was expected to live for only a short time due to advanced tuberculous he claimed he had contracted as a result of the work-related accident 26 years earlier. Judge Liebowitz ultimately committed *The Mad Bomber* to the Matteawan State Hospital for the Criminally Insane.

In the middle of April, Dr. John Bodkin Adams was acquitted following a sensational murder trial at The Old Baily in London. Between 1946 and 1956, more than 160 of his patients had died in suspicious circumstances—132 had left the doctor money or other valuables in their wills.

The trial, specifically concerning the death of Mrs. Edith Morrell, took seventeen days—the longest murder trial in Britain up to that time—and had important legal ramifications. First, it established the doctrine of *double effect*, whereby a doctor giving treatment with the purpose of relieving pain may, as an unintentional result, shorten a life. Secondly, because of all the publicity surrounding Adams's committal hearing, the laws were reformed to allow defendants to ask for such hearings to be held in private. Finally, though a defendant had never been *required* to give evidence in his own defense, the judge under-lined in his summing-up that no prejudice should be attached to Adams for *not* doing so. The judge also stressed that *the act of murder needed to be proved by expert evidence.* Following forty-four minutes of deliberations, the jury found Adams not guilty of the murder charge.

On April 22, John Irwin Kennedy became the first African-American to take the field for the Philadelphia Phillies—the last team in the Major Leagues to integrate, ten years after Jackie Robinson had started his career with the Brooklyn Dodgers. Kennedy played a total of five big league games.

Throughout April, Americans were being constantly reminded of the Soviet Union's regular nuclear arms testing—rejuvenating the efforts of the House Un-American Activities Committee.

At the same time cases of the deadly flu, first identified in East Asia in February, began to appear in the west.

And Edgar Smith was informed that his murder trial was scheduled to begin on May thirteenth—just sixty-eight days after his arrest.

Selser

Attorney Joseph Gaudielle had represented Edgar Smith at both the arraignment and the indictment.

Following the indictment, Gaudielle met with Prosecutor Guy Calissi.

Gaudielle then reported to his client.

Calissi, who Gaudielle described as a *very reasonable and honest man,* had made an offer.

Gaudielle informed Smith that the prosecutor was prepared to accept a plea of guilty to second-degree murder—based on the assumption that this was an *unpremeditated* crime of passion.

Calissi would require, however, that Smith make that plea and render a full confession in open court.

Gaudielle assured his client that even with the imposition of a maximum sentence, Smith could be a free man in eight to ten years.

Gaudielle strongly urged Smith to accept the deal.

Smith adamantly refused to consider pleading guilty to something he did not do.

Two weeks later, Gaudielle visited Smith and informed him that he was withdrawing from the case.

John Selser then became Edgar Smith's attorney.

Gaudielle had bailed out before ever having asked Smith for his side of the story.

Selser, on the other hand, wanted to hear it all.

The attorney asked his client to be very specific about the events from the time when Victoria Zielinski entered the car—up until the time Smith last saw the girl alive.

Over several meetings in April, Smith related his account of events to his new counsellor.

According to Smith he was driving home—after picking up kerosene at Secor's—when he saw Victoria Zielinski on Wyckoff Avenue.

She waved at the car as he passed.

Smith turned around, went back to her, and he stopped. She opened the passenger door and asked for a ride home. Smith said he had given Vickie rides before. She got into the car at about 8:45 that evening, March fourth.

They headed toward her house. She told Smith her sister was coming to meet her, and she didn't want Myrna to see her in the car. When they reached West Crescent, just before her house, Victoria asked Smith to go around the block—back around toward Fardale.

Vickie said she wanted to tell Smith something and so, to get out of the road, Smith pulled into the dirt drive to the sandpit.

Smith pulled into the end of the road and stopped the car.

Vickie was talking about problems at school.

Then, out of the blue, she told him she had heard rumors that Smith's wife had been *playing around* with one of his friends.

He told her it was ridiculous, but she persisted—suggesting his wife was a cheat.

Smith became angry, slapped Vickie, and told her to get out and walk home. She jumped out of the car and ran toward Fardale, and Smith started to leave. He was trying to decide whether to let her go or to apologize and get her safely home. He was having trouble seeing the road as he backed out, and he opened the door so he could lean out to see.

Then he heard a commotion coming from where Vickie had run.

A girl and a man, arguing.

Smith stopped the car and jumped out, losing a shoe. He saw two people coming toward him on the dirt road—and saw a car on Chapel. As they came closer, he recognized Vickie with a man who was holding her arm.

Smith heard Vickie say, "Let me go. Let go of me."

He said he didn't know what to do and instinctively grabbed a baseball bat from the back seat. He walked around to the back of the car and, as they came closer, Smith recognized that the man with Vickie was Donnie Hommell.

Hommell appeared as mad as hell. Vickie was crying.

Hommell said she had fallen and hit her head.

Victoria was bleeding.

She asked Smith to drive her home. Smith told Vickie to get into the car—he would take her to a doctor.

Vickie got into the car and then Hommell grabbed her by the jacket and was trying to pull her out.

She fell on the ground on her side, her legs still in the car, and grabbed Smith around the legs. Her blood got onto his pants. She was hysterical, telling Smith to make Hommell leave her alone. Smith was trying to get her on her feet, and Hommell was pushing Smith away. Hommell finally calmed down.

Smith got Vickie to her feet and tried to calm *her* down.

Hommell said he would take care of her. Smith considered Don her boyfriend. He decided she would be alright and he left.

Smith said he had dropped the bat when he saw Hommell and forgot about it until he was nearly home.

When he arrived home, he changed pants and managed to get the heater going with the kerosene he had picked up. It was still cold in the trailer and his wife wanted to go to her mother's house, so Smith called Joe Gilroy to ask for a ride to Ridgewood.

Smith left to pick up Gilroy, taking the blood-stained pants with him. He stopped back at the sandpit. Hommell and Vickie were gone. He found his shoe but didn't find the baseball bat.

On his way to Gilroy's house he threw the pants out of the window.

When he was passing through Ramsey, he saw Donnie Hommell sitting in his car in front of the bank across from Tony's Amoco garage and he stopped to ask about Vickie.

Hommell said Smith should keep his mouth shut about Vickie—that if Smith said anything about what had happened, Hommell would take it out on Smith's wife and baby.

Smith continued on his way to pick up Joe Gilroy.

He said he didn't take Hommell's threat seriously until he heard about Vickie's death the following day.

Selser met with Calissi.

He related Smith's account to the prosecutor, including Hommell's threat to Smith's family.

Selser maintained that Donnie Hommell needed to be looked at seriously before Edgar Smith could be brought to trial.

Calissi would not buy any of it.

He told Selser they had two choices.

Smith could choose to accept the prosecution's offer, a plea of second-degree murder—including an open confession.

Or choose to face a jury in May.

Victoria Zielinski (left). Victoria and her young sister Myra. They planned to meet halfway between the Nixon and Zielinski homes the night Victoria went missing.

Police from Mahwah and Ramsey, and the Bergen County Prosecutors' Office arrive at the sandpit on the morning of March 5, 1957, after the body was discovered by Victoria's parents.

VICTORIA ANN
SEPT. 6, 1941
MARCH 4, 1957
DAUGHTER OF
ANTHONY & MARY ZIELINSKI

Only 28 miles and just an hour from Manhattan, Ramsey and Mahwah were small, friendly villages in the fifties. A brutal crime like the murder of Victoria Zielinski was rare, and instilled outrage and fear in the communities.

Spots of blood on the seat of Joe Gilroy's Mercury convertible led police to Edgar Smith as a suspect. Smith had borrowed the vehicle on the night Victoria was killed.

Smith was picked up on the following night, March 5, and taken to Mahwah Police Headquarters for questioning.

Smith arrives at the Mahwah police station just before midnight on the fifth and is interviewed through the night. Prosecutors Fred Galda (left) and Guy Calissi escort Smith to the scene asking to be shown the areas where he claimed to have left the vehicle and gotten sick, and where he had discarded his pants. At that time, Smith had not admitted being with Victoria at the sandpit.

Galda would conduct the Q&A that would be known as the "statement" and entered into evidence as a confession of guilt.

Calissi would be the lead prosecutor for the State at the murder trial.

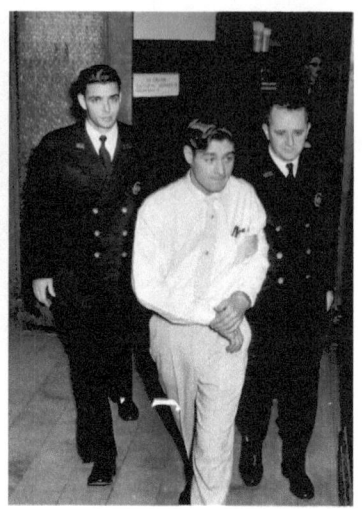

Police display bloodied pants later confirmed to have been worn and discarded by Smith. The suspect escorted to his arraignment the afternoon of March 6, after twenty hours in custody.

Photographs of Smith for police records taken March 7.

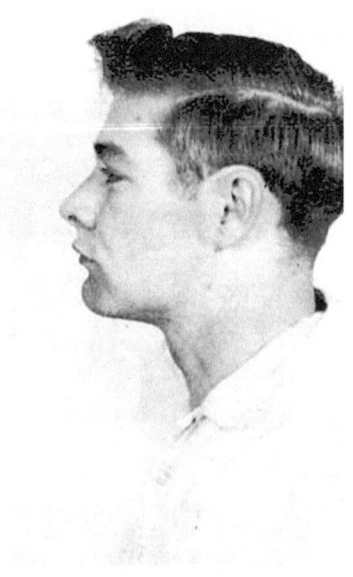

Trial and Error
May 1957 to June 1957

*Guilt always hurries towards its complement, punishment—
only there does its satisfaction lie.*
—Lawrence Durrell

*I have no better way of judging innocence
or guilt than anyone else.*
—Robert Shapiro,
O.J. Simpson Murder Trial Defense Attorney

*Ei incumbit probatio qui dicit, non qui negat.
(Proof lies on him who asserts, not on him who denies.)*
—Julius Paulus Prudentissimus

May

The world did not stand still while Prosecutor Guy Calissi and Defense Attorney John Selser prepared their cases.

On May 2, Mob boss Frank 'The Prime Minister' Costello was shot in the lobby of his apartment building. The assassination attempt, ordered by rival boss Vito Genovese and carried out by Vincent 'The Chin' Gigante, failed to end Costello's life—but did inspire Costello, who now saw himself as a *marked man,* to hand over most of his operations to Genovese.

That same day, Senator Joseph McCarthy, forty-eight-years old, died of hepatitis at Bethesda Naval Hospital—but his ghost would haunt the corridors of the Capitol for years to come.

Four days later, the *I Love Lucy* television program ended its run after six years and 180 episodes.

That same day a little-known Senator, John Fitzgerald Kennedy, was awarded a Pulitzer Prize for his book *Profiles in Courage.*

On the eighth of May, South Vietnam President Ngô Đình Diệm was met at the airport in Washington by President Eisenhower and John Foster Dulles.

The following afternoon, Diệm addressed the United States Congress and he received a standing ovation.

On the 12th, he was honored with a ticker-tape parade in New York City where Mayor Robert Wagner called Diệm *a man who history may yet adjudge as one of the great figures of the twentieth century.*

Later that month, the number of United States military personnel in South Vietnam was increased to seven-hundred-thirty-six.

On the 15th, Reverend Billy Graham began his Crusade before eighteen thousand in attendance at Madison Square Garden. The following day, Graham publicly sent out his prayers for a seven-year-old boy trapped in a well in Long Island.

Also, on the fifteenth, Britain test detonated its first hydrogen bomb.

On the 16th of May, Mickey Mantle, Yogi Berra, Hank Bauer, Whitey Ford, and others took Billy Martin to the Copacabana nightclub in Manhattan to celebrate Martin's 29th birthday. Sammy Davis Jr was the headliner. When another group of men began to heckle Davis and direct racial remarks at the entertainer, the Yankees stepped in to defend Sammy.

A fight ensued between the two groups of men which would come to be known as the *Copacabana Incident*. Although charges against the ballplayers were dropped, Yankee General Manager George Weiss—who had been looking for any excuse to get rid of what he saw as a *bad influence* in the clubhouse—traded Billy Martin to the Kansas City Athletics.

That month, at McKinley Park in Chicago, Lorretta Grimes received an anonymous telephone call from a man who claimed to have undressed and killed her two daughters.

Although the Grimes' family had received numerous hoax phone calls following the girls' disappearance, this man ended his call with information suggesting he may have truly been the perpetrator. *I know something about your little girl no one else knows. The smallest girl's toes were crossed at the feet.*

The caller then laughed before terminating the phone call.

On the twenty-eighth, as the closing arguments were being presented at the Edgar Smith murder trial, the National League approved the relocation of the Brooklyn Dodgers and the New York Giants to the west coast.

Calissi

Jury selection for the murder trial of Edgar Smith began on May 13, 1957.

The jurors would be selected from a pool of Bergen County residents—despite the legitimate concerns of the defense that the extensive publicity concerning the case could prove to be prejudicial.

Newspaper coverage during the two months between the arrest and the trial in the *Ramsey Journal, Herald News, Bergen Evening Record, Ridgewood News, Newark Star Ledger, New York Daily News, New York Post* and *New York Herald-Tribune* was damning, featuring sensational headlines—such as SMITH SAYS CAN'T REMEMBER KILLING RAMSEY GIRL and ADMITS HE PUNCHED SCHOOL GIRL, KNEW THE VICTIM, SAYS SHE RESISTED ADVANCES.

Twelve jurors and two alternative jurors were eventually selected, most of whom admitted to having read about the horrible crime as recently as the day before reporting for duty.

The trial would be held in Room 326 of the Bergen County Superior Court in Hackensack, New Jersey—which was the largest room available.

The room could accommodate 500 people, with spectators both sitting and standing on the main floor and on a horseshoe-shaped balcony.

The courtroom was filled to maximum capacity every day of the trial.

In his opening statement to the jury, Prosecutor Guy Calissi made it abundantly clear he intended to prove—*beyond any reasonable doubt*—the defendant was guilty of first-degree murder and he would be asking for the maximum penalty.

Death by electrocution.

Considering Edgar Smith's testimony during his 14-hour interrogation two months earlier, much of Calissi's description of the events of March 4th—as he described them in his opening statement—was suppositional.

> May it please the Court, ladies and gentlemen of the jury.
>
> From the evidence the State will show that the victim, Victoria Zielinski, was a fifteen-year-old schoolgirl.
>
> Victoria left the Barbara Nixon house at 8:30.
>
> Smith passed her going in the opposite direction. He pulled down a short distance, backed into a driveway, came back and picked her up. Smith turned onto Crescent Avenue, Young Road, down to what is called the sandpit.
>
> He went right into the sandpit.
>
> They talked.
>
> Victoria talked about school but the defendant, Edgar Smith, did not have school problems on his mind.
>
> He molested this girl immediately.
>
> He ripped up her sweater and fondled her breast, this fifteen-year-old girl.
>
> She refused his advances and she tried to get out of the car.
>
> He grabbed her, but she still released herself and started running.
>
> He ran after her. He finally caught up with her down on Fardale Avenue and he struck her

with a blunt instrument, which we will offer into evidence, and which the defendant at that point tried to discard and hide.

He got her back into the sandpit.

He wanted to silence this girl, for while he was trying to molest her in the car she said, *You are like all the other men. I am going to tell my father.*

He was afraid of being exposed, and this man had to silence this girl.

She ran from him, refusing his sexual advances.

He got her back in the sandpit and crushed her head with a very heavy implement.

Her brains were scattered on the sand.

In the sandpit he took that body, that mutilated body, he took it to the top of a knoll and dumped it.

We will prove that this murder was intentional, willful, premeditated murder, a murder in the course of attempting to have sexual relations with this girl, Victoria Zielinski, a fifteen-year-old schoolgirl.

We will show that it was premeditated, that he intended to kill her, to silence this girl.

We will show you that this was a brutal, a savage, a sadistic killing.

If we produce the evidence then I will ask this jury to render a verdict of guilty of murder in the first degree without a recommendation of mercy.

Thank you.

Opening remarks by defense attorney John Selser stated in great detail Smith's own account of events—which was quite different from Guy Calissi's hypothetical reconstruction.

Selser's presentation was three times as long as that of the prosecutor and it was evident the jury was getting impatient for the testimony to begin.

Prosecutor Guy Calissi's first witness was Myrna Zielinski, the victim's younger sister.

Witnesses for the Prosecution

On Wednesday, May 15, Guy Calissi began his questioning—leading Myrna Zielinski through the evening of March fourth.

The last time she had seen her sister, Victoria, alive.

Myrna recounted walking Vickie halfway to the Nixon home at around 7:30, returning home, and then leaving her house again an hour or so later to meet her sister who would be returning around that time. When she didn't cross paths with Victoria along the way, Myrna continued on to the Nixon's house and was told her sister had already left.

It was at this point that the girl introduced the name of a young man who would figure markedly in the story of Edgar Smith throughout the trial—and for years to come.

> Calissi: What time did you get to the Nixon house?
>
> Myrna: About ten of nine.
>
> Calissi: Then what did you do?
>
> Myrna: Then I left her house and walked back home.
>
> Calissi: Did you see anybody in an automobile?
>
> Myrna: Yes, I did.
>
> Calissi: Who did you see?
>
> Myrna: I saw Don Hommell. I was four houses from home when I saw Don.

Calissi: And which way was Don going?
Myrna: Going toward Ramsey.
Calissi: Going slow or fast?
Myrna: He was going very fast.
Calissi: Do you know approximately what time it was when you saw Don Hommell?
Myrna: Between five and ten after nine.

Calissi then brought out, piece by piece, Victoria's blood-soaked clothing for the thirteen-year-old witness to identify.

By the time Calissi finished with Myrna, eliciting tears and requiring rests for her to regain her composure, the girl had identified Victoria's black loafers, white socks, cardigan sweater, blue jeans, and book bag.

Selser's cross-examination centered on the question of Donald Hommell.

Selser: Do you know Don Hommell?
Myrna: Yes.
Selser: You knew that Don was friendly with your sister, Vickie, didn't you?
Myrna: She knew him.
Selser: Had he come to the house for Vickie at any time?
Myrna: He never came. He never took her out.
Selser: He never did?
Myrna: No.
Selser: Now, did I understand you to say that Hommell was driving very fast?
Myrna: Yes, he was driving very fast.
Selser: How fast would you say he was going?
Myrna: About maybe sixty or so.

Selser: What kind of car was Don driving?

Myrna: A Ford.

Selser: A two-tone green Ford?

Myrna: Yes.

Selser: That is all, Myrna. Thank you very much.

The State's next witness was Barbara Nixon, who was asked to establish a timeline of Vickie's arrival and departure, and also asked to identify Victoria's clothing.

Following Calissi questions, Selser cross-examined the witness.

Selser: How do you know exactly when Victoria left your house?

Nixon: Well, she said she had to meet her sister, start meeting her sister, at eight-thirty, and so she left my house around eight-thirty.

Selser: Well, did you look at a clock to see if it was eight-thirty?

Nixon: I don't remember.

Selser: You said you had been listening, I think you said, to the radio, or was it television?

Nixon: Radio.

Selser: Radio. Was there a change of program?

Nixon: I don't remember.

Selser: The only reason then you say eight-thirty is because she said that was the time she wanted to leave?

Nixon: Yes.

Selser: You really don't know if it was that time or not, do you, Barbara?

Nixon: No.

Selser: Was there a clock in the room?

Nixon: Yes.
Selser: You didn't look at it at all?
Nixon: I don't remember.

Mary Zielinski, Victoria's mother, was called next by the prosecution.

Her recollection of her experience at the sandpit was vivid and emotional.

"When did you see Victoria after you had seen her when she left at seven-thirty to go to Barbara Nixon's?" Calissi asked.

"At the sandpit. When she was murdered."

"What did you do when you saw your daughter at the sandpit?"

"What would any mother do?"

At this point, Mary Zielinski broke down and Judge O'Dea called a recess to give the woman time to compose herself.

"Did you go up to the sandpit to make any identification?" Calissi asked when he continued questioning Victoria's mother.

"I did. I went up there."

"What did you see?"

"I saw her red gloves, and a couple of feet away I saw her locket broken, and I saw—it was horrible—I saw her brains scattered on the ground. Then I looked over at my husband and he said, *there she is.*"

"Did you recognize Victoria?"

"I would anyplace. Her campus jacket was not on her, it was alongside her, and her bra was off, but it was hanging down. Her breast was exposed."

"Where was the brassiere on her body, Mrs. Zielinski?"

"Down around her midsection and her sweater was up around her neck."

"I show you a brassiere and ask you if you can identify it."

"That is Victoria's."

"Can you estimate how far from the dirt mound you saw the brains?"

Selser objected to the manner in which the question had been phrased, but Judge O'Dea said he would allow it.

Mrs. Zielinski was unable to estimate the distance.

Calissi then had her identify all of the clothing her daughter had been wearing the night she disappeared.

When Selser was offered the opportunity to cross-examine the witness, he informed the judge that he had no questions.

Calissi's next witness was Anthony Zielinski.

He recounted his activities on the night of his daughter's disappearance, and his discoveries the following morning before and after Captain Wickham had arrived at the scene—with very little of critical value to add to his wife's testimony. He did refer to a map of the area, furnished by the prosecution, to point out specific locations.

Selser had only two questions for the witness.

"You said that the shoe on Fardale, according to your estimate, was about one-hundred-twenty feet from Chapel?"

"Well, approximately, yes."

"And I think you said the scarf or babushka was about twenty feet further away from Chapel."

"In that radius."

"That is all I wanted to straighten out, sir, thank you."

The next witness called was Captain Wickham of the Mahwah police.

Led by the prosecutor, he described how he had been called to meet Vickie's parents at the intersection of Fardale Avenue and Chapel Road.

"I met Mr. and Mrs. Zielinski. They pointed out a scarf and a loafer which was on the side of the road on Fardale Avenue."

"As a result?"

"As a result, on top of the mound of dirt, we found the body of the girl. It was on the north side, down an embankment, about six foot."

"What was the position of the body?"

"The body was in a semi-crouch, mostly on the back, with

the legs up toward the stomach. The clothing had been pulled up over the shoulders, and it had blue dungarees on, no shoes, and white socks."

"Did you notice anything else in the sandpit at the time?"

"Yes. On the way in we noticed, I noticed, tire marks."

Calissi did not pursue that line.

"Anything else?"

"I observed a large rock with a large amount of blood on it, which was partially up on top of the bank, and up on top, also near the rock was a large clump of blood and a white substance which looked like brains to me. The body of the dead girl had a large hole in the head. The whole skull was missing."

"What did you observe about the clothing?"

"The clothing had been pulled up over the shoulders, leaving the middle section of the body bare, and the brassiere was down around the waist."

The remainder of the day was consumed by the identification by Captain Wickham of dozens of photographs of the scene. One by one, the photographs were admitted into evidence.

At four in the afternoon, Judge O'Dea called an adjournment—and he scheduled the proceedings to resume at nine-thirty the following morning.

Thursday

The testimony resumed on May 16th, with Captain Wickham identifying additional photos from the scene at the sandpit—which were then logged in as evidence.

Calissi continued his questioning—asking Wickham if he had seen Edgar Smith at any time on the fifth of March.

It was the first time Smith's name had been mentioned in the courtroom.

Wickham recounted the searches for Smith's discarded pants, and for the locations where Smith claimed he had been ill.

He testified that no pants were found at the time, and no evidence found to confirm that Smith had thrown up at the scene.

When Selser finally cross-examined the witness, he directed Wickham's attention to the tire tracks found at the sandpit.

> "Where exactly did you see the tracks?"
>
> "They were on the driveway, and beyond the driveway, both."
>
> "How far beyond the driveway?"
>
> "Approximately fifty feet, I would judge, or better."
>
> "Running in what direction?"
>
> "Running in a westerly direction."
>
> "How close would you say the nearest blood was that you noticed, to any of the tire tracks?"
>
> "About twenty-five feet."

"Was any blood found between Fardale Avenue and the sandpit area, including the dirt driveway?"

"None that I noticed."

"No more questions. Thank you."

The next three witnesses had been responsible for taking and processing the crime scene photographs. They talked about the technical aspects of their work.

Then, out of sight of the jury, Calissi showed another set of photographs to the judge.

These were copies of the original black-and-white photos of the body at the sandpit that had been enlarged and had been colorized by the Technicolor Corporation in Princeton, New Jersey.

The rendered photos were gruesome, the blood bright red.

Selser objected to their introduction into evidence on the grounds they were inflammatory.

Selser's objection was overruled by O'Dea, and the photographs were admitted and shown to the jury.

Following Wickham's testimony, the prosecutor called Howard Sneider, the mortician who had removed the body from the sandpit to the funeral chapel where the autopsy had been performed.

Once again, the victim's clothing was brought before the jury.

County Detectives James Stewart and Russell Ridgeway—who had supervised the collection of evidence at the scene and could describe the method in which it was handled—were later brought to the witness stand.

At four, Judge O'Dea adjourned the proceedings.

The trial would resume the next morning.

Scheduled to appear on the stand Friday was a witness whose testimony Calissi expected would be of significant benefit to the prosecution's case.

Gilroy

Day three of testimony began on Friday morning.

It was the seventeenth day of May, 1957.

The jury had heard a great deal about Victoria Zielinski, the last hour or so of her life, and her condition when she was discovered.

Now, they would finally be hearing something about the man accused of ending Victoria's life and dumping her battered body at the sandpit.

Joe Gilroy swore to tell the truth, the whole truth, and nothing but the truth.

Prosecutor Calissi began with questions about the evening of March 4th.

Gilroy told of loaning his 1950 Mercury convertible to his good friend, Eddie Smith.

Smith had taken the car at approximately seven that evening.

Later, Smith called Gilroy and asked if Joe could drive him, his wife, and baby to his mother-in-law's home in Ridgewood.

> Calissi: Approximately what time was that call?
> Gilroy: Approximately ten or fifteen minutes after nine.
> Calissi: Then what happened?
> Gilroy: Eddie came to pick me up at my house.
> Calissi: What time did he pick you up?
> Gilroy: About a quarter of ten.

Calissi: And then?

Gilroy: We drove back to his trailer to pick up his wife and baby.

Calissi: From your home to the trailer, did you and Eddie Smith have a conversation?

Gilroy: Yes. Well, he told me he was sick, and he threw up on his pants, and he had to throw them away. We picked up his wife and baby and I dropped them off in Ridgewood.

Calissi: You took your car then?

Gilroy: Yes, sir.

Calissi: Would you describe the interior of your car to us?

Gilroy: I have blue seat covers and, in the back, there was a whole mess of stuff. There were a couple of baseball mitts, a couple of baseball bats, and a lot of junk was back there.

Calissi: What time did you arrive in Ridgewood?

Gilroy: Oh, about a quarter after ten.

Calissi: When did you hear from Smith again?

Gilroy: The next day. Oh, around noon. He called asking for a ride back to his trailer. Donnie and I went out to pick them up with Donnie's car.

Calissi: Donald Hommell?

Gilroy: Yes.

Calissi: What happened when you arrived?

Gilroy: Donnie told Eddie that police were looking for a Mercury.

Calissi: Did Smith react in any way?

Gilroy: He had a startled look on his face. Then, he brought his wife and baby out. They got into the back seat and we started toward Ramsey.

Calissi: On the way to Ramsey, did you have any conversation with Smith?

Gilroy: Well, I don't remember, but Eddie or his wife picked up a lipstick from the floor in back. I don't know which one it was, and they handed it up to Donnie.

According to Gilroy, when they arrived at the trailer Smith said that he wanted to go with Joe and Don to Ramsey. He walked his wife and baby into the trailer and then he came back to the car carrying an old pair of shoes.

In Ramsey, Gilroy and Eddie were separated for a short time.

"Eddie had the shoes when we got to town, and then he didn't have them," Gilroy testified. "I started to suspect him. I wasn't sure. I couldn't believe it."

Calissi turned next to items in Gilroy's vehicle.

Calissi: I show you S-68 for identification, Mr. Gilroy, and ask whether you can identify it.

Gilroy: That's the brown baseball bat that was in the back of my car.

Calissi: What about the other bat?

Gilroy: It was a white bat.

Calissi then produced a second baseball bat, one that was wrapped in paper.

Calissi: I show you S-69 for identification and ask whether you can identify it.

Gilroy: That is the other bat I think was in the car.

Calissi: You think?

Gilroy: That was the other bat that was in the car.

Calissi: Is this the condition the bat was in on

the night or day of March fourth?

Gilroy: I couldn't be sure of that. I see it's cracked. We might have cracked it playing ball. I don't know.

Calissi: What about the color of the bat?

Gilroy: It wasn't dirty like that. It was white.

Calissi: Fine. You may cross-examine, Mr. Selser.

Selser: Now, while you were bowling at the Paramus Bowling Alleys on the afternoon of March fourth, did anything happen to Ed's foot or leg?

Gilroy: When he was bowling, he crossed the ball over and hit his ankle with the bowling ball.

Selser: Was the skin broken at the point where he hit the ankle?

Gilroy: Yes, it was cut a little.

Selser: Now, you said that when you and Don Hommell arrived in Ridgewood to pick up the Smith family, Don said something to Eddie about the police looking for a Mercury. Had you told Donnie Hommell that you had loaned Eddie your Mercury?

Gilroy: Well, I don't know how Don knew, but, no I didn't. I don't think so.

Selser: Now, when you got to Ridgewood, do you remember Don saying anything else to Ed? When he saw Ed?

Gilroy: He said, *Did you hear about the murder?* That's what Hommell said to Eddie.

Selser: Hommell said it?

Gilroy: Yes.

Selser: And didn't Ed say at that time, *Was that Vickie?*

Gilroy: Well, I think so.

Selser: What?

Gilroy: Yes.

Selser: Now, this lipstick that was found in the automobile. Didn't Hommell then say, *It looks like Vickie's.*

Gilroy: No, sir.

Selser: Did Hommell take the lipstick into his hand?

Gilroy: Yes, sir. Donnie said *maybe* it was Vickie's.

Selser: He said maybe *what*?

Gilroy: He said, *Maybe it was Vickie's.* He threw it out the window.

Selser: When did you first examine the back seat of your car, to see whether or not the baseball bats and the other items were still there?

Gilroy: I didn't examine the back seat of my car.

Selser: Do you know whether they were or were not still in your car when you left the car at Tony's garage for the police?

Gilroy: I presume they were in the back seat of my car.

After a series of questions asked primary to clarify points of previous testimony, Selser excused the witness.

Calissi called up three more witnesses that morning.

William Hoehne, an attendant at Secor's Service Station, testified that Edgar Smith had been there on the night of March fourth and had purchased kerosene—departing around eight-thirty.

Gloria Kanreck testified that, on the evening of March

fourth, she had stepped off a bus on the highway in front of Secor's, had entered Secor's, and she had seen Smith leave with a fuel can at around eight-thirty.

Detective George O'Har stated that on March 8th, at about three-thirty in the afternoon, he had gone to the intersection of Fardale Avenue and Chapel Road. O'Har said he had been assigned to search the area. During the search, O'Har discovered a white baseball bat, later designated State's Exhibit S-69.

Then, Judge O'Dea called the recess for lunch.

The afternoon session began with the testimony of Gordon Graber.

Detective Graber was able to provide accounts, in detail, of trips he, First Assistant Prosecutor Galda, and Captain DeMarco had taken with Smith in the very early hours of March sixth.

> Graber: First, we went to Mechanic Street in Ramsey, where Mr. Smith showed us the garbage can where he had put his pair of black shoes.
> Calissi: And did you find the shoes?
> Graber: Yes, a pair of black Oxford shoes.
> Calissi: Then, what did you do next, Detective?
> Graber: From that point, we proceeded to the crime scene where Mr. Smith was going to show us where he had gotten sick. He told us he had left the car and thrown up at that particular point. We searched that spot and found no evidence of anyone throwing up there. We walked back to the gravel pit and Mr. Galda shone a light over to the knoll and he asked Mr. Smith if he knew what was over there. Mr. Smith said he had never been over there in that section at all.

Calissi: In addition to searching the sandpit, did you make any other discoveries or searches?

Graber: He told us he had thrown his pants away. At a little bridge along Pulis Avenue. We could not find his pants.

Graber then testified that he had taken a second trip back to the sandpit some hours later that morning with Smith, Galda and Calissi.

Calissi: Did Smith point out the exact place where he had driven into the pit?

Graber: Yes. He did.

Calissi: While Smith was in the sandpit, and in your presence, did he say what had occurred and what had happened?

Graber: Yes. He told us he had driven Victoria Zielinski back into the sandpit, and that she had slapped his face. She then jumped out of the car, and he said he fell out of the right side of the car.

Calissi: And from the sandpit, where did you go with Smith?

Graber: South on Chapel Road, about 350 feet.

Calissi: And did you discover anything there?

Graber: We looked over in the field and discovered a handbag and some school books.

Calissi: Was there any conversation pertaining to the number of times Smith was at the sandpit?

Graber: Yes, sir. He said he went to the trailer court and changed his pants, and then he returned with a flashlight to search for his missing shoe.

Calissi: You may cross-examine, Mr. Selser.

. . .

Selser's cross-examination was brief and unremarkable.

Calissi then called for the State's next witness, with only twenty-five minutes remaining in the session.

At which point, Selser made a plea to Judge O'Dea.

"May I respectfully ask the Court whether or not it can find it within reasonable convenience to recess now? Frankly, sir, I am anticipating an extensive cross-examination of the following witness and would much rather his examination not be broken into parts. And very honestly, I'm exhausted and should so much be grateful to the Court were we at this time allowed to recess."

O'Dea was at first resistant, but he relented and granted adjournment.

The trial would resume at nine-thirty Monday morning, at which time Calissi would call his next witness.

The first week of the Edgar Smith murder trial received a remarkable amount of media coverage throughout New Jersey and the New York City metropolitan area.

But, that weekend, a seven-year-old boy named Benny Hooper captured the headlines.

Seventy-five miles from the courthouse, sprinting across a field in Manorville, Long Island while at play with friends, the boy fell into a pit.

A dry well, 21-feet deep and one foot wide.

Benny was trapped below, wedged in the narrow space, sand falling down on him, his feet soaked in a foot of water.

His father put down a shovel with rope, but the boy could not hold on.

Soon Benny was no longer answering to calls from above.

Responders decided they could not dig straight down without the sides collapsing and smothering the boy. Instead they dug a parallel pit several feet away. They would then begin digging a horizontal tunnel in an attempt to reach him.

No one was sure if they could get to Benny in time.

The boy's doctor declared that it was *improbable* Benny was still alive, newspapers reported no sign of life from below, and at around 12:30 on the afternoon of the 17th a priest administered last rites near the well.

Just before eight, Friday night, one of the rescue workers clawed his way through and pulled the boy out.

Benny Hooper was still breathing.

At a time when they were few and far between, the press had a feel-good story to report.

A good old-fashioned happy ending.

That weekend Benny Hooper's parents, and many others, may have been celebrating what was being called a *miracle*.

Edgar Smith, in his jail cell, may have been wondering when he would next see *his* daughter—who would be five-months-old in a week.

And Attorney John Selser was more than likely preparing for his cross-examination of the prosecution's next witness, Donnie Hommell.

Hommell

In April, Smith's attorney, John Selser, had pleaded with Calissi to look at Donald Hommell as a person of interest in the murder of Victoria Zielinski.

The prosecutor had brushed him off.

It seemed as if the County District Attorney's Office, and the police departments involved in the investigation, were willing to ignore Hommell completely.

Now, Guy Calissi was calling Hommell as a witness for the State.

It was a strategic move.

It gave Calissi the opportunity to prepare Hommell for what he expected would be an exhaustive cross-examination.

Donnie Hommell was sworn in first thing Monday morning.

> Calissi: Now, on March 5, 1957, did you have occasion to see Joseph Gilroy?
>
> Hommell: Yes, sir.
>
> Calissi: When was the first time you learned that Smith was driving Gilroy's car on the fourth of March?
>
> Hommell: In a conversation between Joseph Gilroy and Tony Saveriano.
>
> Calissi: When was that?
>
> Hommell: Approximately between noon and one, on the fifth.

Calissi: As a result of that conversation, what did you do, if anything?

Hommell: After the conversation, I left for Ridgewood with Joseph Gilroy to pick up Eddie Smith.

Calissi: Whose car did you use?

Hommell: Mine.

Calissi: What did you do in Ridgewood?

Hommell: We picked up Eddie Smith, his wife and baby.

Calissi: Did you have any conversation with Edgar Smith when you met him in Ridgewood?

Hommell: I winked at Gilroy, and I said, *I hear they think it is a Mercury and they are checking all of the Mercurys in Bergen County.*

Calissi: What did Smith say?

Hommell: Well, he just had a funny look on his face, and he didn't say anything.

Calissi: Tell us about the discussion concerning the lipstick. What was all that about?

Hommell: Well, when Eddie and his wife got into the car, I guess one of them picked up the lipstick and handed it over the front seat to Joe or me. Kiddingly it was said it could be Vickie's.

Calissi: Who said that?

Hommell: I don't know.

Calissi: Was it you?

Hommell: I can't remember, sir.

Calissi: What happened to the lipstick?

Hommell: I just threw it out the window.

Calissi: Thank you. The witness is yours, Mr. Selser.

Calling Hommell for the State offered the prosecution an additional advantage.

The scope of the cross-examination—the subject matter of questions the defense would be permitted to ask the witness—would now be limited to what had been introduced in direct.

On top of that, some questions Selser may have planned to ask could be objected to on the grounds they had already been *asked and answered.*

In spite of the restrictions, for Selser it would be the first opportunity to plant a seed of doubt in the minds of the jurors.

> Selser: With regard to the lipstick, you knew that was Vickie's, didn't you?
>
> Hommell: No, sir.
>
> Selser: When did it get into *your* car?
>
> Hommell: I don't know sir.
>
> Selser: Whose lipstick did you recognize it to be?
>
> Hommell: That I couldn't say.
>
> Selser: As a matter of fact, the lipstick was found in your automobile when the front seat was moved, wasn't it?
>
> Hommell: I don't know, sir.
>
> Selser: Wasn't the lipstick found when the front seat of the car was moved back and the lipstick was forward of the front seat?
>
> Hommell: I couldn't say.
>
> Selser: In the front compartment of the car?
>
> Hommell: I can't say. I didn't see it being found.
>
> Selser: Where was it you threw the lipstick out of the car?
>
> Hommell: I couldn't say.
>
> Selser: You had been out with Vickie, had you not?

Calissi jumped up to object. O'Dea overruled.

Hommell: Casually, that's all.

Selser: She had been in your car?

Hommell: Yes.

Selser: When was the last time, before the night of March fourth, that Vickie had been in your car?

Hommell: I would say about a month before that.

Selser: Not since then?

Hommell: That I couldn't say. I don't think so.

Selser: Of course, you knew Vickie pretty well, didn't you?

Hommell: Casually I knew her.

Selser: How many times would you say Vickie went out with you?

Once again Calissi objected and was again overruled.

Hommell: Very few times.

Selser: Can you tell me how many times?

Hommell: I would say about ten times at the most.

Selser: What time did you leave your place of employment on the fourth of March?

Calissi jumped up and objected, O'Dea said he would allow it.

Calissi continued to object—much more vehemently—leading to a long argument between Calissi, Selser and O'Dea.

Calissi insisted that Hommell's whereabouts on the night of March fourth were not relevant.

The exchange became so heated that O'Dea finally asked that the jury be removed from the courtroom.

After a great deal of bantering, Selser agreed to withdraw the question—while Calissi complained that having asked the question was prejudicial.

O'Dea, wanting to move on, called the problem resolved.

When the jury was escorted in, Selser withdrew the question and surprised everyone by then announcing he had no further questions.

Selser had planted the seed—the jury might now be wondering not only when Hommell left his place of employment, but also what Don did later that night.

Calissi had no choice but to re-direct.

> Calissi: Where do you work, son?
> Hommell: Wyckoff Pharmacy.
> Calissi: What are your hours of employment?
> Hommell: That night, it was six to nine.
> Calissi: What time did you leave that night?
> Hommell: About five after nine.
> Calissi: Now, on this particular night of March fourth, where did you go after you left the drug store?
> Hommell: To Pelzer's Tavern in Mahwah.
> Calissi: What time did you get to Pelzer's that night?
> Hommell: About nine-fifteen or nine-twenty.
> Calissi: When you got to Pelzer's who, if anyone, was there?
> Hommell: Charles Rockefeller.
> Calissi: When you travelled the route from the drug store to Pelzer's, did you see anyone you recognized on the road?
> Hommell: Myrna Zielinski.
> Calissi: Did you see Edgar Smith, the defendant, at any time during the evening of March 4, 1957?

Hommell: Definitely not, sir.

Calissi: You may cross-examine now, Mr. Selser.

Since Calissi had now brought up the subject of Hommell's movements after leaving his job, Selser now had the freedom to pursue it.

And the questions Selser asked Hommell suggested that the Defense might later have witnesses who would contradict Hommell's accounts.

Selser: Now, Mr. Gilg is the pharmacist where you are employed, is he not?

Hommell: Yes, he was.

Selser: And he was the man who was on duty the night of March fourth, wasn't he?

Hommell: I can't possibly remember whether he was or he wasn't.

Selser: Now, the pharmacy where you are employed is on Wyckoff Avenue, isn't it?

Hommell: I believe so.

Selser: And the drive from the pharmacy to, say, the Nixon home, at the speed of twenty-five miles an hour, takes how long?

Hommell: That I couldn't say, sir.

Selser: Would you say that it takes more than three and one-half minutes?

Hommell: It might.

Selser: How much longer would you say it takes?

Hommell: That I couldn't say.

Selser: Would it take as long as four minutes?

Hommell: I don't know, sir.

Selser: At what speed would you say you were driving along Wyckoff Avenue?

Hommell: About sixty.

Selser: Were you in a hurry?

Hommell: No, I just normally drive that fast.

Selser: Now, you say you went directly to Pelzer's?

Hommell: Yes.

Selser: Was Mr. Pelzer there?

Hommell: I believe he was. I couldn't positively say.

Selser: Don't you know that when you arrived at Pelzer's that it was a quarter to ten?

Hommell: No. It wasn't a quarter to ten.

Selser: You say you got there at a quarter after nine?

Hommell: Approximately a quarter after nine. It could be twenty after nine. I couldn't say.

Selser: How long did you stay at Pelzer's?

Hommell: I couldn't possibly say, sir.

Selser: What did you do at Pelzer's?

Hommell: I sat around and talked to Rockefeller for a few minutes.

Selser: Rockefeller was playing pool when you got there, wasn't he?

Hommell: I believe so. He may have, and then again, I can't say he was actually there.

Selser: From Pelzer's, where did you go?

Hommell: Well, I think I went to Pellington's, or then I went directly home. I couldn't possibly remember.

Selser: Who did you meet at Pelzer's, other than Rockefeller?

Hommell: I think Rocky was the only person in the place at the time.

Selser: You didn't see anyone else in Pelzer's?

Hommell: I don't think so, not that I can

remember.

Selser: Which Pelzer was behind the bar?

Hommell: Either Herbie Pelzer or his wife, I can't remember.

Selser: Now, what time did you get to Pellington's?

Hommell: I couldn't say for sure.

Selser: Was it after ten?

Hommell: I would say it was before ten, if it was, I don't remember.

Selser: Who did you meet at Pellington's?

Hommell: I don't remember if I was there or I wasn't. I can't say.

Selser: Let's see if we can refresh your recollection. Do you remember Tommy Doyle being at Pellington's?

Hommell: He could have been, I don't remember.

Selser: Do you remember asking Tommy Doyle if he would go with you to Herbie's place?

Hommell: I might have said it. I don't remember.

Selser: Do you remember Dick Schlott being at Pellington's?

Hommell: No, I don't, sir.

Selser: Do you remember John Metzger being at Pellington's?

Hommell: No, I don't sir.

Selser: Do you remember asking John Metzger if he would go with you to Pelzer's?

Hommell: I say I didn't. I don't remember if I did.

Selser: Were you or not over on Pulis Avenue on the morning of the fifth, at the area where the stream crosses Pulis?

Hommell: Definitely not, sir.

Selser: Do you remember Mrs. Woods who lives immediately adjoining the area?

Hommell: Never seen the lady before or ever heard of her.

Selser: And you told her to *mind her own damn business?*

Hommell: Never seen the woman or ever heard of her.

Selser: When did you find out that Smith had thrown his pants away?

Hommell: I believe March fifth, that night, I think.

Selser: How did you learn about it?

Hommell: I think it was from one of the police officers, or I read it in the paper. I don't remember.

Selser: Do you remember saying to Rocky, *Be sure you don't mention my name.?*

Hommell: No, sir, I never said that.

Selser: When did you leave the Navy?

Hommell: September, 1956.

Selser: How long were you in?

Hommell: About nineteen months.

Selser: You had a nervous breakdown, didn't you?

Hommell: No sir, I had a skin rash, a nervous skin rash.

Selser: Now, on the fifth, you talked to Mr. Gilg of the pharmacy, didn't you?

Hommell: I believe so, yes, sir.

Selser: Do you remember asking Mr. Gilg about a solution that would remove bloodstains?

Hommell: No, I asked him about a solution to *test* bloodstains.

Selser: Are you familiar with this baseball bat marked as S-69 in evidence?

Hommell: I don't know, sir.

Selser: *This* baseball bat?

Hommell: I can't remember, sir, no.

Selser: Do you remember, after the police had possession of Gilroy's car, asking whether or not you could get into the car to get the other baseball bat?

Hommell: I believe so. There was something to that effect.

Selser: Who were you with when you went up there?

Hommell: Charles Rockefeller.

Selser: How did you know there was only one bat remaining in the car?

Hommell: I didn't know there was one remaining. I don't know how many.

Selser: Why did you ask about the *other* baseball bat?

Hommell: I didn't know how many were in the car.

Selser: But you did do that, didn't you?

Hommell: I believe so, sir, yes.

Selser: That is all at this time.

Selser had achieved what he had hoped. He had managed to suggest another possible suspect.

What jurors took away from Selser's two cross-examinations of the witness would remain to be seen—but one thing was clear.

Donnie Hommell appeared to have an extremely poor memory.

Time of Death

Attorney Selser's two cross-examinations of Donnie Hommell may have greatly helped his client—but his cross-examination of Raphael Gilady may have completely negated their effect.

Bergen County Medical Examiner Dr. Raphael Gilady performed Victoria Zielinski's autopsy.

Gilady's testimony based on his physical examination of the body would provide the jurors, the Court, and counsel the nearest estimate available as to the time of death of the victim.

After Gilady's qualifications were conceded, Calissi began his direct.

> Calissi: Now, Doctor, on March 5, 1957, were you called to Emburgh's Funeral Home?
>
> Gilady: Yes.
>
> Calissi: Would you explain to us exactly what you did when you got there?
>
> Gilady: I performed a complete autopsy on the body of Victoria Zielinski. The body revealed on inspection a total crushing of the skull. The brain was absent. The subject was decerebrated. Her left eye was totally destroyed. Her lower jaw and upper jaw had multiple fractures. The nose was fractured in two or three places,

with bleeding from the mouth. Most of her teeth were loose. There was not a single mark on her elsewhere. I found very pure nylon panties that were not stained or mutilated, and no marks or bruises on her thighs. I did a rectal examination, which was entirely normal. There was no bleeding from the vagina or the vulva. The hymen was intact. I concluded that the cause of death was due to a total crushing of the skull with traumatic decerebration.

Calissi: Now, can you, Doctor, establish the time of death based on your examinations?

Gilady: I did the autopsy not long after noon, and I estimate she was dead about twelve hours, give or take an hour.

O'Dea asked the doctor for clarification.

O'Dea: What time did you do the examination?

Gilady: I would say it was between twelve-thirty and one. I arrived early. I believe I began work at around one.

Calissi: How certain is your estimate?

Gilady: I would say time of death was twelve hours prior to my examination, perhaps an hour or two less due to the very cold outdoor temperature which can speed the process of rigor mortis.

Gilady's testimony put the time of death at midnight or perhaps later.

Joe Gilroy's testimony accounted for Edgar Smith's whereabouts from ten that night through the following morning.

Selser could have left it at that, with no questions for the witness, and then he could have legitimately submitted a motion to dismiss the charges against Smith.

Instead, he chose to cross-examine Dr. Gilady, which was disastrous.

> Selser: Doctor, from your examination made, you have established that the time of death occurred somewhere around midnight of March fourth?
>
> Gilady: About, give or take an hour.
>
> Selser: So, that in your judgment, I take it that you would be of the opinion that the brain was separated from the head of the girl somewhere in the area of midnight?
>
> Gilady: Yes, give or take an hour.
>
> Selser: So, it was, in your judgment not later than eleven—not earlier than eleven, I mean—or perhaps not later than one.
>
> Gilady: It could have been earlier than eleven.

John Selser's cross-examination had only served to confuse the witness, confuse the jurors, and spring a leak in what for a moment had appeared to be an airtight alibi for his client.

Calissi next called Detective Charles DeLisle.

He was questioned about the statement made by Smith to Assistant Prosecutor Galda on March sixth.

> Calissi: Detective, did you ever discuss that statement with the defendant, Edgar Smith?
>
> DeLisle: Yes, sir. On the eleventh of March.
>
> Calissi: I show you a document and ask whether or not you can identify it?
>
> DeLisle: This is the "statement", the transcription of the statement given by Smith and taken by a court stenographer. I took this statement over to the jail at about ten on the morning

of March eleventh, and I asked Smith to read it.

Calissi: Did Smith read it?

DeLisle: He did read it, sir.

Calissi: How long did he take to read it?

DeLisle: Approximately thirty-five minutes. I asked him to sign the statement. He said he would not sign it because his lawyer told him not to. I asked him if the statement was accurate and he said, *Yes, it is accurate.*

Selser's cross-examination consisted of two questions.

Selser: Who was Mr. Smith's lawyer then?

DeLisle: I think Mr. Gaudielle.

Selser: I was not his lawyer at that time, was I?

DeLisle: I don't think so.

The "statement" was entered into evidence and, over Selser's objections, O'Dea admitted it as a *concession of guilt.*

Then, over a period of two hours, Calissi read the statement to the jury.

The statement that DeLisle testified had taken Smith thirty-five minutes to read takes up more than forty pages in the trial record.

Calissi then called John Brady, the owner and director of Edel Laboratories in Newark.

He testified as an expert in blood sampling and analysis.

The type of blood on Smith's shoes could not be identified.

The blood on Smith's pants and socks was type O.

The victim's sweater was heavily stained with type O blood.

As were her jacket, her brassiere, the red gloves, and the largest stone in evidence. The lower legs of her jeans were stained with blood, unspecified. The blood stain on the seat of Gilroy's car and those on the baseball bat could not be typed.

It was determined that Victoria Zielinski's blood was type O, but at that time DNA testing was a thing of the future.

No fingerprints were found on the rock or the bat.

Smith's gloves, shirt, and jacket had been tested and were found entirely free of blood.

After questioning Brady, Calissi addressed the Court.

"The State rests, your honor."

Selser moved for a judgment of acquittal based on the fact that Smith had not been present at the time of Victoria's death and must therefore be innocent, notwithstanding evidence to the contrary.

O'Dea's ruling, after studying the motion, suggested he may have become as confused during Dr. Gilady's cross-examination as was the jury.

Judge O'Dea's ruling, below, comes from the trial transcript in the public record.

> On motion of judgment for acquittal, the defendant urges that with the testimony of Dr. Gilady as to the cause and time of death—and the previous testimony as to the whereabouts of the defendant on the night of March fourth—it was demonstrated that it would have been impossible for Mr. Smith to have administered the fatal blows.
>
> A review of Dr. Gilady's testimony does not support the defendant's contention in this regard.
>
> The doctor said, in answer to a question, he estimated she was dead about twelve hours before he did the autopsy, give or take an hour, and emphasized it was a very difficult question to decide.

Then the doctor said, *Rigor mortis usually sets in between two and four hours, therefore I would say approximately twelve hours or an hour or two less.*

And on cross-examination, *It could have been earlier than eleven because the prevailing weather was so cold.*

Now, taking all of the testimony of the doctor as to the exact time of death, the exact time of decerebration, it seems clear the exact time of death could not be established from his examination and, according to his own estimate, it could have occurred *earlier* than eleven that night.

Therefore, the time the fatal blow was struck is a question for the jury to determine from all the evidence.

Therefore, the motion is denied.

The trial would continue.

The case for the Defense was set to begin the following morning.

Defense

Attorney Selser called Patricia Smith to the stand.

She testified that her husband, Edgar, had arrived back at the trailer with kerosene at approximately nine on the evening of March fourth—which would have been approximately twenty-minutes after Victoria left the Nixon home.

On cross-examination by Calissi, she confirmed that her husband had told her he had thrown his pants by the bridge on Pulis Avenue. She also testified she had identified the pair of pants while she was being held at the prosecutor's office, but they had been folded and she couldn't see the pants entirely.

Selser called Rosella Wood.

She testified that she had seen two young men near her home at eleven on the morning of March fifth, looking as if they were searching for something.

According to Wood, when she asked the boys if they had lost something, one of them turned to her and said, *Oh, mind your own business.*

When Selser asked if Wood saw that boy in the courtroom, she pointed to Donnie Hommell and said, *That's the boy.*

Wood's testimony contradicted Hommell's insistence during his cross-examination that he had not been there at the bridge that morning and had never seen the woman.

She couldn't identify the boy he was with but was positive

she saw Hommell that morning.

Selser never produced any witnesses who may or may not have seen Hommell at Pelzer's Tavern or at Pellington's on the night of March fourth.

Selser's case was going to rest on throwing suspicion upon Donald Hommell—to create doubt in the minds of the jurors.

He called his client, Edgar Smith, to the stand.

Selser led Smith through the events of March fourth.

Smith related his movements that evening, exactly as he had to his attorney during their pre-trial meetings—from the moment Victoria Zielinski entered Joseph Gilroy's car, until the moment he had left her at the sandpit with Hommell.

Then Selser began a line of questioning designed to paint Donnie Hommell the villain.

He did not get very far.

> Selser: What was your knowledge of Donnie Hommell's activities with respect to violence?

Calissi jumped to his feet.

> Calissi: Objection. Objection. I object to the question as being irrelevant.
> O'Dea: All right, we will excuse the jury.

The jurors were escorted out of the courtroom.

> Selser: I most respectfully urge upon the Court the thought that I have a right to explain the state of mind and basis of fear in support of the statement already made that Hommell threatened to kill the defendant's child if he mentioned Hommell's name, and it is upon this theory that

I offer the evidence.

O'Dea: Isn't that already in? Mr. Smith has already made that statement, that Hommell so stated.

Selser: I have the right to show the basis of fear. If I were to say to someone alongside me, *I would kill your child*, they certainly would not believe it and would not be justified in a fear. But, if Donnie Hommell says it, knowing Hommell as this man does, there is a basis for fear and the state of mind which is hereby prompted in the defendant.

Calissi: If the Court please. This is merely an attempt to paint Hommell as a rascal, as a vicious person, not to show the basis of fear.

O'Dea: All this is a matter for cross-examination.

Selser: I intend to develop, sir, first of all that the witness knew that Hommell was discharged from the Navy under circumstances indicating he was a psychopath.

Calissi: That is absolutely wrong. I don't think you have the right to ask this witness whether a man is a psychopath.

Selser: I intend to show by this witness that Hommell without provocation beat up some youngsters, deliberately ran into a doctor's car and said to the man, *I will bash your skull in*. I will show that on another occasion Don Hommell drove his automobile into that same doctor's garden and when the man complained Hommell said, in the presence of this witness, *You crippled son of a bitch, I'll kill you*. I will show that Hommell, deliberately, without provocation, smashed pool cues and committed acts of violence at Pelzer's Tavern—showing that Hommell is a dangerous, psychopathic creature.

Calissi: I object.

Selser: It is true, Mr. Calissi. These are acts which raised in this witness' mind the thought that the threat made was one which Hommell was capable of committing.

Calissi: And I object.

Selser: I am not only prepared to prove the state of mind, I am prepared to prove the facts.

Calissi: And I object to it. We could bring in any young man, go through his life history, and we could find in this man's character and in this man's reputation something for which he could not be canonized. So, this business of trying to paint Hommell as a vicious, malicious, poisonous type of individual is not proper in this case.

Judge O'Dea stepped in, and for reasons he did not elucidate, he ruled that *the question regarding Donnie Hommell's propensity to violence* would not be permitted.

With that, the vilification of Donnie Hommell ended before it could begin—and the jury was returned to the courtroom.

After a long cross-examination of Edgar Smith by Calissi, one that went over old ground, Selser rested the case for the defense.

It was Friday afternoon, May 24.

Judge O'Dea declared that Final Arguments would be heard at nine-thirty Monday morning.

Last Words

Closing arguments began on Monday, May twenty-seventh—
two weeks after jury selection.

Defense Attorney John Selser was up first.

> "I believe there is a basis for your finding that
> this case has been brought on for consideration
> before this crime has been solved. I believe sin-
> cerely that the truth of the matter is not yet es-
> tablished, factually or otherwise.
>
> "You will recall that the entire area about the
> sandpit where the body was found, where the
> blood existed upon the clothing of the victim,
> upon the rocks, on everything there, there was
> Type O blood, human tissue, and pieces of bone.
> On Eddie Smith's trousers there was no human
> tissue. There were no pieces of bone. There were
> only tiny specks of blood on Smith's shoes that
> could not be typed, they were not blood-soaked,
> no tissue, no bone. Here was a very gory area
> that he is supposed to have been walking over
> and none of these things, which were absolutely
> present, were present on his clothing. How could
> it be possible? Is it possible he could have
> walked through all of this gore and left upon the
> shoes as little blood as was found?"

Selser next turned to the pants, and where they were found.

"They were no longer on Pulis Avenue, where the defendant testified he had discarded them, because at eleven on the morning of March fifth, Donald Hommell and some other person were searching the area and when Mrs. Wood saw those men and asked if she could help she was told by Hommell to mind her own damn business.

"And then where are those pants found? On Oak Street, in such a position that a policeman riding on the street could see them—thrown there that they might be seen, not that they might be concealed, in plain view of the officers riding along Oak."

Selser cited Smith's talk with a priest sometime after he had been picked up by the police.

"If a man were a willing offender desirous of clearing his soul right after, they say, he had a conference with a priest, would he not say he killed the girl and say how he killed the girl?

"Eddie Smith did not."

Selser went over, in great detail, Dr. Gilady's estimate of time of death—emphasizing the short amount of time that Edgar Smith's whereabouts were unaccounted for.

"I may also add that her hands were clutched, her finger nails were bitten very severely.

"Now, before I go on to the reading of the testimony, her finger nails were chewed off. This was not something that had happened in a few seconds or minutes. Whatever happened to the victim took a long period of time."

Selser continued on for hours going over the evidence and testimonies, weighing claims and counterclaims, and pointing out much of what he found *illogical* about the prosecution's theory.

Selser, of course, asked the jury to find the defendant not guilty and took his seat.

The prosecutor rose and approached the jury box.

Calissi immediately began chipping away at the foundation upon which Selser had built his case for acquittal.

"Now, I am not sure what the defense has done here, because in summation it was stated that we have not solved the crime.

"Yet, the defense at the same time seemed to have solved the crime for us by naming Hommell. I thought that was the purpose of the defense to show that Hommell had committed this crime—and the foulest, dirtiest, legal trick that was ever pulled by a defendant was naming his friend as the person to whom we should point the finger and say that he, Don Hommell, had murdered Victoria Zielinski.

"Sympathy should go to Don Hommell and his family. What a disgraceful thing to have to cope with, a friend pointing his finger at you and saying, *You committed this crime.*

"Now, how under God's sun can you blame a thing like that on Hommell? What kind of character, what king of malicious, vicious mind must a person have to concoct and to invent that kind of a story?

"The defense is grabbing at straws.

"This is a very intelligent, cunning person we are dealing with.

"Cold as a cucumber.

"Persons might have cried during the course of this trial, but not Smith. Not Edgar Smith. Edgar Smith sat here as if this was a Hollywood production—cool, calm and collected.

"This is the kind of mind we are dealing with.

"What has the State proved? You have to understand that cases of this kind are not always judged on direct evidence. Smith went into the sandpit. Smith ran down Fardale Avenue, he admits he grabbed a bat. Smith chased Victoria with the bat and struck her on Fardale Avenue with the bat and he threw the bat away."

The week before, a 15-year-old schoolgirl, missing for six days, was found raped and strangled with her own belt several miles from the courthouse.

Calissi chose words specifically as he addressed a jury that had likely heard about the unrelated but similar incident.

"Here was Victoria, a schoolgirl fifteen years of age in the car. The clothing indicates her entire top was exposed. What do you think Smith was doing in the car? What in the light of human experience do you think he was doing in the car? Why would her clothing be all the way up? You know why.

"Because the man, Edgar Smith, was attempting to force himself upon the young girl.

"Where was the brassiere of the girl? Down around her stomach, down around her stomach.

"Now, what happened? He crushed her skull.

"Smith had the bat with him when he chased her down Fardale Avenue. He struck Vickie in the head and got rid of the bat and then brought her back into the sandpit. And then he completed his mission because he did not want to be exposed. She had not conformed—she had not acquiesced to his desires. Smith had to silence her. This is a terrible, terrible crime.

"Again, I say—this has been a horrible, despicable attempt on the part of the defendant to create doubt by concocting, by fabricating, by inventing this terrible story about a friend.

"We are dealing, I say again, with a very cunning man, who sits for two weeks, doesn't bat an eyelash, shows absolutely no remorse, and believes that this is just *one of those things*.

"The justice for Victoria Zielinski demanded by the people of the State of New Jersey, and particularly by the people of Bergen County and the family of this innocent schoolgirl, will be placed on your shoulders. You have a duty to perform.

"The people of this county are looking to this jury. Will the teenagers of the county, the schoolgirls of this county, walk the streets without fear? I again repeat to you that the eyes of Bergen County, especially, are now on this jury. I ask you to do your sworn duty."

Calissi ended his arguments late Monday afternoon.

Judge O'Dea announced he would instruct the jury Tuesday morning and deliberations would begin immediately following.

Verdict

On Tuesday morning, Judge O'Dea instructed the jurors who would be charged to determine Edgar Smith's innocence or guilt.

"You determine from the evidence according to the law what are the true facts as nearly as you can ascertain the truth from the evidence adduced from the evidence you have seen and heard elicited from the witnesses during this trial.

"You may draw proper and legitimate inferences of facts from the facts which you find and with your conclusions of fact, the conclusion of fact that you draw.

"The statutes mentioned in the indictment, 2A:113-1 and 2A113-2 provide: If any person, in committing or attempting to commit arson, burglary, kidnapping, rape, robbery, sodomy, or any unlawful act against the peace of the State, of which the probable consequences may be bloodshed, kills another, then such person so killing is guilty of murder.

"I will refer to the facts from the evidence, from the testimony.

"I am merely taking the facts from the case to

show you, the jury, how to take the facts and apply the law to the facts or the facts to the law.

"When I discuss the facts, I take them at random.

"There is evidence direct and circumstantial that the victim was killed as a result of severe mortal blows.

"The defendant contended with her, struggled with her, was annoyed, startled, alarmed by her remarks regarding his wife, she fled or sought to flee, travelled on foot at the scene, he took the time to retrieve a baseball bat from the rear of the auto. There was evidence of her hair, clothing, a distance from the scene of her body, blood-drenched rocks near her body, blood-drenched foliage, all sufficient for the jury if they find the testimony to these facts credible.

"I have pulled out these facts at random. I am calling that to your attention, citing these facts, solely for the purpose of showing you, helping you, guiding you in your deliberations.

"If you find that the defendant murdered Victoria Zielinski the night of March fourth, 1957, then you determine whether the murderous act, the killing, the bashing and crushing of her head were committed with intent to take her life.

"If you find there was no intent to take her life in dealing the mortal blows, in braining her at this lonely dark scene, then your verdict shall be guilty of murder in the *second degree.*

"If you find that there was intent to kill her, by bashing her face and head with willful, deliberate death-dealing blows, that there was sufficient time and thinking in the mind of Smith as he retrieved a baseball bat from the back seat of the car at the scene, as he pursued the victim who sought relief from his clutches, as he travelled about the scene of the murder, then your findings shall be murder in the *first degree.*

"Now, what do we mean by moral certainty? You don't have to be as sure of guilt, as certain of guilt, as you are that two plus two are four. You don't have to be as sure as you are of death. A moral certainty is something less than those kinds of certainties, and you have to be satisfied only with that lesser certainty.

"Now as to another point of Dr. Gilady's testimony as to the time of death.

"Let me say the element of the time of death is not an essential element of the proof of the State, that the time of the killing on the essential element of the offense is not material or important."

Judge O'Dea then handed the case to the jurors to decide.

The *random* nature of the judge's instructions would be seen in later years as a clear indication that O'Dea had made up his own mind.

O'Dea's instruction to the jury sounded a great deal like the closing argument of the Prosecution.

The jury retired for its deliberations at eleven-thirty on the morning of May twenty-eighth.

They returned after two hours and twenty minutes with a verdict of guilty of murder in the first degree.

June

By 1957, the number of regularly scheduled television shows had been growing exponentially for more than a decade.

Faraway Hill, the first broadcast Soap Opera, premiered on the DuMont Television Network in 1946. *The Guiding Light, Love of Life, As the World Turns, Search for Tomorrow, The Secret Storm*, and *The Edge of Night* were all airing by 1957.

Howdy Doody premiered in December, 1947 and began a flurry of children's programming that included *The Mickey Mouse Club, The Mighty Mouse Playhouse, Romper Room, Winky Dink and You, Andy's Gang*, and *Captain Kangaroo* by 1957.

The Toast of the Town, later to be called *The Ed Sullivan Show*, arrived in 1948. By 1957 there were variety shows hosted by Milton Berle, Dinah Shore, Lawrence Welk, Steve Allen, Jack Benny, Frank Sinatra, and others.

The Goldbergs, appearing in 1949, was followed by a great number of family-oriented TV comedies and dramas—and by 1957 these included *The Honeymooners, The Adventures of Ozzie and Harriet, Lassie, Father Knows Best*, and *Leave It to Beaver*.

By 1957, television westerns, crime dramas, and game shows had hit the small screen in full force.

Between 1955 and 1957 alone, there were nearly one-hundred new television programs brought into American living rooms.

The number of television sets in the U.S. had grown from nine million in 1950, one in every ten households—to over 80 million by 1957, one in every two American homes.

Regularly scheduled broadcast news programming was beginning to mature past infancy.

Meet the Press premiered in 1947 on NBC.

In 1954, CBS introduced *Face the Nation*.

On May 28th—a day after Edgar Smith was found guilty of first-degree murder in New Jersey—Daniel Schorr and Stuart Novins of CBS News and correspondent B.J. Cutler of the *New York Herald Tribune* interviewed Nikita Khrushchev, the First Secretary of the Central Committee of the Communist Party of the Soviet Union, in Khrushchev's office at the Kremlin in Moscow.

For a more than a decade, Americans had been encouraged to fear the Russians.

When the questions turned to *conflicts* and *animosity* between America and the Soviets, Khrushchev made it clear that he and his people considered the adoption by Americans of terms such as *Cold War*, *Red Scare*, and *Domino Theory* to be both nonsensical and dangerous.

The historic interview aired on the CBS news program *Face the Nation* on June 2, 1957.

Americans were presented, for the first time, with another side of the story and, although the Soviet leader offered mixed messages, Khrushchev seemed to be attempting to assure viewers that the Soviets were not *scary monsters out to control the world*.

> "As far as competition between capitalist and socialist ideologies are concerned, we have never made a secret of the fact that there will be a struggle between these two ideologies, but we

never believe this is the same thing as war because it is a struggle in which the system which has the support of the people is the system that will come out on top.

"We believe our socialist system will be victorious, but it does not mean, under any circumstances, that we want to impose our system on anyone.

"We simply believe the people of each country themselves will come to realize that this system is best for them.

"I can prophesy that your grandchildren in America will live under socialism.

"And please, do not be afraid of that.

"Your grandchildren will not understand how their grandparents did not understand the progressive nature of a socialist society."

Although Khrushchev's prophesy may have sounded somewhat ominous to American viewers, the Soviet leader was presenting a picture quite different from the one painted by Presidents Truman and Eisenhower, Senator Joseph McCarthy, and the House Un-American Activities Committee.

Khrushchev went on, addressing the subject Americans had been schooled to most fear.

"God knows how many speeches are being made in your country saying in how many hours the Soviet Union can be destroyed by the power of the United States.

"We do not indulge in such things.

"Our political leaders do not make speeches trying to prove that we can destroy the United States. That would be stupid on our part.

"I do not deny we have said that if some

American generals and politicians say they can destroy the Soviet Union, that if the means of warfare now enable one country to destroy another, then that second country can probably destroy the first one also and, in that respect, we are sure of ourselves. And if any man, who I would call a madman, should unleash war, then we would have to take our steps. It would be a great calamity for mankind.

"We have to live on one planet.

"You prefer the capitalist system. We prefer the socialist system. We will continue to have ideological differences. We will continue to compete, but we must live together on this one planet."

Whether or not this groundbreaking telecast would serve to ease the uncertainties of any in its audience would remain to be seen.

But, regardless, there were still evils demonstrated within their own borders which would continue to unsettle Americans.

Two days after Khrushchev had faced the nation, the fourth of June, 1957, Edgar Smith came before Judge Arthur O'Dea in the Bergen County courtroom.

It was three months to the day since Victoria Zielinski had been murdered.

Smith was sentenced to death by electrocution.

On the sixth, Smith was delivered to death row at the New Jersey State Penitentiary in Trenton.

That same month, another twenty-three-year-old man, born eight days before Edgar Smith in 1934, travelled from South

Carolina to California.

On his journey west, he purchased a handgun in Shreveport, Louisiana.

First Secretary of the Community Party of the Soviet Union Nikita Khruschev interviewed by American journalists at his office in the Kremlin. The historic meeting was broadcast on *Face the Nation* on June 2, 1957.

El Segundo

*He asked us to get out of the car and he said, 'I think
I'm going to kill you.' He marched us out into a field.
I thought it was over. He had the gun. I figured it just
takes four bullets and we're all gone.*
—Robert Dewar, one four teenagers robbed
on the night of the murders

*Officer Phillips appeared to be ready to start a citation.
We stopped and looked the situation over and Phillips waved
the paper at us like everything was all right, so we went ahead.*
—Officer James Gilbert, one of the last people
to see the murder victims alive

*We were high school sweethearts. The first time I saw him
I thought he was beautiful and I said to myself, 'I'd like
to marry that guy.' They woke me up about four
in the morning and they told me that he and his partner
had been shot and killed. I thought, God, since
I went to sleep the world's gone mad.*
—Jean Curtis, twenty-three-year-old wife
of one of the murder victims

Summertime

In the nineteen-fifties, the start and the end of public-school summer vacations were clearly defined.

Families considered *summertime* the nine weeks or so falling between the Fourth of July and Labor Day.

Classes ended no later than the final day of June and began again during the first week of September.

In Brooklyn, particularly in South Brooklyn, summertime was dominated by beach and baseball—daily trips to Coney Island by those in their teens and early twenties, while pre-adolescent boys furiously participated in Little League Baseball contests and girls hopscotched and jump-roped on the sidewalks.

My team, The Brooklyn Banners, was playing flawless ball in the late spring and early summer of 1957.

It looked as if we had a spot in the Borough Championship Playoffs locked up.

It was the last year the Brooklyn Dodgers would play in New York—they were destined to relocate to Los Angeles—and the fate of Ebbets Field was not known. The Borough Championship series was scheduled to be held at Ebbets during a Dodger's road trip.

The prospect of playing on what we considered a mystical *field of dreams* and *sacred ground* was both difficult to imagine and electrifying.

On July sixth, at a church dinner in Liverpool featuring a

band called *The Quarrymen,* Paul McCartney and John Lennon met for the first time.

On the ninth, the Major League All-Star Game was played at Busch Stadium in St. Louis.

The American League roster included Nellie Fox, Al Kaline, Mickey Mantle, Ted Williams, and Yogi Berra—while the National League lineup included Hank Aaron, Stan Musial, Willie Mays, Ernie Banks, and Frank Robinson.

The American League recorded three runs in the top of the ninth inning, taking a 6-2 lead. The National League answered with three runs in the last of the ninth, but it was too little too late to deny their rivals a 6-5 victory.

That same day, *Loving You,* the second film featuring Elvis Presley, hit theaters nationwide—quickly replacing *The Gunfight at OK Corral* as the most popular movie in America.

On July twelfth, Dwight Eisenhower became the first U.S. President to fly in a helicopter.

On the thirteenth, Presley's *(Let Me Be Your) Teddy Bear* reached the top of the Billboard Charts and held the spot for seven weeks.

Three days later, Marine Major John Glenn flew a Vought F 8U Crusader from Los Alamitos in California to Floyd Bennett Field in Brooklyn—setting a transcontinental speed record of 735.55 miles per hour.

On the twenty-first, Althea Gibson became the first African-American to win a major tennis tournament—the Women's Singles title at Wimbledon.

Although I would not learn of the *Lover's Lane Bandit* until more than forty-five years later—the events of July 22, 1957 in El Segundo, California made national news the following day.

My tenth birthday.

Lover's Lane

Shortly before midnight on the twenty-first of July in 1957 two teenaged couples, coming from a summer party, parked their 1949 Ford to watch planes take off and land from Hawthorne Municipal Airport.

And to do what legendary disc jockey and *rock & roll* promoter Murray 'The K' Kaufman would refer to as *submarine race watching*.

The area where they parked, east of El Segundo in Los Angeles County, was known as *Lover's Lane*.

One of hundreds of such secluded areas throughout America where couples stopped to experience their first tastes of kissing and light petting.

"It was getting steamy in the car, so I rolled down the window," one of the boys recalled. "That's when the gun came through the window and a man said, *This is a robbery*. At first, I thought it was a joke—that someone was pulling a prank—but I could see that the gun was real. Then he said, *I don't know what to do with you.*"

The assailant demanded their money and jewelry. He ordered them all out of the car, had them remove their outer clothing, and bound and gagged each of them with surgical tape.

Then the man raped one of the young girls.

A fifteen-year-old high school sophomore.

Much like most girls of her age in that time.

Not unlike Victoria Zielinski.

The *Lover's Lane Bandit*, as he would come to be known, held the high schoolers captive for more than an hour.

Then he marched them all out into a field where, it was later reported, they all believed they would be shot and killed.

Instead he left them there in the field, bound and unclothed, and drove off in their 1949 Ford.

Phillips and Curtis

Just after one in the morning on the twenty-second of July, El Segundo Police Officers Richard Phillips and Milton Curtis were in a parked black-and-white police car when they spotted a 1949 Ford stop briefly for a red light at the corner of Sepulveda Boulevard and Rosecrans Avenue and then proceed through the intersection while the traffic signal was still red.

They followed and pulled the Ford over to side of the avenue.

Officer Phillips left their car, while Officer Curtis remained in the police cruiser to attend to protocol—reporting over the radio that they had stopped a vehicle for a traffic violation.

El Segundo Police Officers James Gilbert and Charlie Porter heard the report over their radio. They were near the location of the traffic stop. They decided to go to the scene.

When they turned onto Rosecrans, they saw the police car and the Ford. Officer Phillips, and a man they assumed to be the driver of the Ford, were out of their vehicles. It appeared as if Phillips was about to write up a citation.

When Gilbert and Porter pulled up and slowed down, Phillips waved them on—indicating that he and Curtis had it handled.

The second police car drove off.

Minutes later Officer Phillips was on the radio calling for an ambulance, reporting that both he and his partner had been shot.

171

Gilbert and Porter raced back to the scene.

They found Officer Phillips on the ground. He had been shot three times in the back. He died before medical help arrived.

Officer Curtis was still in the police car, dead. He had been shot three times in the abdomen.

Richard Phillips was twenty-nine years old. He was married with three young children.

Milton Curtis was twenty-five years old. A rookie, only two-and-a-half months on the job. He was married with two children under the age of five.

It was not until the four stranded teenagers were discovered that police first learned of the events earlier that night at the lover's lane.

Armed robbery, rape, and automobile theft.

By then, Richard Phillips and Milton Curtis had already been murdered in cold blood.

Hundreds of police officers from throughout Los Angeles County were deployed to comb a wide area surrounding the murder scene.

No resource was spared. No request for assistance denied.

The victims were two of their own.

There was no sign of the perpetrator. No one had heard or seen the man.

Then, less than four blocks from the murder scene, police discovered an abandoned 1949 Ford.

The Getaway Car

When the 1949 Ford was discovered, not far from the murder scene, it was quickly determined that the vehicle had been struck by three gunshots.

One bullet had hit the trunk of the vehicle, and two others had travelled through the rear window.

At the scene, investigators learned that Officer Phillips, apparently while on the ground dying, had discharged his service weapon six times. Three of his shots had struck the fleeing vehicle.

The massive ongoing manhunt continued.

There was no sign of the perpetrator.

No one who was interviewed had heard or seen the fleeing suspect.

Howard Speaks, a crime scene investigator with the Los Angeles County Sheriff's Department, hoped the vehicle would supply clues.

"The only thing going through my mind was that I had to be sure to do everything right," Speaks would later say.

Only two of the three bullets that had hit the vehicle were located, suggesting the third shot may have struck the driver.

Officer Phillips may have marked his killer.

Speaks went through the vehicle inside and out. On the steering wheel he found and was able to lift two partial prints of a left thumb.

At the time, before DNA testing, fingerprints were still the most reliable method of identifying suspects.

The two partials did not appear promising. Then a lab technician thought to put the two together and investigators felt confident they had a single thumb print that *might* identify a suspect.

Investigators were able to create sketches of the suspect from witnesses including the teenaged victims who had been robbed, assaulted and terrorized, and Officers Gilbert and Porter who had seen him with Officer Phillips shortly before the killings. The police sketches were printed in newspapers throughout Los Angeles County.

It seemed as if it would only be a matter of time before they located the killer.

Optimism soon turned to frustration.

No match could be found for the lifted thumb print.

No one came forward to identify the suspect from the police sketches.

After days of searching and interviewing there were no new leads.

The man who was responsible for the rape of a teenage girl and the murder of two on-duty police officers had vanished.

The Murder Weapon

Several years after the tragic events in Hawthorne and El Segundo, investigators were no closer to identifying the rapist and murderer.

Five children, still quite young, could not yet fully understand where their fathers had gone.

And month by month, the end of the decade approached.

During those final years of the fifties, the United States and the Soviet Union continued regular nuclear bomb testing.

The United States and Canada created NORAD, the North American Air Defense Command.

President Eisenhower sent federal troops to Little Rock when Governor Orval Faubus used the Arkansas National Guard to block the integration of Central High School.

In God We Trust was first used on U.S. currency.

Elvis was drafted into the Army and stationed in Germany for two years.

The Tonight Show with Jack Paar premiered on national television—as did *American Bandstand, Maverick, The Twilight Zone,* and *Leave It To Beaver.*

On The Road, Dr. Zhivago, and *Lolita* were published.

Albert Camus won the Nobel Prize in Literature in 1957. Boris Pasternak was given the same honor a year later but was pressured by Soviet authorities to decline acceptance of the prize.

The entire Clutter family was killed in Holcomb, Kansas. The events would later be immortalized by way of Truman Capote's *In Cold Blood*.

West Side Story and *The Sound of Music* premiered on Broadway.

Barry Gordy founded Tamla Records, later to become Motown.

Buddy Holly and the Crickets had a string of number one hits starting with *That'll Be the Day* in September, 1957. On February 3, 1959, Holly was killed in a plane crash near Clear Lake, Minnesota.

The territories of Alaska and Hawaii gained statehood.

Edmund Hillary reached the South Pole by land.

Ted Williams became the highest paid baseball player to date when he signed with the Boston Red Sox in February, 1958, for $135,000.

Floyd Patterson dominated heavyweight boxing.

The Bridge on the River Kwai, Ben-Hur, Some Like it Hot, North by Northwest, and *Anatomy of a Murder* reached movie screens.

The Soviet Union successfully launched the first artificial Earth satellite, Sputnik.

Nikita Khrushchev visited California. The Soviet leader met with Shirley MacLaine, lunched with Frank Sinatra, and was later denied admission to Disneyland.

"I would much like to see Disneyland," Khrushchev complained, "but *we cannot guarantee your security,* they say. Then what must I do? What is it? Is there an epidemic of cholera there or something? Or is it that gangsters. who can destroy me, have taken hold of the place?"

A young ex-Marine named Lee Harvey Oswald had travelled to Moscow.

Edgar Smith had spent more than two years on Death Row. An appeal to the State Supreme Court had been denied in May, 1958. The points raised in the appeal concerned the enlarged colorized photographs of Victoria Zielinski's body, which were said to be inflammatory. Judge O'Dea's technical errors of law in his charge to the jury. O'Dea's prejudicial error in telling the jury that time of death was immaterial. And the admittance of Edgar Smith's *unsigned* statement into evidence. The higher court rejected every point.

The date of execution was set for August 19, 1958. An urgent appeal to Governor Robert Meyner to commute the sentence to life imprisonment was denied. A request to the Appellate Division of the New Jersey Superior Court for a stay of execution was denied.

At the eleventh hour, Judge Mendon Morrill of the United States District Court, District of New Jersey signed an order to stay the execution pending the filing of a new appeal.

In 1959, a man digging up weeds in his yard—only a mile from where two El Segundo police officers had been murdered two years earlier—came across the frame of a handgun.

When Doug Tuley discovered the gun, it was badly rusted and missing the cylinder. He thought nothing of it, putting it away with other *junk* in his garage. Nearly a year later he came across a cylinder that matched the frame and finally brought both to the police.

The weapon was identified as a nine-shot Harrington and Richardson .22 caliber revolver.

The serial number on the weapon pointed police to a Sears Department Store in Shreveport, Louisiana, where the weapon had been purchased at the cost of $29.95 in June, 1957.

Two detectives from Los Angeles County travelled to Shreveport and they found the Sears sales clerk who had sold the gun. He dug up the sales record. The buyer was recorded as G.D. Wilson. The sales clerk had filled in all of the information on the paperwork. The buyer was not required to sign his name.

The detectives could find no record of a G.D. Wilson residing in the Shreveport area, nor could they find anyone of that name with a criminal record or wanted for a crime in Louisiana or California.

They assumed the man had been passing through and thought he may have spent a least one night in Shreveport. They checked hotels and rooming houses.

On the day the weapon was purchased, a man who signed the register as George D. Wilson rented a room in the YMCA, just across the avenue from the Sears store. Wilson listed a false home address in Miami, Florida.

The detectives returned to California with little of value to show for their efforts.

By the time the new decade had arrived, after nearly three-thousand possible suspects had been looked at and cleared, the murder of Officers Phillips and Curtis was considered a cold case.

El Segundo, California was the home of both a Douglas Aircraft factory and Nash Automobile factory in the fifties.

After assaulting four teenagers and taking their car, the assailant was stopped by El Segundo police officers Phillips (left) and Curtis for a traffic violation. The perpetrator killed both officers, one on the street and one in the police vehicle, and drove off in the stolen car.

Both Richard Phillips and Milton Curtis were in their twenties. Curtis was a rookie.

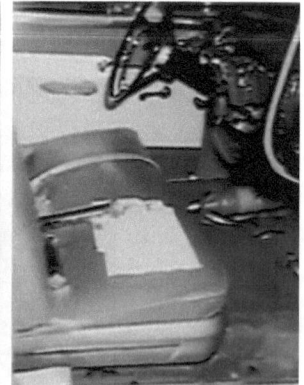

Newspaper headline on July 23, 1957. The search for the killer would be largest in California history at the time.

Two composite police sketches of the killer from descriptions given by one of the Lovers Land assault victims and a police officer who saw him at the traffic stop.

When the getaway car was found, it was discovered that three shots from Phillips' service revolver had struck the fleeing vehicle. Only two bullets could be located, leading investigators to speculate that one shot had struck the killer.

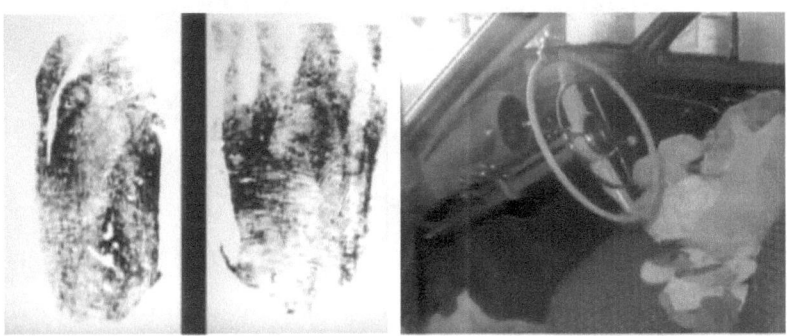

Two partial thumb prints were lifted from the steering wheel, and then the two were combined to produce an acceptable full thumb print. However, no match could be found—and no one came forward who could identify the suspect from the published composite sketches.

Three years after the shootings, a handgun confirmed as the murder weapon was discovered by a man on his property a mile from the murder scene. The serial number led investigators to a Sears store in Shreveport, Louisiana where it was purchased—in June 1957. The name of the buyer had been given as G.D. Wilson. It was learned that a George D. Wilson had checked into a YMCA on the night of the purchase. No man with that name could be found after an extensive national search, and it was decided that it was a false name.

Investigators did, however, now have a sample of the suspect's handwriting. Though of no use at the time, it went into the case file with the thumb print.

A New Decade

If you can remember anything about the sixties,
you weren't really there.
—Paul Kantner

The thing the sixties did was to show us the
possibilities and the responsibility that we all had.
It wasn't the answer.
It just gave us a glimpse of the possibility.
—John Lennon

People today are still living off the table scraps of the sixties.
They are still being passed around—the music and the ideas.
—Bob Dylan

Changes in Scenery

Elvis Presley spent the last two years of the fifties in Germany, far from the music revolution he was instrumental in creating.

Elvis' absence, and the untimely death of Buddy Holly, opened the door to a new generation of pop, rock and R&B artists who would go on to dominate the charts between 1961 and 1967.

Four guys from New Jersey, who might be considered the first *Boy Band*, released what would be their first number one hit, *Sherry*, in 1962. The Four Seasons would follow with three more chart-toppers by 1964.

In 1961, *Please Mr. Postman* by The Marvelettes was the first number one Motown hit. By 1967, Motown groups had captured number one spots sixteen times—including ten chart-toppers by The Supremes.

In early 1964, *I Want To Hold Your Hand* by The Beatles reached the top of the American charts. By 1967, the British Invasion had accounted for more than 30 number-one singles—including fifteen by *The Fab Four*.

At the same time, popular music was progressively focusing on political and social issues—anti-war and civil rights themes. *Blowin' in the Wind, For What It's Worth, Universal Soldier,* and *I Ain't Marching Anymore* became protest anthems.

Moviegoers were still drawn to big budget epic adventures. *Lawrence of Arabia, Doctor Zhivago, The Great Escape, The Magnificent Seven, The Guns of Navarone,* and *Goldfinger* had all been released by 1965. When producer Kirk Douglas insisted that Dalton Trumbo be credited with writing the screenplay for *Spartacus* in 1960, the Hollywood Blacklist was broken.

Lavish film adaptations of Broadway musicals were box office favorites, including *My Fair Lady, The Sound of Music,* and *West Side Story.*

However, the period had also produced its share of films that spotlighted political and social issues. *Dr. Strangelove, Inherit the Wind, The Pawnbroker, Judgment at Nuremberg, To Kill a Mockingbird,* and *In the Heat of the Night* were released between 1960 and 1967.

The popularity of the *historical novel* earned Best Seller status for Irving Stone, Leon Uris, Irving Wallace, Mary Stewart, Harold Robbins, Morris West, and James Michener.

Simultaneously, more topical and off-beat fiction—including Ken Kesey's *One Flew Over the Cuckoo's Nest,* Anthony Burgess' *A Clockwork Orange,* Kurt Vonnegut's *Slaughterhouse Five,* William Styron's *The Confessions of Nat Turner* and Joseph Heller's *Catch 22* captured the imaginations of students in colleges throughout America.

Counter-cultural sentiments were being increasingly represented in film, music and literature.

The times they were a-changin'.

Inauguration Day

On the eighth of November, 1960, John Fitzgerald Kennedy was elected thirty-fifth President of the United States.

The Senator from Massachusetts defeated his opponent, Vice President Richard Nixon, by less than one hundred thousand votes.

At forty-three years old, he became the second youngest man to hold the office. (Theodore Roosevelt was forty-two when he became President in 1901, following the assassination of William McKinley.)

John Kennedy was also the first Roman Catholic to win the Presidency. (Al Smith, the only Catholic to run for President before Kennedy, was defeated by Herbert Hoover in 1928.)

Unlike his opponent, Richard Nixon, and his two predecessors, Dwight Eisenhower and Harry Truman, John F. Kennedy was a member of America's aristocracy.

In his Inaugural Address on the twentieth of January, 1961, the newly elected President made America's goals perfectly clear and stated the price we would be willing to pay to succeed in those goals.

> "Let every nation know, whether it wishes us well or ill, that we shall pay any price, bear any burden, meet any hardship, support any friend, oppose any foe to assure the survival and the success of liberty."

America would stand behind their allies, pledging the "loyalty of faithful friends."

America would support the nations liberated after the second world war, pledging that "one form of colonial control shall not have passed away merely to be replaced by a far more iron tyranny."

America would do everything in her power to aid struggling third-world nations "not because the communists may be doing it, not because we seek their votes, but because it is right."

And, as Nikita Khrushchev had done on *Face the Nation* more than two years earlier, Kennedy stressed that our country was interested only in peace—but would not stand unprepared.

> "To those nations who would make themselves our adversary, we offer not a pledge but a request that both sides begin anew the quest for peace before the dark powers of destruction, unleashed by science, engulf all humanity in planned or accidental self-destruction.
>
> "We dare not tempt them with weakness. For only when our arms are sufficient beyond doubt can we be certain beyond doubt that they will never be employed.
>
> "Let us begin anew—remembering on both sides that civility is not a sign of weakness—and sincerity is always subject to proof. Let us never negotiate out of fear—but let us never fear to negotiate."

Kennedy closed with an appeal to Americans, and to all peoples of the world, to accept shared responsibility for the fate of mankind.

> "In the long history of the world, only a few generations have been granted the role of defending

freedom in its hour of maximum danger.

"I do not shrink from this responsibility—I welcome it.

"And so, my fellow Americans, ask not what your country can do for you—ask what you can do for your country.

"My fellow citizens of the world, ask not what America will do for you, but what together we can do for the freedom of man."

Kennedy did not specifically mention the Soviet Union, but his message was certain.

The doctrines of his predecessors Truman and Eisenhower—declaring America's commitment to safeguard against forced imposition of communist ideology in our hemisphere and beyond—would remain in full effect.

And, although not naming them, there were two countries in particular that the new president surely had on his mind on the day he took office.

A Thousand Days

From the chambers of the Capitol, to the halls of 1600 Pennsylvania Avenue, the *leaders of the free world* were of one mind—America would be devoted to a policy of containment.

The fear of communism became an obsession and the commitment to prevent it from spreading became a national crusade when in November 1956 Khrushchev said, *We will bury you*—and, only two months later, Eisenhower said, in effect, *Go ahead. Try it.*

In July 1950—one month after U.S. ground troops were ordered into Korea—President Truman authorized fifteen million dollars in military aid to the French in Vietnam. In November, Truman created a Military Assistance Advisory Group, MAAG, in Saigon.

Following a resounding defeat by the Viet Minh at Dien Bien Phu in the spring of 1954—resulting in more than three thousand French soldiers killed or missing, nearly five thousand wounded, and eight thousand captured—the French began a total withdrawal from Indochina following sixty-seven years of colonial rule.

The Geneva Accord in July created a Vietnam divided into North and South at the 17th Parallel.

In January 1955, the first direct shipment of U.S. military aid to South Vietnam reached Saigon—with an offer to train the

South Vietnamese Army.

In July, Ho Chi Minh visited Moscow and the North Vietnamese leader agreed to accept Soviet aid.

Four years later, July 1959, two American advisors were killed in an ambush by guerillas at the MAAG compound in Bien Ho.

By the time President Kennedy took office in 1961, there were nearly three-thousand American military *advisors* in South Vietnam.

On the first of the new year, 1959, revolutionary guerillas forced Cuban dictator Fulgencio Batista to flee the country. Fidel Castro, a Marxist-Leninist, soon became Prime Minister.

When Kennedy took the oath of office there was a Communist led nation, supported by the Soviet Union, ninety miles off the coast of Florida.

Kennedy, who was a proponent of the Truman and Eisenhower Doctrines and whose father was a strong supporter of the late Senator Joseph McCarthy, took the *domino theory* seriously—as was indicated in his inaugural address.

The newly elected president quickly surrounded himself with advisors who shared his sentiments.

He chose his younger brother, Robert, for Attorney General.

Dean Rusk, an ardent anti-Communist, for Secretary of State.

And Ford Motor Company President, Robert McNamara, for Secretary of Defense.

Romantics would come to call it *Camelot*.

Arthur Schlesinger Jr. would later refer to it simply as *a thousand days*.

The beginning of a decade-long social and political upheaval—a clash of cultural values and ideology—the likes of which Americans had not witnessed in one hundred years.

During Kennedy's short presidency, from the start of 1961 through the end of 1963, Americans witnessed the birth of the Peace Corps.

The trial, conviction, and execution of Adolf Eichmann.

The first man in space, Yuri Gagarin of the Soviet Union.

The first American in space, Alan Shepard, less than a month later.

The Bay of Pigs fiasco.

The Summit meeting in Vienna between Khrushchev and Kennedy, and the resuming of nuclear testing by both the United States and the Soviet Union which had been suspended since 1958.

A new single season Major League homerun record set by Roger Maris.

The introduction of the birth control pill in Britain.

The first African-American, Jackie Robinson, inducted into the Baseball Hall of Fame.

The first man to orbit the earth, John Glenn.

The Cuban Missile Crisis.

The March on Washington for Jobs and Freedom where an estimated 300,000 heard Martin Luther King Jr. deliver his *I Have a Dream* speech.

The assassination of Ngô Đình Diệm by the Army of the Republic of Vietnam, ARVN.

The assassination of President John Kennedy on November 22, 1963 in Dallas.

And, a month later, a totally different sort of British Invasion arrived on America's shores when a catchy little two-minute and twenty-four-second tune called *I Want to Hold Your Hand* first hit airwaves in the U.S.

. . .

By the end of those first years of the sixties the investigations into the murder of the Grimes Sisters in Chicago, the Boy in the Box in Philadelphia, and the two El Segundo police officers were stone cold.

Edgar Smith and his lawyers continued in their attempts to appeal his murder conviction—hoping for a reversal or, at the least, a retrial.

In April of 1961, after several failed attempts, an appeal built upon the manner of the interrogation of Smith by police investigators in 1957 was heard by the United States District Court. In January 1962, the appeal was denied.

Meanwhile, Smith earned his high school equivalency diploma and was taking correspondence courses from Penn State and the University of Illinois.

In 1963, an article appeared in a New Jersey weekly wherein Smith told the reporter he read and enjoyed *National Review*. Soon after, as Smith entered his sixth year on Death Row, he received a letter offering a free subscription to the magazine. Smith accepted—and so began a long and unusual relationship between the convict and the writer of that letter, William F. Buckley Jr.

Buckley and Lichtenstein

After the United States District Court for the District of New Jersey had denied Edgar Smith's appeal in January 1962, Smith lost confidence in his attorney, John Selser, and lacked the funds needed to retain a commendable replacement.

Smith wrote to the United States Court of Appeals in Philadelphia and explained his situation.

Three days later, a lawyer was appointed by the court. It was the first time an inmate on death row in New Jersey had a counselor appointed by a federal court. Smith's new lawyer was Stephen Lichtenstein.

Lichtenstein argued Smith's appeal before a three-judge panel of the United States Court of Appeals for the Third Circuit in Philadelphia.

Arguments for appeals continued to focus on the bullying interrogation by police investigators in 1957, admitting into *trial evidence* Smith's statement to Assistant Prosecutor Galda in spite of Smith's refusal to sign the statement, and what was considered Judge O'Dea's *prejudicial* charge to the jury.

Additional testimony had been gathered from individuals who could not testify as to Donnie Hommell's whereabouts at the time of Victoria Zielinski's death—but *could* testify Hommell *was not* where he claimed to have been.

In July 1963, the court rejected the appeal by a vote of two-to-one.

The services of Lichtenstein were no longer covered by the

court after the appeal was rejected.

However, the lawyer went one step further at his own expense.

Lichtenstein submitted the case for consideration by the United States Supreme Court. In February 1964, the high court refused to accept the case for review by a vote of eight-to-one.

Following their initial contact by mail in 1963, William Buckley was granted permission to write to Edgar Smith regularly—initiating a frequent correspondence between Smith and Buckley that would continue into the seventies. Buckley told Smith he was looking into means of raising funds needed to retain counsel.

Buckley had been trying to obtain permission to visit Smith for more than two years before he was finally granted a single visit in March 1965.

In November, *The Approaching End of Edgar H. Smith* by William Buckley was published in *Esquire Magazine*. The article inspired a number of readers to make financial contributions to help cover Smith's legal costs.

Buckley then informed Smith that he could have any lawyer he wished.

Smith chose Lichtenstein, who he considered an excellent lawyer and one devoted to his cause.

Lichtenstein began immediately to initiate a new round of appeals.

Subsequent appeals and requests for review of the case submitted to the Federal District Court and the Supreme Court in 1966 and 1967 were denied.

As 1967 drew to a close, Edgar Smith—now in his tenth year on death row—may have felt what Buckley had referred to as *the approaching end.*

1968

Nineteen hundred sixty-eight was arguably the most turbulent year of what was inarguably a tumultuous decade in American history.

There were both revolutionary and civil wars being waged within its borders.

Americans and their children in the Deep South and in rural Appalachia were experiencing poverty, hunger, and a lack of health care as devastating as those of third-world countries.

The federal assistance for the *War on Poverty* promised by President Lyndon Johnson was obstructed by the escalating costs of the conflict in Vietnam.

The war in Vietnam was becoming increasingly unpopular as greater numbers of Americans lost their lives in Southeast Asia.

And the anti-war sentiment reached a boiling point with news of the Tet Offensive in late January 1968 when, in the city of *Huê* alone, American and South Vietnamese forces suffered more than six-hundred dead and nearly thirty-two-hundred wounded—shocking the public who had been led by its political and its military leaders to believe the North Vietnamese were being defeated and incapable of launching such an ambitious military operation.

By this time both Martin Luther King Jr. and New York Senator Robert Kennedy were voicing their opposition to continued American involvement in Vietnam—each concluding that the energy and the finances expended by our leaders in *helping* the citizens of South Vietnam was exhausting the resources needed to address the dire conditions of citizens in our *own* country.

On the Homefront, the racial tensions which had been creating turmoil and controversy since the Watts Riots in 1965 continued.

In February, three African American males were killed and twenty-seven other protesters were injured by Highway Patrol officers in Orangeburg, South Carolina.

On the third of April, Martin Luther King Jr. made his *I've Been to the Mountaintop* speech in Memphis, Tennessee.

"Trouble is in the land—confusion all around. But I know, somehow, that only when it is dark enough can you see the stars. And I see God working in this period of the twentieth century in a way that men, in some strange way, are responding. Something is happening in our world. The masses of people are rising up. And wherever they are assembled today—whether in Johannesburg, South Africa; Nairobi, Kenya; Accra, Ghana; New York City; Atlanta, Georgia; Jackson, Mississippi; or Memphis, Tennessee— the cry is always the same.

"*We want to be free.*

"Well, I don't know what will happen now. We've got some difficult days ahead. But it really doesn't matter with me now because I have been to the mountaintop.

"And I don't mind.

"Like anybody, I would like to live a long life. Longevity has its place. But I'm not concerned about that now. I just want to do God's will. And He's allowed me to go up to the mountain. And I've looked over. And I've seen the Promised Land. I may not get there with you. But I want you to know tonight, that we, as a people, will get to the promised land.

"And so, I am happy tonight.

"I'm not worried about anything.

"I'm not fearing any man."

It would be King's last speech. The following day he was assassinated by James Earl Ray.

Robert Kennedy learned of Dr. King's death shortly before a scheduled speech in Indiana. He sadly gave the news to the crowd, urging whoever was listening to control their emotions and remain peaceful—as King would have wished.

Nevertheless, riots broke out in cities across America.

On the sixteenth of May, Kennedy announced he would be seeking the nomination for the Presidency—shocking Democrats by challenging a sitting president from his own party.

"I have seen the inexcusable and ugly deprivation which causes children to starve in Mississippi, black citizens to riot in Watts. young Indians to commit suicide on their reservations because they've lacked all hope and they feel they have no future, and proud and able-bodied families to wait out their lives in empty idleness in eastern Kentucky.

"I have traveled and I have listened to the young people of our nation and felt their anger about the war that they are sent to fight and about the world they are about to inherit.

"I cannot stand aside from the contest that will decide our nation's future and our children's future."

Kennedy was also challenging Senator Eugene McCarthy who, as an outspoken critic of the Vietnam War, had been gaining great support among students at college campuses from coast to coast.

On the thirty-first, Lyndon Johnson shocked both his political party and the American people with a nationally televised declaration.

"I shall not seek, and I will not accept, the nomination of my party for another term as your president."

On the fifth of June, McCarthy and Kennedy faced-off in the California Primary. It was a foregone conclusion that the victor would be the Democratic candidate in the General Election.

Senator Kennedy won the primary and was then shot several times at the Ambassador Hotel in Los Angeles following his victory speech.

Kennedy died shortly after one in the morning on the sixth of June.

The year moved toward its end with the bloody confrontations between protestors and police during the Democratic National Convention in Chicago—where Vice President Hubert Humphry became the party's candidate, defeating anti-war advocates Eugene McCarthy and George McGovern.

And then, in November 1968, Richard M. Nixon was elected and would become the thirty-seventh President of the United States.

That same year, a book was published that I would stumble upon at a yard sale—twenty-five years later.

Brief Against Death

Brief Against Death was published by Alfred A. Knopf in 1968.

The author was a man who was in his eleventh year on Death Row at the New Jersey State Penitentiary in Trenton.

His name was Edgar Herbert Smith Jr.

The book describes the 1957 murder of a fifteen-year-old girl from Ramsey, New Jersey named Victoria Zielinski.

The narrative is an account of the crime and of the arrest, interrogation, first-degree murder charge, indictment, trial, conviction, and sentencing of the author—and of many failed appeals during the first decade of his incarceration.

In the opening pages of the book, which Smith titled *Author's Notes*, he stated the following:

> 1/ All dialogue between attorneys, the judge, and the witnesses found within the portion of my book dealing with my trial is directly quoted from the official printed transcript of the trial.
>
> 2/ All dialogue between myself, my attorneys, the police, and any other persons, except where otherwise noted, is reconstructed from my memory of the original conversations, supplemented in some instances by the memories of other persons involved.
>
> 3/ All dialogue that took place other than in my presence is constructed from three major

sources: (a) trial testimony of persons involved; (b) newspaper and magazine accounts of the case; and (c) statements made either to me or to my attorneys by one or more of the persons involved.

4/ Descriptions of events that took place not in my presence were reconstructed for the most part from sources mentioned above, with heavy reliance on the trial record.

Some of this can be verified through existing records. Some cannot.

Statements made by Smith himself in 1957, attributed in 1968 to his memory and otherwise undocumented, cannot be clearly judged as having been true or false in the first place.

And Smith concludes his opening notes with a qualification.

"Obviously, after so many years have passed since the actual events described, no one's memory could be letter-perfect as to every detail. I am confident, however, that nothing of substance has been misrepresented."

Brief Against Death, written in the first person, is far from objective.

Throughout the narrative Smith editorializes about the injustices of the police and the court—and the blunders of his counsel.

But, with all that, his arguments were compelling and the book became very popular—raising questions and influencing opinions.

And much of its notoriety was due to the support of the man who had become Edgar Smith's *champion,* William F. Buckley Jr.

Buckley was invited to write an introduction to the book.

Buckley agreed and titled his contribution *A Friend in the*

Death House, which concluded with the following:

> "And then an incredible telephone call from
> an editor at Knopf. They had received a manu-
> script from one Edgar Smith, at the Death House
> in Trenton, New Jersey. He has read the manu-
> script, and the book is now scheduled for publi-
> cation. I was astounded. I asked Smith why he
> hadn't advised me he was writing a book. *Didn't
> want to get you into any trouble*, he said. *You
> have enough to worry about.*
>
> "Nothing, I judge, to compare with the worry
> that the jurors are likely to feel on reading this
> book by the man they condemned."

Buckley had obviously decided Smith was innocent—and the
publication of Smith's book created doubts about his guilt in
the minds of many.

I asked Mr. Buckley, years later, what it was that led him to
believe in Smith's innocence.

He was unable or unwilling to answer the question.

Nevertheless, *Brief Against Death* initiated a new chapter in
the Edgar Smith story—and eventually led to extraordinary results.

The decade came to a close with a Civil Rights Act passed by
Congress and with Paris chosen to host proposed Vietnam
Peace Talks.

The Beatles bowed out—and were replaced by Led Zeppelin
as the most popular music group in the world.

And an estimated half-million people congregated for *Three
Days of Peace and Music* at Max Yasgur's farm in New York
State where only two deaths were reported—both non-violent
accidents—and Jimi Hendrix closed the Woodstock Festival

with his haunting interpretation of *The Star-Spangled Banner*.

An anthem to the tragedies and disillusionment—but also to the hopes and dreams of a generation.

In his inaugural address on January 20, 1961 John F. Kennedy reiterated the commitment of the United States, as Truman and Eisenhower had before him, to support our allies and stand firm against Soviet aggression through strength.

We dare not tempt them with weakness. For only when our arms are sufficient beyond doubt can we be certain beyond doubt that they will never be employed.

Fidel Castro took power in Cuba in January 1959. So, when JFK took office, there was a Communist-led nation only ninety miles off the coast of Florida—supported by the Soviets. On April 17, 1961, the failed Bay of Pigs invasion raised tensions in the hemisphere. In October, 1962 the US and USSR stood at the brink of war when Kennedy ordered a blockade of Soviet ships heading for Cuba during the thirteen days that would come to be known as the Cuban Missile Crisis.

Contributing to fear among Americans that peace was becoming more tenuous was the increase in the number of American military advisors sent to South Vietnam, already exceeding three thousand.

The space race was in full swing. Soviet astronaut Yuri Garga-
rin (above, left) was the first man in space in April, 1961. In
May, America's Alan Shepard followed.

It was a scientific contest—but the military considerations were
obvious.

William F. Buckley Jr., seen here at his *National Review* office and joining in a mayoral debate with John Lindsay and Abe Beame, began corresponding with Edgar Smith by mail in 1963 and became a staunch supporter.

His November 1965 article in *Esquire Magazine* helped raise funds to retain attorneys for Smith's state and federal court appeals.

Buckley wrote the introduction to Smith's book, *Brief Against Death*.

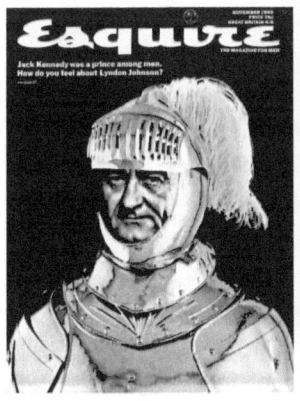 

On September 15, 1963 a bombing of the 16th Street Baptist Church in Birmingham, Alabama injured 22 and killed four young girls. Racial tensions mounted.

Tha assassination of President Kennedy in November shocked the nation. Although many theories would arise, including suspicions of participation by organized crime and the government itself, the public was still fed on the fear of the Soviet Union and its reach into nearby Cuba—and a majority of Americans were ready to blame the Commies.

President Lyndon Johnson set his sights on fighting a War on Poverty, and signed into law the Civil Rights Act of 1964. Johnson's efforts to alleviate internal unrest and violence were compromised by the increased American commitment to the Vietnam conflict. Meanwhile, the Republican Party was shifting to the right under the leadership of William F. Buckley and Arizona Senator Barry Goldwater.

Anthems by songwriters Bob Dylan and Phil Ochs, like *Masters of War, A Hard Rain's A-Gonna Fall*, and *I Ain't Marchin' Anymore*, rallied youth to the causes of civil rights and anti-war protest. The Tet Offensive in January 1968 changed the perception of America's ability to resolve the Vietnam quagmire.

The assassination of Martin Luther King Jr. in April, and of Robert Kennedy in June, followed by the violent Democratic Convention in Chicago, was dividing America along racial, political and ideological lines. Youth against the old establishment. North against South. The threat of civil war became as palpable as the threat of Communism.

Edgar Smith, in his 11th year on death row and isolated from the significant changes in the world outside the prison walls, continued his fight for a new trial through appeals to the state and federal courts. All appeals had been denied until the publication of *Brief Against Death* in 1968. The renewed attention it brought to his case, and William F. Buckley's support, provided a ray of hope.

Thirteen Years

One of the many lessons one learns in prison is things are what they are and will be what they will be.
—Oscar Wilde

To be in prison so long, it's difficult to remember exactly what you did to get there.
—Jack Henry Abbott

As long as you have capital punishment there is no guarantee that innocent people won't be put to death.
—Paul Simon

It is surely easier to confess a murder over a cup of coffee than in front of a jury.
—Friedrich Durrenmatt

Lost Battles

Edgar Smith was arrested on March 6, 1957.

Smith was indicted on March 8, and arraigned on the indictment on March 11. His trial began on May 14.

The trial ran for two weeks.

The jury deliberated for two hours and twenty minutes, including a lunch break, and delivered a verdict of guilty of murder in the first degree.

On June 4, sentence was pronounced by Judge Arthur J. O'Dea.

> For the reason that the statute N.J.S. 2A: 113-4 mandates that every person convicted of murder in the first degree shall suffer death unless the jury by its verdict recommends life imprisonment, you are sentenced to the judgment and punishment of death at the hand of the Principal Keeper of the New Jersey State Prison at Trenton during the week commencing Monday, July 15, 1957.

The process of appealing a conviction in a state court, particularly in a death penalty case, although a guaranteed right of the incarcerated convict, is an arduous and more often than not unsuccessful endeavor—as Edgar Smith would come to learn over his subsequent fourteen years and nine months on death row.

Initially, the death sentence pronounced by Judge O'Dea was stayed automatically by a mandatory appeal to the New Jersey Supreme Court.

That court *affirmed* the conviction and the sentence one year later.

Following that affirmation, a petition to the United States District Court for a Writ of Habeas Corpus was denied without prejudice due to a failure to exhaust every state court remedy.

Immediately after, Smith's attorneys moved in the Bergen County Court for a new trial on the basis of newly discovered evidence.

The motion was denied by Judge O'Dea, and his denial was upheld by the New Jersey Supreme Court in June 1959.

In November 1960, the United States Supreme Court denied review of Smith's case.

A second attempt to secure a Writ of Habeas Corpus in the United States District Court was denied in January 1962.

Following this denial, Smith was no longer able to pay for legal services and his attorneys withdrew from the case.

Smith wrote to the Chief Judge of the United States Court of Appeals in Philadelphia, pleading for the assignment of an attorney.

The court assigned Stephen Lichtenstein.

Another appeal to United States Court of Appeals in 1963 was denied two votes to one—another loss, but it was the first time that *any* judge had voted in Smith's favor.

A petition for reconsideration was denied by a vote of 5-2.

In late 1963, following a second appeal to the United States Supreme Court, that court again refused to review the case.

Following those loses, having exhausted every avenue of federal appeal, the courts would no longer pay for attorney services and Smith found himself again without counsel in the spring of 1964.

By that time, he had served seven years on death row.

Then, William F. Buckley Jr. came to the rescue.

An Unlikely Ally

William Francis Buckley Jr. was an internationally renowned journalist, author, and commentator.

In 1954, Buckley co-wrote *McCarthy and His Enemies*—a book that strongly defended Senator Joseph McCarthy as a patriotic crusader against communism.

The author of more than fifty books of non-fiction and fiction, Buckley founded *National Review* in 1955.

Buckley also hosted more than 1,500 episodes of the public affairs television program *Firing Line.*

In 1960, Buckley helped form the Young Americans for Freedom. In 1962, he began a nationally syndicated newspaper column, *On the Right.*

For an entire generation, Buckley was the preeminent voice of American conservatism. His primary contribution to politics was a fusion of traditionalist conservatism and classical liberalism, a synthesis which laid groundwork for a rightward shift in the Republican Party, as exemplified by Barry Goldwater and Ronald Reagan.

In 1965, Buckley ran for mayor of New York City—as a candidate for the new Conservative Party, hoping to restore momentum to the conservative cause in the wake of Goldwater's defeat in the 1964 presidential election and to steal votes away from the relatively liberal Republican candidate, John Lindsay, who later became a Democrat.

Also, in 1965, Buckley met with Edgar Smith at the prison in

Trenton to discuss strategy in Smith's continued efforts to appeal his conviction.

Buckley and Smith had first come into contact in 1962, and by 1965 Buckley was firmly convinced of Smith's innocence.

And William F. Buckley Jr. was not a man who kept his opinions to himself.

Habeas Corpus in simplest terms is a *recourse in law* through which a person can report an *unlawful detention or imprisonment* to a court and have the court determine the lawfulness of the incarceration.

Examples of *writs of habeas corpus* have been cited as early as during the reign of Henry II in Twelfth-Century England.

In modern times, a writ of habeas corpus is primarily identified as a plea to the court to review the legality of a criminal conviction which led to a prison or death penalty sentence.

The goal is to have the conviction overturned.

The process begins at the municipal or state level.

Traditionally, arguments concerning *wrongful* conviction revolve around factors such as a poorly executed case by defense attorneys, the failure to fully investigate other suspects, inappropriate interviewing methods used by police or prosecutors, discovery of new evidence, and the prejudice of the trial court.

All attempts for review on the state level had been summarily denied.

Prosecutor Calissi and Judge O'Dea were sticking to their guns.

Smith and Buckley agreed that Smith's only chance for reversal or retrial would lie in federal courts but, in order to succeed there, every possible avenue of state court review would need to be exhausted.

By this time, Smith was acting as his own attorney.

The two men reached a decision.

Smith would again file an appeal to the Bergen County

Court, this time for a writ of habeas corpus—making certain it contained every argument for a new trial that could later be taken to the federal court.

Meanwhile, Buckley would write an article about the case for *Esquire,* with hopes of inspiring readers to contribute funds for Smith's defense at the federal level.

In April 1965, Judge O'Dea denied Smith's petition for a writ of habeas corpus, and subsequently the New Jersey Supreme Court denied an appeal to overturn O'Dea's ruling.

A petition for reconsideration was also denied.

On April 16, Good Friday, Associate Justice William Brennan of the United States Supreme Court issued a stay of execution in order to permit Smith to appeal in federal court.

Judge Brennan's order came four days before Edgar Smith's scheduled execution date.

In July, Smith filed in the United States District Court for the District of New Jersey the petition denied by Judge O'Dea which the New Jersey Supreme Court had refused to consider.

As a result of Buckley's article in *Esquire Magazine,* sufficient funds were collected to enable Smith to secure a lawyer of his choice—he chose Stephen Lichtenstein.

In June 1966, the United States District Court ruled Smith's petition presented nothing new, and the writ of habeas corpus was denied.

The ruling was affirmed by the United States Court of Appeals by a vote of two-to-one.

The next step, which would likely be Smith's last appeal, would be a fourth attempt to convince the United States Supreme Court that the case merited review by that court.

And then, in the fall of 1968, Alfred A. Knopf published Edgar Smith's book, *Brief Against Death.*

Certiorari

The term *certiorari* goes back to Roman law—used in regard to reviewing a court case. In the United States, it is a process seeking judicial review—and a *writ* issued by a court that *agrees* to review.

A *certiorari* is issued by a superior court, directing an inferior court or other public authority to send the record of a proceeding for review.

As Associate Justice James Wilson, the person primarily responsible for the drafting of Article III of the United States Constitution in 1789, explained:

> In every judicial department, well arranged and well organized, there should be a regular, progressive, gradation of jurisdiction—and one supreme tribunal should superintend and govern all the others. An arrangement in this manner is proper for two reasons:
>
> 1. The supreme tribunal produces and preserves a uniformity of decision through the whole judicial system.
>
> 2. It confines and supports every inferior court within the limits of its just jurisdiction.
>
> If no superintending tribunal of this nature were established, different courts might adopt different and contradictory rules of decision—

and the distractions springing from these different and contradictory rules would be without remedy and without end. Opposite determinations of the same question, in different courts, would be equally final and irreversible.

In the United States, *certiorari* is most often seen as the writ the Supreme Court of the United States issues to a lower court to review the lower court's judgment for legal error—*reversible error*—where no appeal is available as a *matter of right*.

Since the passing of the *Judiciary Act of 1925*, most cases could not be appealed to the Supreme Court of the United States as a *matter of right*.

Therefore, a party who wishes the Supreme Court to review a decision of a lower court is required to file a *Petition for Writ of Certiorari* in the High Court.

If the Supreme Court grants the petition, the case is scheduled for the filing of briefs and for oral argument.

A minimum of four of the nine Supreme Court justices is required to grant a *writ of certiorari*, referred to as the *rule of four*.

The Supreme Court denies the vast majority of these petitions, and thus leaves the decision of the lower court to stand without review.

Buckley and Smith agreed that the chance of becoming one of the small number of cases accepted for review by the Supreme Court would require a high-profile litigator. Stephen Lichtenstein, aware of his lack of expertise in performing on that kind of *national* stage, agreed as well.

Smith therefore retained the services of the prestigious Washington law firm of Williams and Connolly.

The first task would be the writing of the petition upon which the Supreme Court would decide whether Smith's case merited review.

The task was delegated to Steven M. Umin, who would also

take full charge of the case.

Umin's résumé was impressive.

Summa cum laude graduate of Yale University; a Rhodes Scholar; articles editor of *The Yale Law Journal*; law clerk to Chief Justice Roger Traynor of the California Supreme Court— followed by a year as a law clerk to Justice Potter Stewart of the United States Supreme Court.

Steven Umin filed the petition for a *writ of certiorari* to the Supreme Court of the United States on August 12, 1968.

Hearts and Minds

Three weeks after the filing of the petition to the United States Supreme Court, *Brief Against Death* was released.

The reaction to Edgar Smith's book was nothing less than sensational.

The book introduced an eleven-year-old crime in a small New Jersey town to a national audience.

For those newly introduced to the events in Bergen County in 1957, *Brief Against Death*, albeit narrated through the perception of a convicted murderer, presented compelling arguments for Smith's innocence.

For those already acquainted with the crime and the subsequent trial, it raised doubt where little doubt of Smith's guilt had existed previously.

On top of that, as a result of Smith's description of life on death row in Trenton, the book inspired an examination of the living conditions in the New Jersey State Prison—ultimately resulting in reforms.

But, above all, was the reaction of the media.

In 1957, all newspapers in northern New Jersey, from the *Bergen County Record* to the *Hudson News,* and from the *Herald-Dispatch* to the *Newark Star Journal,* were firmly in the prosecutor's corner—and published pre-trial pieces which could easily have prejudiced prospective jurors.

"A 23-year-old Mahwah father of one child,

shortly after noon today, confessed to having killed 15-year-old Victoria Zielinski."
—*Herald News,* March 6, 1957

"Smith, questioned since early yesterday morning, finally signed a statement."
—*Bergen Evening Record,* March 7, 1957

"Admits he 'punched' school girl. Knew victim. Says she refused advances."
—*Hudson-Dispatch,* March 7, 1957

Over the two months between Smith's arrest and trial, similar damning articles appeared in local newspapers as well as in the *New York Daily News, New York Post,* and *New York Herald-Tribune.*

Following the publication of *Brief Against Death,* more than eleven years later, the news media displayed a remarkable change of heart.

Smith's book had raised questions which the media could no longer ignore.

Brief Against Death was given a great amount of publicity in the press and became a best-seller.

If and in what way Smith's personal account would impact the Supreme Court response to the petition for a *writ of certiorari* remained to be seen.

The Highest Court in the Land

Although the Supreme Court reconvened in October, the body was slow getting down to business due to the impending Presidential Election.

On November 5, 1968, Richard M. Nixon was elected Thirty-Seventh President of the United States.

A few days later, Attorney Steven Umin wrote to Edgar Smith suggesting that the Supreme Court Justices would likely rule on the petition for a *writ of certiorari* on the day they returned from recess.

On the afternoon of the 12th of November, Attorney Stephen Lichtenstein visited Smith at the prison.

Lichtenstein's news shocked Smith.

The Supreme Court had accepted Smith's case for review, granted the *writ of certiorari*, summarily reversed the Court of Appeals, and remanded the case to the federal court for a full habeas corpus hearing on the merits of the claims of *illegal police conduct*.

The ruling was 8-1.

The ruling generated a great deal of press coverage—including front page notice in *The New York Times*—inarguably influenced by William F. Buckley's article in *Esquire Magazine* and Smith's *Brief Against Death*.

It marked the first ruling in favor of Edgar Smith after nearly 12 years of motions, appeals, and petitions.

It also marked the beginning of Smith's most critical battle.

First, the mandate would have to come down from the Supreme Court to the Federal Court of Appeals. Afterward, an order for a hearing would go down to the District Court.

Attorney Lichtenstein estimated the hearing could begin sometime in the spring—April or May, 1969.

The Waiting

The Court of Appeals letter requiring the federal court to hold Edgar Smith's hearing was dated February 14, 1969.

On April 9, when there was still no word, Attorney Umin wrote to Judge Lawrence Aloysius Whipple of the United States District Court for the District of New Jersey suggesting the hearing be held on May 19—a date agreed to by the state.

A week later, Whipple wrote to Umin, *If and when my schedule allows, I shall contact you immediately.*

May arrived with no further word. Edgar Smith entered his thirteenth year on death row.

On July 15, Umin wrote to Chief Judge Anthony Augelli pointing out that the case had been dragging without action for five months and suggesting that the hearing be scheduled for November—one year after the Supreme Court had sent the case down to be heard.

A week later, Augelli replied to Umin—stating *Judge Whipple has agreed to assist in every possible way to expedite a disposition of this case.*

Another month passed.

Umin wrote again to Judge Whipple, requesting a *show cause order*—a formality requiring the prosecutors to reply to the petition Smith had filed in 1965, which had never been answered by the state.

All Judge Whipple was required to do was sign the order.

Then, both sides could finally begin their preparations for

the hearing.

Whipple stalled again.

On October 1, Steven Umin wrote again to Whipple asking why the letter requesting the signing of the *show cause order* had not to date been signed and returned, reminding Judge Whipple of his pledge to assist in every possible way to expediate the process.

"I respectfully submit this action should be taken now so that necessary delay does not become *undue* delay," Umin added.

Which was tantamount to warning Judge Whipple that the defense was prepared to go over his head.

A few days later, the *show cause order* was signed and delivered.

On October 22, with a hearing date not yet set, Umin wrote once again to Judge Whipple—suggesting that a hearing date be set at once, with a minimum of forty days for preparation.

Nothing happened—and once again a new decade had begun.

In January of 1970, two judges were appointed to the federal court in New Jersey by President Nixon.

Umin wrote to the Chief Judge asking that Smith's case be assigned to one of the new judges for action.

Several days later the case was assigned to Judge George Barlow, newly seated in Trenton.

On February 6, not having heard from Barlow, Umin wrote Judge Barlow and suggested April 20th as the date to begin the hearing.

Judge Barlow replied promptly, agreeing to a pre-hearing conference in his chambers sometime in March, and added, "*If circumstances permit*, we will be able to establish a hearing date at the time of the pre-hearing conference."

Umin's reply to the judge made it clear that leaving the case subject to *other commitments* and promising an early hearing only *if circumstances permit* was not good enough.

And on February 25, Edgar Smith himself wrote a lengthy

letter to Judge Barlow, in which he included:

> I realize, Your Honor, that the popular notion is that men in prison are not overly principled, but some of us do have principles and mine tell me I cannot accept status as a second-class petitioner—nor can I accept this altogether novel concept that habeas corpus is a second-class writ. I must ask this court to reconsider its priorities. I do not ask this court to believe I am innocent simply because I said so in a book, or to believe I was illegally convicted and confined simply because my petition makes that claim, but I firmly believe that when a petitioner comes before a federal court and claims that he has been illegally convicted and confined under sentence of death for more than thirteen years, more than one-third of his life, then this court has no greater priority, no higher duty, than to determine promptly and effectively whether those claims are true.

Judge Barlow did not respond directly to Smith. Instead Barlow wrote to Steve Umin and said, in part: "I appreciate Mr. Smith's concern. As you know, I regard the setting of a hearing date now as impractical and premature. Please advise Mr. Smith that any further communication to the Court should be made through counsel."

What Is and What Should Never Be
July 1969 to May 1970

The process of plea bargaining is not one which any student of the subject regards as an ornament to our system of justice.
—William Hubbs Rehnquist

We cannot hold that it is unconstitutional for the State to extend a benefit to a defendant who, in turn, extends a substantial benefit to the State and who demonstrates by his plea that he is ready and willing to admit his crime.
—Brady v. United States, 1970

So, I called to the Captain, "Please bring me my wine." He said, "We haven't had that spirit here since nineteen sixty-nine."
—Eagles, "Hotel California"

Summer of '69

When spring became summer in June 1969, I was twenty-one-years-old—a senior at the City College of New York, majoring in Sociology with a minor in Education.

Martin Luther King Jr. and Robert F. Kennedy had been gone for more than a year.

Richard Nixon was President of the United States.

The Vietnam War was costing lives in ever increasing numbers.

By June, the number of Americans killed-in-action since the beginning of the year exceeded six thousand.

South Vietnamese military deaths surpassed eight thousand, and the enemy death toll was estimated at more than seventy-five thousand.

And there was no end in sight.

On July 20, two Americans walked on the moon.

Two days after the historic moon landing marked twelve years since the murder of El Segundo police officers Richard Phillips and Milton Curtis.

And investigators were no closer to identifying the killer than they had been when the murder weapon was identified in 1960.

Investigators did not give up. The victims were two of their own. But the case became colder and colder throughout the sixties, and hopes of ever finding the *Lover's Lane Bandit* continued to fade.

. . .

August arrived.

Edgar Smith was now in his thirteenth year on death row, waiting for the courts to honor the Supreme Court *writ of certiorari* and schedule a hearing.

Smith had turned thirty-five-years-old in February.

Another thirty-five-year old, Charles Manson, would later be convicted of first-degree murder and conspiracy to commit murder for the deaths of Sharon Tate Polanski, Abigail Folger, Wojciech Frykowski, Jay Sebring, Steven Parent, Leno LaBianca, and Rosemary LaBianca—all brutally killed in Los Angeles in August. The sensational Tate-LaBianca murders instilled fear throughout the country unequaled since the Clutter Family murders in 1959.

Americans were reminded once again to check their doors and windows.

Later that month, the Woodstock Music Festival in upstate New York drew nearly a half-million people

In September, The Beatles' *Abbey Road* was released.

Butch Cassidy and the Sundance Kid premiered.

The New York Mets clinched the National League East Championship.

And the summer of '69 came to an end.

Turning Seventy

It was quickly evident that the seventies would be as culturally and artistically unlike the sixties as the sixties were unlike the fifties.

The new decade kicked-off a considerable change in what Americans were watching on television.

Green Acres, The Beverly Hillbillies and *Petticoat Junction* bowed out, making way for *All in the Family, Saturday Night Live, Sesame Street* and *Masterpiece Theatre*.

The mini-series was born—with *Roots, Holocaust, Centennial,* and *Rich Man, Poor Man.*

Monday Night Football made the sport an entertainment spectacle, and *ESPN* gave sports coverage its own home.

And a seemingly ludicrous idea—pay television—became a revolutionary reality when HBO was launched in 1972.

In movie houses, blockbusters of the sixties—including *Lawrence of Arabia, Doctor Zhivago* and *Spartacus,* and a wave of movie adaptations of musicals such as *West Side Story, The King and I, My Fair Lady* and *Oliver,* seemed to have had their day—giving rise to a new generation of film-makers including Robert Altman, Martin Scorsese, William Friedkin, Brian De Palma and Francis Ford Coppola who were presenting a view of the world *not* seen through rose-colored glasses with films like *Mean Streets, The Godfather, The Exorcist, Obsession,* and *M*A*S*H.*

In the seventies, music suddenly became the biggest entertainment moneymaker—earning twice the revenue of the movie box office and three times that of sports.

Sixties music had been dominated by The Beatles and the first wave of the British Invasion, the rich output of R&B from Motown, *psychedelic* rock, and the *protest* songs of Bob Dylan and fellow folk-artists.

The top albums at the start of January 1970 were *Abbey Road* and *Led Zeppelin II*—a premonition, perhaps, of the subsequent changing of the guard.

On April 10, Paul McCartney publicly announced the dissolution of The Beatles. Ten days later, he released his first solo album, *McCartney,* playing all of the instruments and handling all of the vocals. The album reached number one on the U.S. Charts.

Before the end of the year, both Jimi Hendrix and Janis Joplin were gone—casualties of drugs abuse.

Jim Morrison was sentenced to serve six months in jail for indecent exposure at a concert in Miami. Out on bail awaiting an appeal, he travelled to California to complete the album *L.A. Woman* with The Doors. From there, he flew to Paris to avoid incarceration—where he died in July 1971.

In November, George Harrison released *All Things Must Pass*. The three-record album—featuring nearly thirty musicians including Eric Clapton, Ringo Starr, Peter Frampton, and Dave Mason—reached number one worldwide.

Two weeks later, John Lennon's *Plastic Ono Band* with Klaus Voormann on bass and Ringo Starr on drums reached number six on the U.S. Charts.

The decade, however, would be highlighted by experimentation and new forms of music.

From England, *heavy metal, progressive rock, punk, glam*—the works of Led Zeppelin, Black Sabbath, Pink Floyd, Genesis, The Clash, Jethro Tull, Yes, and David Bowie.

While in America—the blue-collar anthems of Bruce Springsteen, *country* rock of The Eagles, jazz-oriented work of Steely Dan, and the phenomena of the Ramones and Talking Heads.

And Disco.

And on record album shelves, placed alongside original cast albums showcasing the talents of Rogers and Hammerstein, Lerner and Lowe, and Bernstein and Sondheim, were soundtracks of films like *Harold and Maude,* featuring music by Cat Stevens and *McCabe and Mrs. Miller,* with songs by Leonard Cohen.

But the sixties had passed Edgar Herbert Smith by—and the seventies threatened to do the same as he waited in a prison cell on death row in New Jersey for anything resembling good news.

Unacceptable Terms

Finally, a date for a pre-hearing conference was set.

Edgar Smith was granted permission to sit in on the pow-wow.

On the morning of April 10, 1970, the day Paul McCartney informed the world that The Beatles were quits, and more than seventeen months after the Supreme Court ruling, the conference was scheduled to commence at ten in the Federal Courthouse in Trenton—a ten-minute ride from the prison.

Smith was transported in handcuffs, attached to a belt around his waist, to the office of the United States Marshal—and was placed in a detention cell to await the start of the proceedings.

It was the first time Smith had been outside the walls of the prison in nearly thirteen years.

Smith later shared his initial impressions with Bill Buckley.

> The outside world is filthy. The air stinks, the new buildings look like cheeseboxes, and the new cars look like toys made in Japan. The dirt is what amazed me, I cannot remember the world being so dirty and I wonder if I notice it only because I was seeing it—almost—for the first time. I wonder if others, who are out there every day, realize how filthy the buildings and streets are and how rotten the air smells. Believe it or not, in the big parking lot across the street

from the courthouse, the most astonishing thing was not the designs or the bright colors of the new cars lined up in rows, but the fact that I did not see one clean car in the entire lot. Every car was filthy, the colors muted by a film of dirt. The streets are the same way, dirty, littered, and filled with bumps and holes and cracks. The people were clean, all dressed in the wildest, brightest colors one could imagine, and the girls were wearing skirts that almost weren't, but they weren't smiling. Everyone was walking around looking as if they had just flunked algebra.

Smith was soon informed there would be an indefinite delay.

Attorneys Lichtenstein and Umin had gone *somewhere* to meet with Assistant Prosecutor Edward N. Fitzpatrick.

In November, William Cahill had been elected Governor of New Jersey—the first Republican to hold the office since 1954—leading to the appointment of new prosecutors throughout the state. Guy Calissi, who had been fighting Smith's appeals tooth and nail since the conviction, was out.

Umin and Lichtenstein returned to Trenton from their *secret* meeting with Fitzpatrick shortly before two that afternoon and met with their client.

Fitzpatrick had stated at the outset that the Bergen County Prosecutor's Office and the State of New Jersey thought it would be to everyone's benefit if Smith's case were *terminated*.

Brief Against Death had cast serious doubts among public officials and in the media with regard to the fairness and the integrity of the judicial system in general, and the County Prosecutor's office in particular.

In addition, defending the state's case against Smith's appeals would be extremely costly to taxpayers.

For these reasons the state would be willing to reach a settlement which would grant Smith his freedom in the shortest possible time and, at the same moment, preserve the respectability of the state's conviction record.

All Smith needed to do was to plead guilty to second-degree murder for a crime he had insisted, for thirteen years, he had not committed.

The sentence could then be reduced from death to life imprisonment with the *possibility* of parole.

It was the same offer Calissi had presented to Smith in 1957.

Since the parole board had absolute discretion to deny parole for as long as it wished and without reason, the uncertainty was unacceptable to Smith.

After further discussions, Fitzpatrick stated that he would be willing to write to the parole board recommending parole at first eligibility on the grounds that he felt Smith was fully rehabilitated and the state should use Smith as an example of the *success* of the rehabilitation process.

Fitzpatrick had consulted his superior, Prosecutor Robert Dilts.

Dilts agreed that if Smith accepted a life sentence, and Fitzpatrick wrote to the parole board as promised, the prosecutor would *not* oppose parole.

In addition, the prosecutor would agree to make available to the parole board certain *confidential* information in the form of investigative reports that would clearly indicate that Smith's case should *never* have been a first-degree murder case in the first place and Smith should *not* be serving a life sentence.

For his part, Smith was to agree to withdraw his appeal to the federal court and agree to forego any further challenges to his conviction.

Again, since the neither the prosecutor or the judge could *guarantee* parole, Smith was strongly opposed to signing on.

Hard Bargains

Edgar Smith remained adamant.

He continued to insist he was not responsible, in any way, for the death of Victoria Zielinski.

Smith's attorneys presented persuasive arguments for pleading guilty to a lesser charge of second-degree murder—but he would not consider accepting a reduction of sentence that would not *guarantee* the possibility of parole, and a sentence of life imprisonment offered no such guarantee.

It appeared as if only a new trial could provide the prospect of a lesser sentence which would include any *certain* hope of getting out alive.

Lichtenstein and Umin developed a strategy which could conceivably offer a solution Smith would consider.

If Smith agreed, they would request the pre-hearing conference before Judge Barlow be moved to May 8, in order to get all of their ducks in a row.

Then, the prosecutor *and* Smith's attorneys would go to Barlow to argue whether Smith's conviction was legal under *Greenwald v. Wisconsin*—a 1968 case in which the Supreme Court had voided a conviction and ordered a new trial due to the use of a confession obtained in circumstances similar to those in which the police had obtained statements from Smith following his arrest.

No *habeas corpus* hearing would be required prior to the argument—a decision would be based strictly on the record compiled in the state court.

The state would argue against applying the *Greenwald* standard, *just for the cameras,* but Judge Barlow would be informed in advance of the arguments that a ruling favorable to Smith would result in *the termination of Smith's case through agreement.*

If Judge Barlow voided Smith's conviction, and ordered a new trial, the prosecutor stipulated that to avoid dragging the case out the state would *not* appeal the ruling *if* Smith would immediately return to Bergen County, waive his right to a new trial, and plead *non vult* to the indictment.

In New Jersey, all indictments were so-called *open indictments.* They do not specify any *degree* of murder, rather a *general* charge of murder—with the determination of the degree left to the trial jury to decide after being presented the evidence. The prosecutor may *ask* the jury to return a first-degree verdict, but it is left to the jury to decide on a first-degree or second-degree conviction. Due to the *open indictment* policy, the New Jersey statutes permit the *non vult* or *no defense* plea to the indictment. Then, it is up to the judge accepting the plea to decide whether to impose a life sentence—or a sentence not exceeding the maximum sentence permitted for second-degree murder, which was thirty years.

A minimum sentence must also be set.

Smith's attorneys felt confident that Judge Barlow would play along and take the sentence of life imprisonment without parole off the table.

Edgar Smith's attorneys walked their client through the math—using a hypothetical sentence of twenty-one to thirty years for second-degree murder.

With such a sentence, Smith could be eligible for parole—considering time served and credits for work time and *good time*—in several months.

Worst case, Smith would *max out* after doing two-thirds of the *maximum* sentence and could be eligible, with time served, to walk out of the prison with *no parole* requirements in as few as three years.

Edgar Smith could be free before his fortieth birthday.

Edgar Smith had been battling the State of New Jersey for thirteen years, with a single goal in mind.

To have his murder conviction overturned, be granted a new trial, and win acquittal.

His attorneys presented Smith with the worst-case scenarios if he chose to *reject* the proposed arrangement.

Whether or not Barlow would order a new trial *without* the proposed stipulations was impossible to predict.

If Barlow did so order, there was no certainty as to how long Smith would have to continue to wait in prison for a trial to be scheduled.

And there was no guarantee that a new trial would successfully lead to acquittal.

If Smith was convicted again, sentencing would *still* be at the discretion of the court—and Smith might never again see short skirts and filthy cars.

Smith's attorneys argued that the surest and quickest way to freedom was to plead guilty to a crime he insisted he had not committed.

Umin and Lichtenstein urged Smith to seriously consider and accept the irony of the situation.

The attorneys also impressed upon their client the urgency of the matter.

They argued it was vital that the media and the public remain interested in the case.

Continued watching—to keep the state accountable.

Talk on the street of Smith's possible innocence, and the allegations of police and prosecutorial misconduct, served to pressure the state to be rid of Smith as soon as possible.

But time was not on Smith's side.

The light focused on the case by *Brief Against Death* was beginning to dim—and the Addonizio scandal threatened to extinguish it completely.

Former Newark, New Jersey Mayor Hugh Addonizio, and nine former or current officials of the Newark Municipal Government, had been indicted by a federal grand jury for taking *kickbacks* from city contractors after the Newark riots of 1967.

Their trial would begin on the first of June in federal court—with Judge Barlow presiding.

And the Addonizio case would then steal the spotlight.

The attorneys pressured Smith to make a decision.

A quick decision.

Smith agreed to take the first step and Barlow granted a continuance.

The hearing was set for May 8, 1970.

Leap of Faith

During the weeks Smith waited for the May eighth hearing, he grew to trust the proposed arrangement less and less.

The wheeling and dealing seemed to Smith like a poker game between the prosecutor and his own attorneys—where his future was the buy-in and the state held all of the high cards.

Too many *what ifs*—which Smith delineated in his own words.

> How did I know that once I had made the plea, and it was too late for me to back out, the judge wouldn't double-cross us and tap me with a life sentence?
>
> How did we know the prosecutor wouldn't double-cross us and refuse to recommend second-degree sentencing?
>
> How did we know that even if the judge went along with the deal and granted me second-degree sentencing, he wouldn't give me the maximum and then he and the prosecutor oppose parole for me?

Lichtenstein tried to assure his client. Everything had been agreed upon and, although parole might be delayed, he felt the judge and prosecutor would honor their side of the bargain.

Lichtenstein told Smith, *We need to take their word.*

245

Smith continued to voice his reservations to his lawyers.

The way he saw it, he would be giving the state everything the prosecutor wanted—the plea, the conviction, the withdrawal of his appeals, the illusion of the *integrity* of the judicial system—and all that he would receive in return was an *imprecise* promise that after he had sold himself out, and it was too late to change his mind, the state would come through with something *specified but not guaranteed*.

He was being asked to trust those who he insisted had been deceitful from the very start.

On May 8, Smith was transported from the prison to the Federal Court Building.

There was very little media coverage of the hearing—there were other, more critical events dominating the news.

Ten days earlier, on April 29, U.S troops invaded Cambodia—instigating widespread anti-war demonstrations.

On May 4, four Kent State students had been killed on campus by Ohio National Guardsmen.

And on the day of the hearing, *Let It* Be—the final album by The Beatles—was released.

In the courtroom—while waiting for Judge Barlow to enter—David Webster, Umin's co-counsel, told Smith he needed to make a decision.

A final decision.

If Smith wanted to back out there was still time, but the judge would need to be informed before the arguments began.

Smith asked for some last opinions from Webster.

"What do you think, David? Is it a good deal?"

"I think so, but you're the one who has to decide."

"Do you trust them?"

"I wouldn't put it quite that way. I would say that all things considered, it would be to the state's advantage to keep its word. They would have nothing to gain by double-crossing you at this stage. The state wants this case closed as much as anyone does."

"You really think it's the best we can do?"

"I think so."

"Okay."

Judge Barlow entered the courtroom.

The roles had been assigned.

Attorney Steven Umin would present the *Greenwald* argument for a new trial.

Assistant Prosecutor Fitzgerald would argue against, with a dramatic performance designed to look convincing to the press and the public.

Judge Barlow would take the matter *under advisement,* and in short time make a ruling in favor of Smith.

The hearing would simply be a matter of going through the motions.

A stage for the performance, as scripted by the defense attorneys and the prosecution, to be acted out.

And if everyone stayed on script, Smith's first-degree murder conviction would quickly be overturned in exchange for a guilty plea to a lesser charge.

His penalty would therefore be reduced from a death sentence to no more than thirty years.

And Edgar Smith could soon become an *ex-convict.*

Attorney Umin and Prosecutor Fitzgerald both expected a ruling from Judge Barlow *before* the judge was scheduled to preside over the Addonizio Trial, set to begin on June 1.

But May came to an end, Americans rolled out the hamburgers and hot dogs to celebrate Memorial Day, and no word had come from Barlow.

Tipping the Scales of Justice

*At his best, man is the noblest of all animals—
separated from law and justice he is the worst.*
—Aristotle

*Nobody gets justice.
People only get good luck or bad luck.*
—Orson Welles

Punishment is justice for the unjust.
—Saint Augustine

*There is a higher court than courts of justice
and that is the court of conscience.
It supersedes all other courts.*
—Mohandas Gandhi

From Barlow to Gibbons

On August 4, Judge Barlow threw a monkey wrench into the works.

Barlow rejected the *Greenwald* argument and, in doing so, negated the possibility of the case being settled out of court.

Smith would, therefore, be forced into a *habeas corpus* hearing after all— and the arrangement worked out between Smith's lawyers and the prosecutor in May went out the window.

The defense decided to file an *interlocutory* appeal of Barlow's ruling. If the United States Court of Appeals overruled Barlow's ruling no hearing would be necessary and a new trial would be ordered. If the Court of Appeals did not overrule, Smith's attorneys would then prepare for the Supreme Court-ordered habeas corpus hearing—a hearing ordered nearly twenty-one months earlier.

Barlow, most likely in an attempt to avoid scrutiny by an appeals court, came back with an offer. If Smith agreed to postpone the interlocutory appeal, the judge agreed to rehear the *Greenwald* argument.

More delays, and by the beginning of October Smith's attorneys decided they would get nowhere with Barlow unless they played his game or, if that failed, tried to go over his head. So— as a *first resort*—Umin withdrew the interlocutory appeal, and proposed January 15, 1971 as the date to finally begin the habeas corpus hearing. Barlow agreed to accept January 15, but only as a *target* date.

There was no commitment.

In addition, nearly a year after the case had been assigned to Barlow, he had failed to address essential *guidelines* for the habeas corpus hearing.

—Which side had the burden of proof?

—What would be the scope of the hearing?

—What issues would the judge permit to be raised?

—What evidentiary rules would be followed?

—What pre-hearing discovery would be permitted?

—Would the defense be bound by federal rules of criminal procedure since Smith's was a criminal case or by the rules of civil procedure, since habeas corpus is a civil proceeding?

Until Barlow answered those questions, neither Smith's attorneys nor Assistant Prosecutor Fitzpatrick could prepare for January 15.

Finally, nearly two years after the Supreme Court sent the case back down to the lower court to be heard, Umin lost patience and decided it was time to file a *writ of mandamus* seeking to have Judge Barlow *ordered* to act without further delay and, if he failed to do so, asking for Barlow's removal from the case.

The petition for the writ of mandamus was filed in the United States Court of Appeals for the Third Circuit in Philadelphia.

It was the fire under the bench that got Judge Barlow moving.

Barlow rushed to his own defense—laying out the rules for the habeas corpus hearing.

Declaring that the burden of proof would be on the state, defining the issues that would be heard, and agreeing to permit full discovery under the *civil* rules of procedure.

It was everything the defense was hoping for when filing *mandamus* to force Barlow's hand—short of a confirmed start date.

Mandamus was denied on December 3, 1970, but the court stated the denial was *without prejudice in the appellant's right to renew the motion if the hearing in the District Court for the District of New Jersey is further delayed.*

When Judge Barlow still failed to confirm a date, Attorney Umin took the matter to Associate Justice Brennan of the Supreme Court, who supervised the New Jersey federal court and the Third Circuit Court of Appeals.

Shortly after, Barlow was replaced by Circuit Judge John Gibbons.

Gibbons was designated to sit as district court judge for the sole purpose of hearing Smith's case, and he immediately ruled that the hearing would begin on January 18, 1971.

Preparation

With the rules of engagement and a date set, after a delay of more than two years, Smith's attorney, Steve Umin, could finally initiate preparation for the habeas corpus hearing—now only three weeks away.

Umin was unrelenting—by the end of December he was working seven days a week, twelve to eighteen hours a day.

Going through records of the case. Reading transcripts, petitions, and briefs from earlier appeals. Interviewing prospective witnesses. Travelling to Colorado to take a deposition from Smith's ex-wife, and then to Florida for a deposition from one of the detectives who had participated in the post-arrest interrogation. Interviewing past and present members of the Bergen County prosecutor's office and going through all of the files made available under the rules of civil discovery. By the second week in January, with over a thousand hours of preparation put in, Umin was ready to begin working with his client—preparing Edgar Smith for *his* testimony.

At the outset, it was decided that Smith would *not* be permitted to look over any of the police reports compiled at the time of the investigation in 1957, including those recounted in Smith's own book, *Brief Against Death*.

Umin felt the story Smith told on the witness stand at the hearing had to be Smith's story exactly as he remembered it fourteen years later, uncolored by the police reports, in order to stand up under cross-examination. The lawyers would prepare

Smith for his testimony by taking *his* story, going over it again and again, shaving it down to the essentials, eliminating unnecessary details, and coaching him in answering *only* the questions asked. Smith was advised, when called by Umin, to take his story from the moment of his arrest up until the arraignment on the murder charge—in chronological order.

Keep it neat and simple.

It was arranged that Smith would be transferred to federal custody while the hearing was in progress, at the Federal Detention Center in New York City.

It was also arranged with Judge Gibbons and the United States Marshals Service to provide Smith and his attorneys a private room in Newark each night after court, for consultation purposes, before he was returned to New York City for overnight detention.

On Sunday, January 17, 1971, the Baltimore Colts defeated the Dallas Cowboys, 16-13, in Super Bowl V.

The followed morning, Edgar Smith was issued a worn, ill-fitting suit, and was handcuffed to a belt around his waist, for the ninety-minute drive from the New Jersey State Prison in Trenton to the Federal Courthouse in Newark.

Hearing at Last

The proceedings were held in what was actually a bankruptcy hearing room—the only room available. It was a small room with bench seats.

The front row was just eight feet from the judge's perch.

Judge Gibbons was already at his roost when Smith was brought in.

Smith sat at the cramped defense table—Lichtenstein on his left, Umin and Webster on his right.

Gibbons reiterated the ground rules.

The prosecutor, Edward Fitzpatrick, called Joseph Gilroy as his first witness. His testimony was the same as it had been at the original trial.

Fitzpatrick next called Detective Vahe Garabedian, a member of the team that had taken Smith into custody and interrogated him in March 1957.

The detective testified to the discovery of spots on the seat of Gilroy's car which appeared to be blood, and to a pair of khaki trousers stained with blood. He further testified that when Smith was asked about the trousers, he claimed they were not his. Last, he stated that scrapings were taken from underneath Smith's fingernails to test for *blood or fibers of the victim.*

In cross-examination, Umin jumped at the opportunity to establish that, at the start, Smith was not merely a suspect—but *the* suspect.

Umin: Did you ever take fingernail scrapings from Joseph Gilroy?

Garabedian: No.

Umin: To your knowledge, were fingernail scrapings taken from any other person apart from Edgar Smith?

Garabedian: On that evening, no.

Umin: When you picked Edgar Smith up, and took him to the Mahwah Police Headquarters, did anyone there tell Mr. Smith that he was free to leave at any time?

Garabedian: I don't know. Not while I was there.

Gibbons: Did you have any instructions to inform suspects they had an option to refuse to go with the police?

Garabedian: I would have to say no, sir, no specific instructions as to that.

Gibbons: You didn't so inform Smith?

Garabedian: That's right. We did not.

Gibbons: Did you tell Smith he was being picked up because the First Assistant Prosecutor had told you to pick him up after receiving information about the blood spots in Gilroy's car?

Garabedian: No.

In the afternoon, Detective Gordon Graber was called to the stand.

Detective Graber had been one of the detectives who had been sent to bring Edgar Smith into police headquarters.

He was questioned by Assistant Prosecutor Springstead, and recounted the course of the investigation—offering no help to either side.

Court recessed at 4:30.

Smith and his lawyers remained in Newark to confer, continue to work on his testimony, and await the delivery of the typed transcript.

Then Smith was taken to the Federal Detention Center on West Street in Lower Manhattan, where he would spend the night.

The foundation of the defense's case to overturn the conviction was to demonstrate that the interrogation of Edgar Smith, from the evening of March 5 into March 6, had violated procedures as stipulated in the Supreme Court ruling in *Greenwald v. Wisconsin.*

When Detective Graber was recalled to the stand the following morning, the prosecution's questioning gave the defense a leg up.

Asked to describe Smith's *attitude* at the various times Graber had seen Smith, the detective testified that Smith had seemed *cool, calm and collected* at two in the morning of the sixth. But, by two that afternoon—following twelve continuous hours of interrogation—Smith was *subdued and very quiet, which he had not been previously.*

Umin capitalized in his cross-examination.

Umin had served as clerk to Justice Potter Stewart when the Warren Supreme Court heard *Miranda v. Arizona*—and he got right to it.

> Umin: Did you tell Smith he didn't have to say anything to you?
>
> Graber: No, I did not tell him that.
>
> Umin: Did you tell him that anything he said might be used against him?
>
> Graber: I did not tell him that.
>
> Umin: Did you give him any information about his legal rights?

Graber: No, sir, I did not.

Umin then turned the questioning to the shoes Smith had discarded, and the recovery of the shoes.

Umin: Can you tell us what your observation of Smith's shoes were?

Graber: There appeared to be some stains on the shoes that could be blood. And there was a red fiber adhered to the sole of one of the shoes that appeared similar to the texture of the sweater the Zielinski girl was wearing.

Umin: On the trip at two in the morning on March 6 to locate the shoes, was Edgar Smith a suspect in the murder of Victoria Zielinski?

Graber: Yes, I would classify him so.

Umin: Would you say he was the *prime* suspect at the time?

Graber: I would say he was the only one who had been with the victim the evening before.

Umin established that by nine on the morning of March 6, while Smith was being interrogated in the county courthouse, judges were available in the building before whom he could have been charged and arraigned.

Instead, detectives continued to question him for seven more hours.

When Umin completed his cross, Judge Gibbons held the witness to ask if during the time Smith was being questioned in the prosecutor's office he had been dressed in a *uniform from the jail.*

Graber admitted that Smith had been dressed in such a uniform after his own clothing had been taken from him.

. . .

The state called Walter Spahr, who had been the Chief of Bergen County Detectives in 1957.

Umin was not worried about what Spahr might say during direct.

Spahr had retired after his name came up in tapes of bugged telephone conversations between members of organized crime and he would not be seen as a *reliable* witness if his testimony was detrimental to Smith.

Instead, Spahr's testimony helped Smith's cause.

During direct, Spahr volunteered that he had been briefed by County Prosecutor Guy Calissi prior to meeting Smith.

Prosecutor Fitzpatrick quickly changed the subject—but the horse was out of the barn—the door was open for Umin's follow-up in cross-examination.

In line with the strategy developed by Smith's legal team, Steve Umin continued his efforts to suggest to Judge Gibbons—through carefully chosen questions to witnesses—that, from the start, the attitude of the prosecutors and of the police in 1957 was *we have our man, no need to look any further, now let's get a confession.*

> Umin: When you met with Calissi in his private office, what did he tell you about the status of the investigation?
>
> Spahr: He said, *We have a pair of pants with blood on them.*
>
> Umin: Did he say who's pants he thought them to be?
>
> Spahr: He said, *We think we may have the man.*
>
> Umin: Did he tell you where the man was at that time?
>
> Spahr: Yes, he said the man was in the office.
>
> Umin: Did he tell you the man was free to leave?

Spahr: I don't believe he mentioned whether the man was free to leave or not.

Umin: Were you told by Captain DeMarco to interrogate Edgar Smith?

Spahr: I think he used the word *talk*, go talk to that fellow.

Umin: Did you use that word when you made your report?

Spahr: Yes, I did.

Umin: What word?

Spahr: Interrogate.

Spahr then testified that Captain DeMarco asked everyone to leave the room so that Spahr and Detective DeLisle could be alone with Smith.

Then, after explaining what he and Detective DeLisle had agreed on in advance as a technique to be used on Smith, Spahr said, *In my opinion, from looking at and hearing about the crime, I felt this was not a deliberate or a pre-meditated thing.*

Umin: Did you know at this point that Edgar Smith had been with Victoria Zielinski the night of the murder?

Spahr: I think I did at that point, yes. It was, and still is my contention, that this was not a well-planned, laid out thing. I believe it hap-pened on the spur of the moment.

Umin: Do your notes contain any indication that you told Edgar Smith that the act must have been done with great provocation?

Spahr: No, they don't, sir.

Umin: But you did tell him that?

Spahr: Yes.

Umin: At any time during that period did you show Edgar Smith a legal file?

Spahr: Yes.

Umin: Can you tell us what that legal file was?

Spahr: I believe the name was *State v. Ludon,* or Ludwin, a homicide case.

Umin: And what did you tell Edgar Smith about it, if anything, when you showed him the file?

Spahr: Yes, I explained that it was my impression, and I think it was correct, that all murders are *presumed* to be second-degree and the prosecutor would recommend a degree of murder at the opening of Smith's trial. I told Smith, *Now, here is a case where this man killed his brother, and look what he got.* Or something to that effect.

Umin could not be more pleased.

Spahr's testimony suggested they were hoping to get a statement from Smith by implying that even though they had the evidence they needed to put Smith at the scene—cooperation could go a long way toward determining the *degree* of the charge.

In redirect, Fitzpatrick again asked a poorly thought out question.

Fitzpatrick: Did anyone in the prosecutor's office say to you, *Go in and talk to this guy and get a confession?*

Spahr: No. And he *never* made a confession.

Testimony on the following day did little, if anything, to advance the state's *or* the defense's case—however, an incident at the close of the day earned Smith a warning from his lawyers.

Twelve minutes before the session was set to end, Fitzpatrick asked the judge to recess early. He had an appointment, he said, and added that to stay twelve minutes longer *would be somewhat of a hardship.*

Edgar Smith then said, loud enough for everyone in the courtroom to hear, *It's been a hardship for me for fourteen years.*

Smith's attorney, David Webster, apologized to Fitzpatrick—and then lectured Smith against doing anything to embarrass the prosecutor again.

"Fitzpatrick is not doing very well, not giving us a very difficult time, and we're far out in front," Webster said. "Let's not get him angry. He may get better if he's angry."

The Return of Fred Galda

Frederick Galda, former First Assistant Prosecutor for Bergen County, now a judge for the Bergen County District Court, was called to testify.

Galda had been in charge of the Zielinski investigation and had led the questioning of Edgar Smith in the spring of 1957.

During direct, Fitzpatrick focused on the bloodied pants, how Smith had denied they were his, and his wife had later identified them *as* his—which led to the question about the moment when Galda first believed he had sufficient evidence to charge Smith with the crime.

It was exactly the line Umin wished to pursue in cross-examination.

Umin began by asking Galda what standards the prosecution had used to determine whether or not to *charge* Smith with the crime. A crucial point, because when the police have sufficient evidence to make an arrest and bring formal charges, they *must* make those charges—regardless of whether or not they feel they have sufficient evidence to get a conviction.

To continue to interrogate a suspect to obtain *more* evidence, to build a stronger case, is not permissible except under rigid controls—the most critical of which is that suspects *must be advised of their rights* and *given access to an attorney*. The suspect has, according to law, ceased to be a *mere* suspect—the evidence has made the suspect the person *in fact* charged with the crime even though formal charges have not yet been brought and, at that point, he or she is entitled to all the protection afforded to those *formally* charged.

Galda explained that when he spoke of *evidence* he felt was needed to bring formal charges, he meant *evidence* with which you could go to trial.

This was clearly a misinterpretation, and Umin jumped on it.

> Umin: If you had sufficient evidence to convince yourself that Smith committed the crime, but insufficient evidence to get a conviction, would you have charged Smith with the crime?
>
> Galda: Many people entered into this phase of the discussions about whether or not to charge Smith. I felt that once it had been established that the pants were Smith's, that we could go no further—that this was now in the *accusatory stage*. This was where we now *had* to accuse him.

But, as the record of the hearing already showed, the prosecutor did *go further*. At least another seven and a half hours interrogating Edgar Smith in the attempt, Umin would argue, to collect evidence supporting a *first-degree* indictment.

The prosecutor had not brought Smith to court for a formal arraignment or informed him of his rights once the investigation had reached the *accusatory stage*—as the Supreme Court ruling in *Escobedo v. Illinois* required.

This again spoke to the defense argument that both the police and the prosecutor had used highly improper—if not illegal—tactics in bringing Edgar Smith into police headquarters and interrogating him through the night—and then continuing to question him through the following afternoon without allowing him the opportunity to have counsel present.

Umin continued to drive this essential point home, playing primarily to the man he considered an *audience of one*—Judge Gibbons.

Umin: When in your mind the investigation reached what you called the *accusatory stage*, what did that mean?

Galda: Can I hear that again?

Umin: What consequences does the decision that the investigation has reached the *accusatory stage* have?

Judge Gibbons: What do you mean by *accusatory stage*?

Galda: We were in a position at that time, when the pants were identified, as I saw it, to formally charge Edgar Smith.

Umin: Did you at that time formally charge Edgar Smith?

Galda: He was formally charged in Mahwah.

Umin: At what time of day?

Galda: Pretty close to five in the afternoon.

Umin: At what time did the investigation reach the *accusatory stage*? Was it around nine-thirty that morning when Edgar Smith's wife identified the pants?

Galda: That would be substantially correct. We were satisfied at that time that was it, and there was nothing more that could be done.

Umin: Did you advise him of his rights at that time?

Galda: I did not.

Umin: Do you know whether he was advised at that time of any of his rights?

Galda: When you say any of his rights—we didn't do that. His rights. He could go to the bathroom, he couldn't leave the building—we didn't say *your rights are X, Y, and Z*, if that's what you are driving at.

Umin: Since you were in the county court-house, it would have been possible at the *accusatory stage*, at around nine-thirty on the morning of March 6, to arraign and charge Smith right there before a county judge—rather than delaying the arraignment and continuing to interrogate him before finally taking him to Mahwah for arraignment at five.

Galda: Is that a question?

Umin: No, sir, merely an observation. I have no more questions, your honor.

Edgar Smith's attorneys unanimously agreed that it could hardly have gone any better.

They had done their best to sell the argument, to Gibbons, that in 1957 the prosecutor and police detectives had violated legal requirements by failing to inform Edgar Smith of his rights and, failing to do so, effectively *denied* him his rights.

Now it would be up to their client to close the deal.

Closing

Edgar Smith had been picked up by police and brought to Mahwah Police Headquarters shortly before midnight on March 5, 1957.

Nearly nine hours later, he sat at the Bergen County Court Building with Detective Charles DeLisle.

To that point, Smith had not been arrested or charged with a crime.

He had asked more than once for an opportunity to call his wife, and to contact a lawyer.

Instead, his wife was brought to the court building in Hackensack to identify a pair of pants, and he was assured he did not need counsel.

Detective DeLisle worked on convincing Smith to make a statement.

"Smitty, your wife is here asking to see you," the detective said. "If you cooperate with us, we'll let you see her and she can go home. You have a little baby. Your wife should be home with the baby, not here answering questions that *you* should be answering. But she cannot leave until we get the answers. All you have to do is cooperate, that's all."

"How?"

"It is very simple. Just give us a statement. If there are some things that you don't want to say, you don't have to. You're a smart boy. You know you can say *I don't want to talk about that* or *I don't remember*."

"You've got to be kidding. You people are not looking for cooperation, you want a confession."

"No, not a confession. We don't want that. Just a statement. You won't even have to sign it. Think it over, I'll give you a few minutes."

"Okay, I'll give you a statement," Smith said after several minutes. "If I don't have to sign it and I can see my wife."

The *statement* was actually a Q&A—with Assistant Prosecutor Fred Galda asking all of the questions, and Edgar Smith providing the answers.

Smith had not been *formally* arrested or charged.

He had not been arraigned, though the means to do so were available at the courthouse.

He did not have counsel present.

The statement was recorded on the sixth of March by court stenographer Arthur Ehrenbeck.

It was never signed by Smith.

Nevertheless, it was admitted into evidence at the 1957 trial by Judge O'Dea—over the strong objections of Defense Attorney John Selser—and read to the jury.

Moreover, it was admitted by O'Dea as a *concession of guilt*.

The statement became a critical piece of the State's case against Smith.

The circumstances leading up to the Q&A, and the manner in which it was introduced and treated in court, were Umin's central arguments for the appeal to Judge Gibbons to overturn the first-degree murder conviction and order a new trial.

All of the preparation for Smith's testimony at the habeas corpus hearing had been directed by Smith's attorneys toward those arguments.

Steve Umin called Smith to the stand and brought his client directly to the point where Smith could plead his own case.

> Umin: There came a time later that morning
> of March sixth, Edgar, when you participated in

a question and answer session—conducted by Mr. Galda and recorded by a stenographer.

Smith: Yes.

Umin: Why did you do that?

Smith: That is a very difficult question to answer. It involves everything that happened to me all night long. When I had first been taken into police custody, I felt *compelled* right off the bat to answer their questions. I felt that if I didn't answer the questions then that in itself was going to be suspicious and perhaps they would take it as incriminating against me. And during the night I had lied to the police. I had given them misleading information, and once having told them something and once they had found out that not everything I had said was true, then I felt compelled to explain, to talk some more. And this went on through the night, and by morning I had gotten myself so tied up in contradictory stories and at that point I was beginning to feel a whole range of pressures on me that I didn't really feel I had any choice other than to attempt to give them one more explanation. I was there. I was not being allowed to contact anyone. All through the night there had been pressure, like a little pressure from being asked to take a lie detector test, or Mr. Calissi wanting me to go to the morgue. I don't know, it's sort of an overwhelming feeling of being in police custody, that was the thing that bothered me more than anything else. It was like being in a cocoon, you are cut off from everyone, you are cut off from everything, you do only what they want, you go where they say you go, you do what they say you do, you can't even go to the bathroom without asking, and when they do allow you to go to the bathroom they send somebody with you to stand in the open doorway as if they're afraid you're going to commit suicide or try to escape. It was the now and then glimpses of my wife that I was given and the attempts to contact my attorney—they let me call my wife and then they would take it away from me. All these pressures in addition to the feeling that I was *compelled* to answer the questions. At some point, I couldn't take it any longer. I knew that unless I went along with them I was going to sit there and they were going to keep hitting me with questions, and keep hitting me with more questions, and my wife was going to sit in an office. And they told me she was being questioned, and that she had identified my pants. They told me she was going to stay there until I *did* give them what they wanted, until I did cooperate with them. They told me if I wanted a lawyer I would have to cooperate with them. If I wanted *anything* I had to cooperate with them. If I wanted a cigarette, I had to cooperate with them. And at some point, I just gave in and gave them what they wanted.

Umin: Did you think that would help you in some way?

Smith: I just didn't know what else I could do. I just don't think it mattered at that point. What mattered was getting out of it, getting out of that office, getting away from the questions, getting to a lawyer, getting to see my wife. Just doing what they said. It is difficult to explain to anyone who hasn't gone through it. You are in a box and there is no way out of it.

Umin: No further questions.

The hearing ended.

Edgar Smith was ordered back to the State Prison at Trenton to await the decision.

Judge Gibbons ruled there would be no closing arguments in court.

Instead, each side would submit closing arguments in brief form by the seventeenth of March.

Rulings

The closing arguments brief ordered by Judge Gibbons was filed by Edgar Smith's defense team before the March seventeenth deadline.

Weeks went by without any sign of Prosecutor Fitzpatrick's brief, which was due to be filed at the same time.

Smith's lawyers informed their client that Judge Gibbons was already at work on his opinion and predicted that as soon as Fitzpatrick filed the State's brief, Gibbons would immediately hand down his ruling.

Fitzpatrick finally filed his brief and on May 17, 1971, Gibbons ruled.

Judge Gibbons voided Smith's conviction and ordered that the *writ of habeas corpus* freeing Smith would issue *unless within 60 days the State of New Jersey shall grant to the petitioner Edgar H. Smith Jr. a new trial on the indictment charging him with the murder of Victoria Zielinski.*

The ruling came down fourteen years after the death of the victim.

Gibbons found that the period of Smith's interrogation on the evening of March 5, 1957, and continuing through the morning and afternoon of March 6, was *coercive in nature* and that the statements elicited from Smith during that period had been *unconstitutionally obtained* and could *not* be used at a retrial.

The judge also ruled that the actions of the police in 1957 were *illegal and unconstitutional under 1957 law*, independent

273

of any *new* constitutional rules established *after* Smith's conviction.

In other words, what the police did was wrong *when* they did it.

Less than a week after Judge Gibbons' ruling, Smith's attorneys filed an *Application for Bail* under the federal rules allowing bail where a habeas corpus petitioner has been successful.

A hearing on the bail application was then set for early June.

On the morning of the bail hearing, Smith was taken from the prison to the federal court building—handcuffed wrists attached to a leather belt around his waist as usual.

The courtroom was crowded with media and spectators—Gibbons ruling in May had made the front page of *The New York Times*.

William Buckley sat in the first row with Warren Steibel—the producer of Buckley's television show, *Firing Line*.

Smith shook hands with Buckley. It was the first time they had physical contact in the many years Buckley had been championing Smith's cause. When Buckley had visited Edgar Smith at the prison, they had always been separated by a glass window and had spoken over a telephone.

Umin presented a short but effective argument in favor of granting bail—citing that Smith's fourteen-year accomplishment in prison had shown that the defendant *would not be a danger to society if released*, that Edgar Smith had *no intention of fleeing*, and that if Smith was retried there was *no fair likelihood he could be convicted of first-degree murder* a second time. He concluded that *one more unconstitutional day in prison would do irreparable harm to Edgar Smith*.

Judge Gibbons appeared impressed.

Fitzpatrick in turn argued that *the federal court had no authority to grant bail to a state prisoner*, that Smith was *guilty of the crime* and *the state would retry him*, and that if Edgar

Smith was set free he would *flee or go into hiding* and *be a danger to the community.*

Judge Gibbons rendered his decision—he would issue an order granting Smith bail in the amount of five thousand dollars.

Fitzpatrick asked that Gibbons restrict Smith's freedom to within the state of New Jersey. Gibbons said there would be no travel restrictions.

Fitzpatrick asked that Smith be denied the right to appear on television. Gibbons said he could not repeal the First Amendment.

Fitzpatrick asked that the order be held up to give the State time to appeal. Gibbons agreed to hold the order for twenty-four hours.

Smith was transported from Newark to the Federal Detention Center in New York City where he would be held until his expected release the following afternoon.

Hurry Up and Wait

The next morning, June 9th, Smith was transported from Manhattan to Newark by United States marshals.

He was placed into a detention cell.

Smith was waiting to be released on bail as ordered by Judge Gibbons.

At noon, Anthony Greski, Chief United States Marshal for New Jersey, took Smith into his office.

Greski said Smith could leave as soon as the bail was posted, and he let Smith use a phone to call Bill Buckley's office.

Buckley's secretary told Smith that someone would be on the way with the five-thousand dollars to cover bail. She said the money was waiting to be picked up and should be there by one in the afternoon—which was when the twenty-four-hour hold granted by Gibbons to Fitzpatrick would expire.

Smith was returned to the detention cell.

At twelve-fifteen, Greski came to the cell.

"I have a telegram I have just received from the clerk of the United States Court of Appeals. I have to read it to you. *No one is to disturb the custody of the prisoner until further order of this court.*"

Thirty minutes later a second telegram arrived. It read as follows.

It is further ordered that the relator, Edgar Smith, is remanded to the custody of the State of

276

New Jersey pending disposition of the appeal on the merits or further order of this court without prejudice to the relator's rights to apply to the courts of the State of New Jersey for release on bond.

Fitzpatrick had gone to Philadelphia to file a motion in the United States Court of Appeals for the Third District to revoke Judge Gibbons' rulings on the conviction reversal, order for a new trial, and granting of bail.

The next step, according to Smith's attorneys, was to wait for the Court of Appeals to rule on Fitzpatrick's motion and hopefully uphold Judge Gibbons' rulings.

The lawyers felt that the Court of Appeals would expedite the process.

It was ordered that typewritten briefs be filed, by both sides, within two weeks—and oral arguments would be heard within thirty days.

There was an *implicit* understanding that a decision would be handed down within a month or two of the oral arguments and, if at that time Smith's lawyers were successful, he could again seek bail.

Edgar Smith was returned to death row in Trenton to await the Court of Appeals ruling.

Wait again.

The State's appeal was argued before the United States Court of Appeals for the Third District in Philadelphia on July 14th. A ruling was expected to come down from that court in early August.

On August 3rd, in a brief two-and-a-half-page opinion, the Court of Appeals held that all of Judge Gibbons' findings of fact and law were correct and that the order reversing Smith's conviction and of requiring a new trial would stand as issued.

Smith and his attorneys decided to test how anxious the State was to close the case by negotiation, conveying to Fitzpatrick the position that they "were preparing for trial and *not* looking for a deal—but that they *would* be willing to listen if the State had something to say."

Meanwhile, Fitzpatrick was going ahead with an appeal to the United States Supreme Court—arguing that the Court of Appeals had been wrong in upholding Gibbons' rulings.

To counter Prosecutor Fitzpatrick's delaying tactics, Smith urged his lawyers to file a *bail application* to the United States Supreme Court.

The attorneys, who were hoping for an audience with the New Jersey Attorney General, felt to do so would put the Attorney General in a position that would make it difficult for him to make a deal of *any* kind.

They argued that the Attorney General would feel *compelled* to *oppose* bail, if only for appearance sake, and to do so successfully he would have to argue that the State could still get a first-degree conviction in the event of a new trial since bail is *permitted* but *not a matter of right* in first-degree cases and the courts rarely grant bail in such cases.

Edgar Smith was not enthusiastic about his attorneys' proposed course of action.

He articulated his concerns in a letter to Buckley.

> I generally object to any discussions with the state, and my objections have been expressed to Steve Umin. I do not think we should have initiated the discussions, nor do I think we should be talking *while I remain in prison*. At least we should have required some show of *good faith* by the State, either a holding back of its appeal to the Supreme Court or an end to the opposition to bail.
>
> I think we must make it clear to the State that

the longer it keeps me in prison, the harder my position will become, and the more determined I will be to *demand* a retrial.

I simply have the feeling that this has become the *lawyers'* case, and at this point the lawyers are thinking only in terms of *dealing.*

It may be incipient paranoia, but I remain convinced that Steve Umin has so committed himself to making a deal with the State that he will not consider anything else, and that his reluctance to file a bail application to the Supreme Court is the result of his belief that he can best sell a deal to *me* if I remain in jail, that the longer I wait, the more anxious I will be to get out of here by accepting *anything* the State offers—if it offers anything.

Smith's lawyers finally met with the New Jersey Attorney General in early September. The result of the meeting was an agreement to meet again *after* the United States Supreme Court ruled on the State's appeal.

The Attorney General seemed willing at that point to settle the case through negotiation, but not until the State had exhausted every avenue of appeal with regard to Judge Gibbons' rulings.

Near the end of September, the State's appeal to the Supreme Court was filed—the State's last chance to prevent Gibbons' habeas corpus order from going into effect and therefore requiring the State to grant Smith a new trial.

Umin immediately filed a petition with United States Supreme Court Associate Justice Brennan, asking that Smith be released on bail pending the outcome of the State's appeal.

Brennan decided *not* to exercise his authority on the bail question, ruling instead that *the question was one of such importance that it should be decided by the full Court rather than by an individual Justice.*

The full Court was out for summer recess, and would not return until the second week in October.

Smith was forced to wait, again, to find out what would happen.

What happened was that the Supreme Court—which tends to avoid *difficult questions* whenever possible—moved the State of New Jersey's appeal to the top of their calendar. The Court dismissed the petition at once and, in doing so, ended the federal role in the case and consequently gave jurisdiction back to the state courts.

At that point, the Supreme Court could ignore the question of bail on the grounds that the case was no longer in the federal courts—and therefore the highest court in the land had no say in the matter.

The Approaching End

When you reach the end of your rope,
tie a knot in it and hang on.
—Franklin Delano Roosevelt

The end of law is not to abolish or restrain,
but to preserve and enlarge freedom.
For in all the states of created beings capable of law,
where there is no law there is no freedom.
—John Locke

I have a wish. It is a fear as well.
That in my end will be my beginning.
—Che Guevara

Fall 1971

While Edgar Smith remained on death row in New Jersey, trapped on a legal see-saw, and a constitutional merry-go-round, other events were stealing headlines—including stories of other prison inmates and other murders.

On August 21, George Lester Jackson, a Maoist-Marxist revolutionary, attempted an escape from San Quentin State Prison in California.

Jackson, like Edgar Smith, had written a book, *Soledad Brother: The Prison Letters of George Jackson,* which had become a best-seller.

Jackson and five hostages were killed as a result of the failed prison break—capturing national attention.

Less than three weeks later, on the ninth of September, approximately one-thousand of the more than twenty-two-hundred prisoners at the Attica Correctional Facility in New York State rose up, gained control of the prison, and took forty-two hostages.

The leaders of the takeover were demanding better living conditions as well as equitable liberties and human rights.

During four days of negotiations, twenty-eight of the prisoners' demands were conceded.

However, authorities would not agree to *complete amnesty* from criminal prosecution for the insurgents—nor would they agree to the removal of Prison Superintendent, William Kirwan.

Negotiations broke down.

On September thirteenth, an assault by New York State Police Troopers to retake the prison facility resulted in the deaths of thirty-three inmates and eleven correctional officers.

In 1971, there were more than thirty bona fide *serial killers* stalking human prey from coast to coast.

Not all of the victims had been discovered or identified at that time.

Many of the predators would not be identified, or recognized as multiple murderers, until sometime later.

But reports of missing persons, and the discovery of corpses, were being continually pronounced in the media—and homeland insecurity was mounting in cities and towns across America.

Among those active in the Fall of 1971 were *The Freeway Phantom, The Houston Mass Murderers, The Zodiac Killer,* Juan Corona, and Ted Bundy.

Between April and November, 1971, five girls between the ages of ten and eighteen were abducted in the District of Columbia area.

Most if not all of the victims had been raped and strangled.

The bodies were dumped along freeways.

The Freeway Phantom was never identified.

In Texas, eight boys went missing and were later found murdered.

The Houston Mass Murderers were later identified as Dean Corll, David Brooks, and Elmer Henley—only after Henley shot and killed Corll in 1973.

Brooks and Henley were tried and received life sentences.

The trio were credited with twenty-eight murders.

In Northern California a mass murderer, who would come to be known as *The Zodiac Killer,* claimed a total of 37 victims between 1968 and 1974.

Zodiac was never identified.

In 1971 a farmer in Yuba City, California—north of Sacramento—noticed a freshly dug hole in a peach orchard.

The next day, the hole was filled with dirt and he notified police.

Investigators uncovered a man's body that had been stabbed and hacked to pieces—and a grocery receipt with the name Juan Corona.

A search warrant for Corona's home was issued, and he was arrested when investigators began finding human bodies buried on his property.

A total of 25 victims were discovered.

Corona was tried and sentenced to life imprisonment.

Theodore Bundy's killing spree is said to have begun in 1971 in Seattle.

By the beginning of 1974, female college students began disappearing at the rate of nearly one per month.

Bundy's homicidal activity later moved to Idaho, Utah, and Colorado.

He was tried and convicted of a kidnapping in Utah, and was later sent to Aspen, Colorado to face a murder charge.

Bundy escaped twice from Colorado jails.

First for six days, before being recaptured. Then, following his second escape, he fled to Florida where he assaulted five more women—killing two.

Bundy was tried and convicted in Florida in 1978, and executed in the electric chair in 1989. He had confessed to 30 murders in seven states.

Also, throughout 1971, the murder trial of Charles Manson and three accomplices had both shocked and oddly fascinated an entire nation.

As did Stanley Kubrick's film adaptation of the Anthony Burgess novel, *A Clockwork Orange*, released in December.

The film received an *X-rating* for its excessive sex and violence and should have been sidestepped for its graphic reminders of the fears predominant at the time, but instead strangely became a box-office and critical success—cited for a number of awards including an Oscar nomination for Best Picture of the Year.

That prize went to *The French Connection,* a film reminding Americans of the increasing specter of their children's exposure to and abuse of drugs.

From the East Coast to the West Coast, minors were finding their freedoms progressively limited by their parents.

There were many more less than pleasant distractions that Fall.

On September 3, a break-in at Daniel Ellsberg's Watergate office began an investigation that would continue for nearly three years and result in the resignation of President Richard Nixon.

Distrust of the government by the governed was no longer reserved to rebellious American youth.

On September 9, John Lennon released *Imagine.* The song pictured a peaceful planet where *all the world could live as one*—which could simply be achieved through man's *good will.* However, due to continued nuclear testing by China and the USSR, Americans had trouble *imagining.*

On September 13, while New York State Police Troopers were storming Attica Prison, Nikita Khrushchev died of a heart attack—leading to a general uncertainty as to what the new leadership might mean to American-Soviet relations.

On the sixteenth, six Ku Klux Klansmen were arrested in connection to the bombing of ten school buses in Pontiac, Michigan—a few days before the buses were to be used to initiate school integration.

On the twenty-second of September, the Organization of the Petroleum Exporting Countries, OPEC, directed member nations to increase oil prices to offset the devaluation of the United States dollar.

On the twenty-fourth, ninety Russian diplomats were expelled from Great Britain for spying.

On the ninth of November, John List killed his mother, wife, and three children in Westfield, New Jersey—and vanished. List would not be captured and brought to justice until 1989.

On November 23, the People's Republic of China was given a seat in the United Nations Security Council.

On December 3, Charles Manson was convicted of first-degree murder, imprisoned, and sentenced to death. The animal was caged, but there was no doubt that Manson continued to have power and influence over his followers on the outside.

And in 1972, the case *California v. Anderson* ruled the death sentence unconstitutional in California—which would make Manson eligible for parole after seven years of incarceration.

There were a great number of events to cause worry in the homeland and, consequently, the approach of Edgar Smith's last stand at the end of November 1971 went somewhat unnoticed.

At the same time, questions of Smith's guilt and of granting him freedom had become debatable.

The State of New Jersey had been fighting vehemently for nearly fifteen years to keep Smith incarcerated, arguing he was *a cold-blooded killer* and *a danger to society.*

However, although the death of fifteen-year-old Victoria Zielinski was no small matter, there had been a change of perspective—both in public opinion and in the media.

A man who had spent more than one-third of his life behind bars, had been a model prisoner, who was articulate enough to write a compelling book, who may or *may not have* committed a crime which appeared unpremeditated and possibly accidental could hardly be considered—by the public, the media, and particularly the State—in the ranks of other *truly* scary monsters running loose in America and the world.

Or so Edgar Smith's attorneys hoped.

Let the Games Begin

Following the Supreme Court's dismissal of the State's appeal of Judge Gibbon's decision, the business of negotiation—or plea bargaining—began once again. With all appellate avenues now closed to the State of New Jersey, the office of Attorney General had either to make a deal with Edgar Smith or obey Gibbon's order for a new trial. Smith's lawyers again held back on petitioning for bail for fear it would upset negotiations.

There were reasons why the State preferred to avoid a new trial.

Witnesses were scattered throughout the country, some had since died, the family of Victoria Zielinski had relocated and the prosecutor was reluctant to reopen old wounds with another trial.

On top of that, the image of New Jersey jurisprudence was under close scrutiny. The State *needed* a conviction—and there was a genuine risk of an acquittal if Smith was retried.

Smith continued to insist, at least in public, that *no deal could ever be good enough to make me plead guilty to this crime. I expect to be retried, and I expect to be found not guilty.*

But, privately, he expressed his own reasons for evading a new trial.

A major concern was the cost in legal fees and expenses—which would require approximately $50,000 he did not have.

Smith's wife, Patricia, had been granted a divorce not long

after his sentencing. She had relocated to Colorado, and remarried.

Smith allowed her new husband to legally adopt their daughter—who was just three months old when Smith was arrested. She was now nearing fifteen-years-old, and her mother's second husband was the only father she knew.

A new trail would require Patricia's testimony, and Smith had no desire to put her or his daughter through such an ordeal.

Finally, there were pragmatic considerations.

A new trial held no *guarantee* of acquittal.

And waiting for a retrial to be scheduled could mean months, perhaps years longer, in prison.

On October 20, 1971, Attorneys Steve Umin and Stephen Lichtenstein came to visit Smith with the first offer from the New Jersey Attorney General.

It was presented by the Attorney General as follows.

PROPOSED PLEA PROCEDURE

I. Presentation of the defendant and the reading of the indictment.

Placing the defendant under oath. Questions as to representation:

Are you represented by counsel?

If so, who are they?

II. Query by the Court as to how the defendant intends to plead to the indictment, and the defendant will respond that he wishes to plead *non vult*.

III. The Court will then question the defendant as to the voluntariness of the plea and his understanding of the plea:

1. You are charged with the crime of murder. Do you understand the nature of this offense?

2. Have you discussed with your counsel the charge of murder and the nature and the conse-

quences of the plea of *non vult* to this charge?

3. Do you understand that a plea of *non vult* is tantamount to a plea of guilty?

4. Do you understand that the Court may impose such sentence as in his discretion he considers appropriate subject to the limits prescribed by law, but in the event the sentence exceeds the recommendation of the prosecutor, you will have the right to retract your plea?

5. Are you entering the plea of *non vult* voluntarily?

IV. The Court will proceed to ask the prosecutor the nature of the facts the prosecutor intends to prove at trial:

1. That the defendant was driving the car of Joseph Gilroy on the night of the murder—March 4, 1957—and that this car was at the scene of the crime.

2. That front portions of the interior of the Gilroy automobile were spotted with blood.

3. That the State will offer several items of clothing stained with blood connecting them with the decedent and identified as belonging to the defendant.

4. That there was adhering to an item of the defendant's clothing a thread similar in color to the sweater the decedent was wearing the night she was killed.

5. That moulage footprint impressions were taken at the scene of the crime which correspond to the size of the defendant's shoes.

6. That in subsequent writings defendant admitted the following:

(a) His presence at the scene of the crime with the decedent in Gilroy's automobile; and

(b) That defendant discarded items of clothing he had worn that evening.

V. Following the presentation by the prosecutor, the Court addresses the following questions to the defendant:

1. Do you understand that a plea of *non vult* is tantamount to an admission of the facts the State has just outlined?

2. Do you admit that you killed Victoria Zielinski?

VI. The Court accepts the plea of *non vult* in the indictment.

VII. The Court asks the defendant and his counsel if they have anything to say as to the Judgment of Conviction to be entered or the sentence to be imposed. Mr. Umin will respond briefly.

VIII. The Court will then ask the prosecutor if he has a recommendation.

The prosecutor shall then answer he does have a recommendation, and his recommendation is that Judgment of Conviction be entered of murder in the second-degree and that the sentence imposed be of the time served by the defendant. The prosecutor will then comment briefly on the reasons for his recommendations.

IX. Entry of conviction of murder in the second-degree, and imposition of sentence of time served.

The entry of the plea of *non vult* in accordance with the above procedure is conditioned upon the entry of Judgment of Conviction of murder in the second-degree and an imposition of sentence of time served without any form of continued supervision.

. . .

Edgar Smith was given a few days to decide.

The choice seemed clear.

Continue to insist on his innocence and remain in prison for an indefinite time awaiting scheduling of a retrial—or accept a conviction of second-degree murder and possibly walk out of prison immediately.

Smith continued to have doubts about the integrity of the Court—continued to fear a *double-cross*.

Smith expressed his reservations and his decision in a letter to Bill Buckley on October 24.

> As you know by now, I saw Steve Lichtenstein again on Friday and told him to go ahead on the understanding that I must have an *iron-clad* guarantee against a double-cross, and that everything must take place exactly as agreed upon.
>
> I have to tell you, Bill, that you are in very exclusive company, since the only people who favor this thing are Umin, Lichtenstein, and yourself. I think it is the wrong thing to do—I am doing it for entirely selfish reasons, not because I think it is right.

When asked later what his *selfish reasons* were, Edgar Smith simply replied: *I wanted out.*

Delay of Game

Shortly after Smith had made the hard choice, agreeing to accept the settlement as outlined in the written plea proposal, Steve Umin advised his client that a new condition had been added.

The Attorney General represented the request as *beneficial* to Smith's cause. He asked that Smith agree to submit to a psychiatric examination, to certify to the judge that Smith could be released *safely* into society. It would, according to the Attorney General, make it easier to persuade the judge that the deal was an acceptable one from the standpoint of public safety—and it would also allay any public fears.

Smith disliked the idea, but acquiesced.

Morris Pashman was the Bergen County judge assigned to the case.

Pashman flatly refused to subscribe to the settlement, and it wasn't until the middle of November that Smith's lawyers were able to ascertain what it was that the judge wanted—what would persuade him to go ahead.

Pashman informed Smith's lawyers that he would not be satisfied unless as part of the proceedings in court—when Smith entered the *non vult* plea—he *confess the crime.*

The judge would accept no less than a *direct admission of guilt.*

Smith protested. He had reluctantly agreed to accept a second-degree murder conviction through a *non vult,* or *no-defense* plea in exchange for his freedom but an *admission of guilt* was something he had denied and battled against for nearly fifteen years. He argued that it would be a betrayal to all those who had believed in his innocence and supported him throughout his incarceration.

Smith's lawyers, and Bill Buckley, continued to maintain that his best hope for freedom was to play along. They argued that whatever the outcome, all who believed him guilty would continue to do so—and those who believed him innocent would also continue to do so, and that they would understand why *he had* to make the hard decision.

Smith gave in.

Judge Pashman must not have expected Smith's quick acceptance of the terms. He seemed unprepared for the decision, and appeared uncertain about how to proceed. He stalled.

Every effort to discuss the delay with Pashman, to determine what *else* he wanted from Smith in return for Smith's freedom, was futile.

As the end of November approached, it was decided there was no way a bail application to the state courts could be avoided.

The application was filed, forcing the judge's hand.

Pashman scheduled a hearing at the Bergen County Courthouse for the twenty-ninth of November.

Meanwhile, Judge Pashman had chosen Dr. Ralph Brancale to conduct a psychiatric evaluation, ordered by the Court—to address the question of if, or if not, Smith's release would pose a *danger to the community*.

Brancale's report included the following *professional* opinions.

> There is nothing in the personality pattern that would suggest the probability of a recurring similar offense, or that manifests any antisocial behavior.

The overall picture looks quite promising and the prospects for the future are good.

No manifest disturbances in either his emotional make-up or his mental processes. It is quite evident that the defendant examined today is a different man than the one who entered the Death House fifteen years ago.

There is no evidence of serious psychiatric pathology and he does not appear to have any malignant psychosexual process. The examiner feels this defendant may be returned to the community without posing a danger to the public.

Smith's attorneys assured their client that Brancale's testimony was a great victory.

However, Judge Pashman continued to delay initiating the outlined plea procedure which would effectively end the long and bitter battle between Edgar Smith and the State of New Jersey.

The hearing entered its third and fourth days with no resolution.

Finally, on Friday, December 3, 1971—after heated discussions between County Judge Pashman, Circuit Judge John Gibbons, the Attorney General of New Jersey, and New Jersey Supreme Court Chief Justice Joseph Weintraub—it was determined the outlined *plea procedure* would go ahead on Monday.

Edgar Smith was returned to Trenton for another weekend on death row.

End Game

On the morning of Monday, December 6, 1971, Edgar Smith arrived at the Bergen County Courthouse in Hackensack at nine-thirty.

Smith was accompanied by transport guards, and an additional escort provided by the New Jersey State Police.

The proceedings did not begin until five-thirty that afternoon.

The courtroom was filled to capacity.

Reporters, spectators, and walls lined with armed guards.

William Buckley had just flown in from Washington, DC on a private jet.

Judge Pashman asked Prosecutor Edward Fitzpatrick if he had *a matter to present to the Court.*

Fitzpatrick informed the judge that the State was bringing Edgar Smith before the Court on his indictment for murder.

Pashman asked Steve Umin if the defense was ready to proceed.

> May it please the Court, Your Honor, the defendant at this time wishes to withdraw his plea of not guilty to the indictment and enter a plea of *non vult* subject to the conditions negotiated and jointly agreed upon with the State of New

Jersey, which will be articulated by Mr. Fitzpatrick in his recommendations to the Court.

Umin's statement was followed by Fitzpatrick's recommendations.

> If Your Honor please, the State has an agreement with counsel and the agreement arrived at is that upon acceptance of a plea of *non vult* to this indictment, the State will recommend a sentence for Edgar Smith as would provide for his immediate release from incarceration under the terms of whatever probation the Court might wish to impose.

Pashman then asked the representative of the Attorney General if that office was in accordance with Fitzpatrick's recommendations.

The reply was that the Office of the Attorney General *concurred wholeheartedly.*

Finally, the judge called Smith to the stand to ask the *big question*—the question to which Pashman had demanded an affirmative answer.

> Pashman: Mr. Smith, did you and you alone kill Victoria Zielinski?
> Smith: I did.
> Pashman: Was anyone else there, Mr. Smith, when you killed her?
> Smith: No.
> Pashman: Did you see anyone else in the area during the time you were with Victoria Zielinski?
> Smith: No.
> Pashman: How did you get to the sandpit, Mr. Smith?

Smith: By automobile.

Pashman: And whose car was it?

Smith: Joe Gilroy.

Pashman: And approximately what time did you get to the sandpit?

Smith: Nine P.M.

Pashman: Would you tell us briefly how did it happen that Victoria Zielinski got into the car.

Smith: She asked me for a ride.

Pashman: Was there any kind of prearranged meeting?

Smith: No.

Pashman: After arriving at the sandpit, Mr. Smith, and a space of time thereafter, did you strike Victoria Zielinski?

Smith: I did.

Pashman: At that time were you wearing tan khaki pants when you killed her?

Smith: I was.

Pashman: Where and when, where and when, Mr. Smith, did you discard those tan khaki pants?

Smith: Same night. Oak Street. Ramsey.

Pashman: Did you leave the sandpit after this and go home?

Smith: I did.

Judge Pashman had quite a lot to say before finally getting around to his ruling—most of it directed at trying to salvage the somewhat tarnished view of the Bergen County police departments and prosecutors' office, and the judicial system in general, which many in the public and the media were looking at as imperfect if not manipulative.

"I do not necessarily agree," Pashman stated, "that the crime had to be more than a second-degree murder."

Pashman went on to say he did not believe there had been any intent or premeditation involved, and Smith had been charged with first-degree murder *simply because he had stated he had left the girl alive and with another man.*

"I truly believe," Pashman said, "I believe that you and you alone, Mr. Smith, brought on the first-degree murder charge and that you alone, as it were, are responsible for the ultimate jury verdict of death."

The judge went on, and on, with a grand speech that included reference to Jean Paul Sartre.

> Perhaps the wheels of justice grind too slowly and we do despair at times. But grind they must, and they must grind with determination regardless of the continuing costs. This is a price, we hope, for a reasonably safe Bergen County. I do not advocate the expenditure of any public funds for the harassment of a defendant, whether it is Mr. Smith or anyone else. That is not the goal of the State of New Jersey. It is not the goal of the County of Bergen and certainly it is not the goal of this Court.
>
> I think it is fair to say that it is normal for any man to attempt to gain his freedom, and it is ludicrous to believe that one will not contend that he is innocent. But in an effort to gain one's freedom, it is no answer to say that the life of Victoria Zielinski cannot be restored and that Edgar Smith cannot be tried for his life under existing law. And we are not seeking to restore the fourteen years and nine months that Edgar Smith has spent in prison. From my vantage point he brought that upon himself. Vicky Zielinski did not. That cannot be the test to determine whether Edgar Smith can be released at this

time. The test is whether the interest and ends of justice have been served by his fourteen years and nine months of confinement and by his thorough and productive rehabilitation of himself.

This is a man who developed from a high school dropout to a self-educated writer. It may be said that Edgar Smith is an outstanding example of the meaningful changes a prisoner may undergo as to render him a useful, productive citizen upon his return to society.

We hope for this.

I think Edgar Smith's example can give us reason to be optimistic about the very beneficial function of our correctional system, and I say that *even* during these days when that system is—unjustifiably in many respects—under criticism.

Mr. Smith, it has been said that a man is the sum total of his actions. If a person's actions have changed, then we now have a *new* person. Well, Jean Paul Sartre had this to say and I will pass it along to you. I am paraphrasing his observations.

Man is the only being in the universe who is totally free. His freedom is a promise as well as a frightening burden. On the one hand, man's total freedom implies that he can be anything, he can do anything, he can change himself into any form. This same freedom is also a terrible weight. It is the weight of responsibility. To be totally free in each act is to be totally responsible also. There are no more excuses for man. He must bear the total consequences of his free acts, for he and no one else performs them.

But along with the tremendous burden of responsibility, let us not forget the promise of that freedom. *I can do better. I can change. I define myself anew.*

Would you please stand, Mr. Smith.

Pashman: Before imposing sentence, Edgar Smith, the Court is required to Comply with *Rule 3:21-r (b)*. In accordance with that rule, do you wish to make any statement in your own behalf and to present any further information at all of any kind concerning this matter?

Smith: No, sir.

Pashman: And you do understand the nature and the meaning of this offense and the plea that has been taken, which is tantamount to a guilty plea?

Smith: Yes, sir.

Pashman ruled.

Therefore, Edgar Smith, on Indictment S-276-56, charging you with murder, it is the sentence of this Court that you serve not less than twenty-five years, nor more than thirty years at the New Jersey State Prison in Trenton. You have spent 90 days in the Bergen County Jail in the year 1957. You have spent 5,296 days in the Death House at the New Jersey State Prison. You will receive credit for all time spent in those institutions. In addition, in accordance with law, you are to be credited with 3,966 days for what is called *good time*. This gives you a credit of 9,352 days. The expiration date for your sentence under this formula is April 26, 1976. The remaining

301

balance of that sentence is 4 years, 4 months, and 20 days. The balance on the 30-year sentence is hereby suspended. You are placed on probation for that period of time, 4 years, 4 months, and 20 days. During that time, you will be subject to the rules and conditions of probation, all of which have been fixed by the court pursuant to N.J.S.A. 2A:162.2, except that I have agreed that there will not be travel restrictions outside the State of New Jersey so long as there is full compliance with the rules and conditions of probation. You will return to the State Prison forthwith for processing out forthwith.

Twenty minutes later, Edgar Smith was in a limousine with his attorneys and William F. Buckley, heading from Hackensack to Trenton to go through the formality of processing out of prison.

Less than two hours later, Smith was a free man—fourteen years, nine months, and two days after the death of Victoria Zielinski.

Freedom Is Just Another Word

Freedom is nothing but a chance to be better.
—Albert Camus

Most people do not really want freedom,
because freedom involves responsibility,
and most people are frightened of responsibility.
—Sigmund Freud

Freedom is what you do with
what's been done to you.
—Jean Paul Sartre

Man is free at the moment he wishes to be.
—Voltaire

Freedom is not enough.
—Lyndon Baines Johnson

Getting Out

On Monday, December 6, 1971, Edgar Smith walked out of the New Jersey State Prison in Trenton for the last time after nearly fifteen years on Death Row.

He was immediately confronted by a few dozen rain-drenched television and press reporters, cameramen and photographers, all fighting to get close—snapping pictures, shooting film, and firing questions.

Smith forced his way to a limousine waiting at the curb, and escaped into the back seat.

Bill Buckley handed him a paper cup of Rosé wine and a deli roast beef sandwich.

"Welcome back to the free world," said Buckley, lifting *his* cup in a toast.

They were heading to a Manhattan television studio where two segments of *Firing Line* would be taped.

The first, an hour with Smith and Buckley alone. The second, an hour with Smith, Buckley, and a panel of three newsmen and an attorney.

The taped programs would be aired on consecutive Sundays.

Reaching the studio, Buckley's chauffeur ushered Smith in through a rear door to avoid the crowd of reporters and rubberneckers out front.

After a quick stop for makeup, Smith joined Buckley on the set and the taping of the first segment began.

Firing Line

The two parts of "The Edgar Smith Story" on *Firing Line with William F. Buckley Jr.* were taped ninety-minutes after Smith was released from prison, after having done more time in a penitentiary *death house* than anyone had previously done in America. Ever.

The first segment featured Edgar Smith and his host, alone on stage before a live studio audience.

Buckley began with a review of the case for the benefit of viewers—with general details of the 1957 crime, the murder trial, and Edgar Smith's endless attempts to overturn the murder conviction.

Buckley made it abundantly clear where he personally stood by closing his introduction with the following statement:

"I can say on behalf of myself, and of the many others who have studied the case and the circumstances, and who know the man who is here tonight, that we believe profoundly that on March 4, 1957, Edgar Smith left Victoria Zielinski alive."

Buckley began by asking why both Smith and the State were inclined to avoid a new trial. Smith reiterated the thoughts and opinions he had expressed to his attorneys and to Buckley before accepting the *non vult* plea agreement.

For his part, the reasons included the lack of financial resources to fund a retrial, unwillingness to expose his ex-wife (who could possibly be called as a State's witness) to the reopening of old wounds or expose his teenage daughter to events she knew nothing about, and the indeterminable period of time he would have to remain in prison awaiting the scheduling of a new trial.

As for the State's motivations, Smith believed New Jersey was anxious to *get done* with him, that they wished to *save face* by getting an *open confession* to murder, even if it meant settling for a *second-degree* conviction. The State may also have been reluctant to put the Zielinski family through the ordeal of another trial. And Smith believed the prosecutors were concerned about the *strength* of their case, since much of the evidence introduced in the first trial had since been ruled inadmissible in a retrial—including the infamous *Q&A* with Prosecutor Fred Galda of March 6, 1957, which was admitted by Judge O'Dea as a *concession of guilt* at the first trial.

Buckley then went on to touch upon *delicate* matters such as the nature of truth in the judicial system, the identity of Victoria Zielinski's murderer, the often misconstrued or ignored legal right of *presumption of innocence,* opinions about capital punishment, and what the future might hold for Edgar Smith.

These are selected excerpts from the transcript of the televised interview.

> WB: What is your position on the correspondence of that which a court *finds* and that which is actually true? Is it coincidence, or just a little better than that?
>
> ES: I'm not certain the law is designed to bring out *truth*. It is to bring out such truth as may be brought out within the rules. Not all of the truth is always brought out, only what can be brought out within the narrow *rules of evidence*. Quite often it is difficult to bring out the truth. Even if you bring out what *you believe* to be the true facts, there's always the chance that a jury is not going to see it the same way. Won't see it the way *you* see it. Won't see it the way the

prosecutor sees it. Won't see it the way the *judge* sees it. It is not necessarily true that if you bring out the truth, and the truth proves A, that the jury is going to come in and say *we find A.* They might find B.

WB: Do you think the jurors who convicted you in 1957 acted responsibly?

ES: I believe that within what they were given, they did. And, taking into consideration what they were instructed by the court, I think they did what they *thought* was right. Whether they did the *right thing* is something else.

Buckley asked Smith what he thought *really happened* in court earlier that day.

ES: They got what they wanted. They got their conviction. They vindicated their system.

WB: You say they vindicated their system even though the federal court *threw out* the conviction because of their disapproval of the way in which New Jersey proceeded against you. And, point number two, here you were in an ambiguous situation in which it seems awfully obvious to me, and to a lot of other people, that when you stepped forward this afternoon and said, *Yes, I killed her,* what you were doing was executing an agreement with the Court rather than adding to the sum of human knowledge. So, their *vindication* is formalistic, isn't it?

ES: That is all I think they ever required. I think all the State of New Jersey ever really wanted was to be able to go to the public and say, *Look, we started this case, we made a lot of mistakes, we did a lot of things wrong, but we got the right guy in the end and therefore our system works.* I think that is really what happened today.

WB: But, don't they nevertheless suffer under the rebuke of the federal court for having introduced into evidence answers, by you, to questions that were coercive in character under the circumstances—as was the finding of the federal court?

ES: Yes. But, then again, they come around with this and say, *Well, we got the answers the wrong way, but Smith just proved today that we got the right answers.*

Buckley then moved on to the elemental question of *who was responsible* for the death of Victoria Zielinski, if *not* Edgar Smith.

WB: We all obviously know that *somebody* killed Victoria Zielinski. Some who have read your book wonder why it is you haven't devoted more attention to trying to get the man who did it.

ES: I never directly said that *this* person, or *that* person, or another person committed the crime. I said in the book, as I recall in a letter to you, that *I left her there alive.* What happened after that, I don't know.

WB: Why was it never worthwhile to attempt to find the guilty person? Why were your efforts not directed toward doing that—during the late fifties and sixties?

ES: It's impossible to do that and keep yourself alive at the same time. I had a choice. To keep myself alive when the State was trying to execute me, or try to solve the case *for* the State.

I couldn't do both.

WB: Is it your intention to find the killer now?

ES: I don't think it's possible. I think this is one of those crimes where only the person who did it knows.

Buckley asked Smith what he thought were the deficiencies in the legal system which found him guilty in 1957.

Smith said he believed all criminal defendants were at a disadvantage, since the State had greater resources—funds, investigators, laboratories.

Smith also expressed lack of confidence in the principal of *presumption of innocence.*

ES: Presumption of innocence, I don't think means too much in a courtroom. You arrest a man, and put him in jail, hold him for seven, eight months, a year. Then bring him to trial. Bring him into a courtroom in handcuffs. Sit him down in front of the jury, with a few guards standing behind him. It's very difficult to say to that jury, *This man is innocent. He hasn't done anything.* The jury looks at him and thinks *why has he been in jail for a year, why is he handcuffed, if he didn't do anything. He must have done something.* Presumption of innocence is a very difficult thing to believe in anymore.

Later, Buckley asked if Smith could say anything about what death row inmates thought of the death sentence.

WB: Is it possible to have conversations in the death house to the point of being able to explore the attitudes of other prisoners on the subject of capital punishment?

ES: When you get into a discussion with men who are on death row, it tends to get very emotional and they tend to be opposed to it. It's really a very difficult subject to explore with people who are subject to it.

WB: How were you able to converse with other death row inmates?

ES: For the first nine-and-a-half years I was in my cell twenty-four hours a day, except for fifteen minutes on Friday when I went to take a shower. Conversations were shouted back and forth. We never saw each other except walking past each other to and from the shower. After my first nine-and-a-half years, we moved to a new death house and there was more contact among the prisoners. Solitary confinement doesn't really exist anymore.

WB: What would have probably happened if by the late fifties, two or three years after your conviction, you simply despaired of trying to win the support of the federal courts? Would you have been executed?

ES: Certainly. As soon as I gave up, I would have been executed.

WS: When does your probation terminate?

ES: Nineteen-seventy-six.

WB: What *can't* you do between now and 1976?

ES: I don't know yet. I have to call the probation officer on Thursday morning and we will talk that over. The only thing I know is that I *can* travel. But about the specific conditions, I'm not really sure. I don't believe they will be very difficult.

WB: What formal difficulties lie in your way of a professional nature?

ES: Well, I couldn't be a lawyer, or a police officer. I certainly could not be a judge. I really haven't even thought about that right now. At the present time, I'm trying to believe the fact that I'm not still in the death house. I would have liked to become a lawyer at one time, but there's no chance of that now. Legal work interests me. I would like to write about the law. Write about prisons and prison reform. Write about criminal cases. It's something I know, something I know how to do. I have some idea about how the people involved in such cases think and feel—after having gone through it myself. The first thing I have to do is complete the final story of this case. *Brief Against Death* covered my case from the time that I was arrested until 1968, and I am just completing a book now which will take the case from 1968 through today. And thereafter, I hope I never have to write about myself again.

WB: Do you feel any sense of bitterness towards the judge who sentenced you or the prosecutors who arranged the deal?

ES: No. I think all of us, the judge, the prosecutors, the Attorney General, my lawyers and myself, we all did what we felt needed—what we felt *had* to be done.

The Fickle Finger of Fame

The second part of Edgar Smith's *Firing Line* appearance was taped on the same evening, December 6, 1971.

Both parts were aired at a later date, one week apart.

For this segment, Buckley and Smith were joined onstage by a four-man panel—three journalists and a lawyer, who had been present at the courtroom earlier that day. Generally, none of the panelists expressed the level of support for Smith's *plea*, or the confidence in his innocence, as had Buckley.

Consequently, Smith found himself having to more vigorously defend his decision to plead guilty to *second-degree* murder. At the same time, due to the rules of the court, he was prohibited from openly declaring his innocence.

Following the taping of the two programs, Smith was taken by limousine to the Buckley home on Park Avenue where Buckley had arranged a reception complete with handshaking and champagne.

At four in the morning, nearly twenty-four hours after leaving Trenton for his court appearance, Smith checked into the landmark St. Regis Hotel on 55th Street, where Buckley had arranged for a suite. It had been nearly fifteen years since Edgar Smith had slept in a dark room—the lights were never turned off in his prison cell.

Smith had to force himself to turn the lights out and he finally fell asleep with—as he later reported—a smile on his face.

The press continued to follow Smith's story, but not for very long—and the coverage tended to be unsympathetic, often unflattering.

An editorial in the Trentonian on the 8th of December stated:

> Well, Edgar H. Smith is free. But it wasn't the truth that got the job done, according to Edgar Smith.
>
> It was a lie. To be accurate, it was several lies.
>
> The way he tells it, the price of his freedom was the admission that he bludgeoned a 15-year old girl to death in a Bergen County sandpit on March 4, 1957. "It was a difficult decision," says Edgar, "but I wanted to be free."
>
> So, his face reddened, his voice low, he told Judge Pashman he killed the girl, and he told the judge how he killed her. It was a hell of a convincing performance.
>
> But after all, he couldn't afford a new trial, so better to be a free liar than a jailed martyr. The judge gave him his freedom because the judge was convinced that Edgar will not kill again, that he is thoroughly rehabilitated. The judge is also convinced the evidence against Smith was *devastating*.
>
> Devastating enough to make a liar out of an honest man, make a confessed murderer out of a professed innocent?
>
> If Edgar Smith's next book doesn't answer that one to your satisfaction—Buckley's next book will.
>
> . . .

And from the *Asbury Park Evening Press* on December 12:

There is something about the release of Edgar H. Smith, Jr. on probation which offends one's sense of truthfulness and honesty.

There is precedent for bargaining with a convicted person to save the State the expense of a second trial, which had been ordered in Smith's case because a federal court had ruled that the confession upon which he had originally been convicted had been coerced. Smith was still maintaining his innocence of the crime.

But in open court, under the questioning of Judge Pashman, Smith said that *he and he alone* had killed the victim, Victoria Zielinski, in a Bergen County gravel pit. Pashman then stated, *The defendant admits this to be a fact. The facts in the case firmly and convincingly establish that the defendant caused the death of Victoria Zielinski. An impartial mind must conclude this.*

Now William F. Buckley Jr. says that the confession Smith made before Judge Pashman was *simply court theater,* and was made only to achieve Smith's immediate release from the Death House.

Yet, if Smith were really innocent of the murder charge, but confessed it under oath, he was guilty of perjury.

Will he stand trial for that? Not likely, says a state prosecutor, who predicted that state officials—and the courts—would probably be content to let events *cool off* in the likelihood that public furor over the case would eventually subside. As no doubt it will.

But, the record of bargaining and cynical dis-

315

regard of the truth remains—to cause distress to
all those to whom the legal process should be
conducted on a far different, and more admira-
ble plane.

For a time after his release, Smith was offered speaking en-
gagements—but before long the requests stopped coming.

Smith rented an apartment in Ridgefield Park in Bergen
County, New Jersey, and continued working on his follow-up
to *Brief Against Death*.

At the same time, there were many events and news stories in
1972 of more concern to Americans than Edgar Smith.

And more disturbing.

In February, the increased fear of plane hijackings led to the
mandatory inspection of passengers and baggage at national
airports.

Also, that same month, sales of the Volkswagen Beetle surpassed fifteen million in the United States—more Beetles sold
than the Ford Model T during its time.

There was a growing fear that the American auto industry
could be in some trouble.

On the 17th, the State of California abolished capital punishment and, as a result, Charles Manson's sentence was com-
muted to life imprisonment with the chance of parole—not a
pleasant thought.

Divisions within the American public were flaring.

Racial tensions escalated—fueled by the Angela Davis murder trial, the revelation of the *Tuskegee Study of Untreated
Syphilis in the Negro Male* which had been kept secret for forty
years, the attempted assassination of Alabama's Governor
George Wallace, and the failure of the Republican administration to support and enforce civil rights legislation initiated by
Lyndon Johnson.

The generation gap also widened.

The young continued to protest America's involvement in

Vietnam—while Nixon was ordering bombings of North Vietnam and, as a result, North Vietnam officials walked out of the Paris Peace Talks.

In late July, there was a shocking story in *The New York Times* reporting that there had been 57 murders in a period of one week in New York City.

In addition, there were serial killers on the loose.

And in November, Richard Nixon was re-elected even as the Congress was investigating the break-in at Washington's Watergate Office Complex—looking to discover if the five men arrested had any ties to the White House.

Smith completed his book, *Getting Out,* and it was published in 1972.

It took his story from where *Brief Against Death* had left off—up to the taping of the *Firing Line* programs.

It did not have the kind of impact as had the first book.

By the end of the year, Smith was out of sight and out of mind.

And, when he later left New Jersey, his short tenure as a *celebrity* was a thing of the past and Edgar Smith literally vanished.

On December 6, 1971, Edgar Smith escorted to a courtroom where, as arranged in the plea bargaining agreement, he would admit to killing Victoria Zielinki, accept a conviction of second-degree murder, and be sentenced to time already served. He was returned to the state prison in Trenton for processing out, and two hours later he was at a television studio in Manhattan with Bill Buckley for a taping of two episodes of *Firing Line*.

Edgar Smith's short-lived celeb-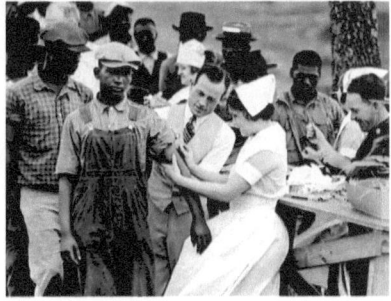
rity was overshadowed by ma-
jor political and social events of
1972 including the bombing of
Haiphong and Hanoi that
stalled the Paris Peace Talks,
the Watergate break-in leading
to a Congressional investiga-
tion, the 40-year Tuskegee Study that left syphilis in African-
Americans untreated, and the end of capital punishment in California that effectively offered Charles Manson a chance for
freedom.

Lies and Truth

Three things cannot be long hidden.
The sun, the moon, and the truth.
—Buddha

The truth is incontrovertible.
Malice may attack it, ignorance may deride it,
but in the end—there it is.
—Winston Churchill

The pursuit of truth will set you free,
even if you never catch up with it.
—Clarence Darrow

It is no wonder that truth is stranger than fiction.
Fiction has to make sense.
—Mark Twain

Yard Sale

In the early nineties, I operated a café and used book shop on the Town Green in Guilford, Connecticut.

One day a week was devoted to book hunting—hopping into the orange 1979 Toyota pickup and stopping into thrift shops and at house sales in New Haven, East Haven, Branford, Clinton, Madison, and other neighboring towns.

On one such excursion, at a yard sale, I ran across a cardboard box full of books. I was pressed for time. I quickly checked the titles on top and spotted five or six books I knew I could sell for three to four dollars apiece.

I asked the sellers what they wanted for each individual book, and I was told I could take the entire box for five dollars.

Sold.

Back at the shop, I dropped the box in a back room where—when I found the time—I would price and shelve the *new* used books.

Two weeks later, I finally got around to exploring the contents.

I discovered a signed first edition of *Triumph and Tragedy* by Winston Churchill, which included a *letter of authentication* by Churchill's secretary dated November 18, 1953.

I later sold that book for nine-hundred-fifty dollars.

There was also a book written in 1968 by a prison inmate. I had read several books of the kind—including *In the Belly of the Beast* by Jack Abbott, *Burn, Killer, Burn* by Paul Crump, and *Soul on Ice* by Eldridge Cleaver.

It was the sort of autobiographical discourse that had intrigued me since I had studied Fyodor Dostoyevsky's *Notes From Underground.*

I decided I would read it before putting it out for sale.

The book was *Brief Against Death,* and it introduced me to Edgar Smith.

The book, written by Smith while he was incarcerated in the *Death House* at New Jersey State Prison in Trenton, captured my interest.

I attempted to learn how the story ended.

The internet was still in its infancy, and all I could discover was that Smith had later written a second book, *Getting Out,* published in 1972.

It took more than two years to locate a copy.

Getting Out was, in essence, a treatise—and a rather cynical one—on how the legal system often works.

It was the story of a man who was locked-up in prison for nearly fifteen years while professing his innocence, and then immediately released when he admitted guilt to a murder for which he continued to deny responsibility.

Smith saw it as the only way to *get out.*

My interest was once again aroused. I was curious about what became of Edgar Smith after his appearance with William Buckley on *Firing Line*—but once again my attempts to learn of Smith's fate were unsuccessful.

Lies

Little is known about Edgar Smith's activities during the four years and ten months following his release in 1971.

And most was not learned until much later.

Smith cashed in on his celebrity during the first few years. *Getting Out* was published, and he sold a number of articles about prison reform to newspapers and national magazines. But his message soon grew redundant. And the Edgar Smith now living in suburban New Jersey was not as fascinating as the Edgar Smith facing the electric chair.

Smith's wife, Patricia, had divorced him in 1964, remarried, and moved to Colorado. His daughter, who was not yet three months old when Smith was arrested, knew nothing about him.

In 1974, Smith—now forty-years-old—married Paige Hiemier.

"I was nineteen-years-old and was very naive," Hiemier later said. "I was impressed with him. He was friends with William Buckley and all these other famous people. And he'd written three books. In all of them he proclaimed his innocence. I believed him."

The newlyweds relocated to San Diego in 1974. Smith found work as a security guard for an exclusive apartment building in La Jolla. Apparently, his background was never checked. He later worked as a public relations director for a small business in Chula Vista but, when the company disbanded, he was out of work again.

According to Hiemier, their marriage was strained—because

she was going to nursing school while working full-time as a bank teller and Smith made no effort to find another job.

"He never once hit me. He was never violent at all around me," Hiemier said. "The one time I was really concerned was one night when we were rough-housing in the living room, just having fun. He suddenly grabbed me around the neck, and he was actually choking me. I was really scared. I shouted that he was hurting me, and he stopped."

Smith finally resumed his job search in the fall of 1976. He approached an editor at the *San Diego Union*, a friend of Bill Buckley, about a job—but he was told there were no openings.

Americans had somehow managed to remain optimistic in spite of the fears instilled by the ideological conflicts of the fifties—and the political and sociological turbulence of the sixties.

Korea, the *Red Scare,* horrific crimes against children and young adults, mass demonstrations leading to deadly violence on our city streets, the *Cuban Missile Crisis,* the assassinations of John F. Kennedy, Martin Luther King Jr., and Robert F. Kennedy, the 1968 Democratic Convention in Chicago, the *Tet Offensive,* Kent State.

If there was one thing that helped Americans remain hopeful through these frightening times, it was confidence.

Confidence in their government.

Confidence in their leaders.

Trust in the truth of what they were being told.

And then, the lies began to surface.

In November, 1970, a court-martial charged fourteen United States Army officers with covering-up what came to be known as the *Mỹ Lai Massacre*—the execution of at least 350 unarmed civilians in two South Vietnamese hamlets in March, 1968.

The news of the mass murder, and cover-up, sent shocks

waves through the ranks of even the strongest supporters of our involvement in Vietnam.

On June 18, 1971, *The New York Times* and *The Washington Post*, using classified government documents leaked by Daniel Ellsberg, began publishing portions of what would be called *The Pentagon Papers.*

The *Pentagon Papers* revealed that the United States had expanded the war with the bombing of Cambodia and Laos, coastal raids on North Vietnam, and Marine Corps attacks, none of which had been reported by the American government or the media.

The most damaging revelations revealed that the Eisenhower, Kennedy, and Johnson administrations had misled the public regarding their intentions.

The Eisenhower administration had actively worked against the *Geneva Accords.*

The Kennedy administration was aware of the plans to overthrow South Vietnamese leader Ngô Đình Diệm before his death in a November 1963 coup.

Johnson made the decision to expand the war while, at the same time, promising *we seek no wider war* during his 1964 presidential campaign—a decision which included plans to bomb North Vietnam well before the 1964 election.

In July, 1972, the shameful details of the *Tuskegee Study* were revealed.

The United States Public Health Service started working on the study in 1932, in collaboration with Tuskegee University in Alabama.

Investigators enrolled 399 African-American sharecroppers from Macon County, Alabama, who had contracted syphilis before the study began.

The subjects were offered free medical care, free meals, and free burial insurance for participating in the study. The men were told the study would last just six months, but it went on for 40 years. After funding for treatment was lost, none of the subsequent subjects were told they had the disease and none were treated with penicillin, even after the antibiotic was proven to treat syphilis successfully. The revelations horrified and incensed the generation of post-war twenty-somethings who recalled nervously standing in lines in grade school auditoriums for *experimental* polio vaccinations.

On June 19, 1972, the press reported that one of the Watergate burglars was a Republican Party security aide. Former Attorney General John Mitchell, head of the Committee to Re-Elect the President at the time, flatly denied any involvement with the *Watergate* break-in—or knowledge of the five burglars.

In July, 1973, White House aide Alexander Butterfield testified, under oath to Congress, that Nixon had a secret taping system which recorded his conversations and phone calls in the Oval Office. These tapes were subpoenaed by Watergate Special Counsel Archibald Cox. Nixon provided transcripts of the conversations but not the actual tapes, citing *executive privilege.*

With the White House and Cox at odds, Nixon had Cox fired in October in what became known as the *Saturday Night Massacre.*

In November—a month following Vice President Spiro Agnew's resignation after being convicted on charges of bribery, tax evasion, and money laundering during his tenure as governor of Maryland—Nixon's lawyers revealed that a tape of conversations in the White House in June, 1972, had a gap of eighteen and a half minutes.

The gap, while not conclusive proof of wrongdoing by the President, cast doubts on Nixon's statement that he had been unaware of the cover-up.

The House Judiciary Committee opened impeachment hearings against the President on May 9, 1974.

In a statement on August 5, 1974, Nixon accepted blame for misleading the country about when he had been told of White House involvement, stating that he had experienced *a lapse of memory.*

Shortly after, Nixon was told by congressional leaders from both houses, and both parties, that he faced certain impeachment and likely conviction.

Nixon resigned his office on August 8, 1974.

The last Americans in Vietnam were evacuated on April 30, 1975, when Saigon fell to the Viet Cong. It marked the end of the conflict that had cost more than 58,000 American lives. The end of U.S. involvement in Southeast Asia should have been universally considered *good news.*

However, it also marked a victory for and a spread of *communism.*

A concern that had guided United States foreign policy for thirty years, and had fueled the fears of an entire generation.

On July 4, 1976, citizens throughout the nation took a welcomed break from whatever worried them, a chance to put the fears and the lies out of mind temporarily, in order to celebrate the two-hundredth birthday of what was, for better or for worse, *their* America.

After reading *Getting Out,* my curiosity about the fate of Edgar Smith was rekindled, but once again my efforts at discovery were unsuccessful.

I decided there was only one person who might possibly enlighten me, so I wrote a letter to William F. Buckley Jr.

I received a reply on March 17, 1995.

Buckley's letter informed me that after more than fourteen years of lies, Edgar Smith had *actually* told the truth on December 6, 1971.

And the truth had set him free.

Truth

Three months after Americans celebrated the birth of their nation, four years and ten months after being released from prison, and just one day after being denied a job with *The San Diego Union*—Edgar Smith stepped back into the spotlight.

Lefteriya Lisa Ozbun, 33, a seamstress at a Chula Vista garment factory, was walking toward the company's parking lot, where her husband was waiting to take her home.

Before she reached the lot, a man jumped out of his car, put a butcher knife to Ozbun's neck, and said, *Keep your mouth shut or I'm going to cut your throat right here.*

Her assailant threw Ozbun into the front seat of his car, taped her wrists together, and drove off.

"I started yelling, *What are you doing? What do you want with me? Where are you taking me?*" Ozbun later recounted. "He just said, *Shut up. I'm going to take your money and I'm going to stick this knife into you.* I told him that I had three children and, if he wanted the money, he could take it. He said, *Don't be stupid,* and he kept driving."

Ozbun knew she had to fight her way out of the car before her abductor reached his destination because once he stopped, Ozbun said, she was certain he would kill her.

"I could see it in his eyes. I'd never seen eyes like that. They were so cold and filled with hate. I knew if I didn't fight, I

330

would never see my kids again."

As they headed south on Interstate 5, Ozbun, who was five-foot-one-inch tall and weighed one-hundred pounds, kicked out the windshield, managed to free her hands, grabbed the steering wheel, and punched at the horn.

The man stabbed her, up to the handle of the butcher knife, piercing her liver and diaphragm and missing her heart by a quarter of an inch.

But Ozbun continued to struggle, lunging with her feet for the brakes, and fighting for control of the steering wheel.

The car weaved onto an exit ramp and the driver hit the brakes.

As the car skidded to a stop at the bottom of an embankment, Ozbun managed to open the passenger door and crawl out of the car—falling to the ground, the knife sticking out of her side.

As her kidnapper sat dazed in the car, a man selling flowers nearby ran over to Ozbun.

She looked up and weakly asked him to get her purse from the front seat because her paycheck was in the purse.

After the man grabbed the purse, the driver regained his composure and sped off. But witnesses had noted the license plate.

It led police to Edgar Smith's door.

When they arrived, Smith had already fled.

Smith evaded capture for several weeks, borrowing money and staying at friends' apartments on the East Coast.

Smith eventually ended up in Las Vegas and called Buckley, who was out of town. He left a phone number and room number with Buckley's secretary.

Buckley made arrangements for Smith to turn himself in.

At Smith's trial in California, he admitted molesting an 11-year-old girl when he was a teenager, and also admitted killing Victoria Zielinski.

Smith said he had struck Victoria inside the car after she resisted his advances, chased her when she ran away, and hit her with a baseball bat.

"Then," Smith said, "I picked up a very large rock and hit Vickie on the head."

San Diego Assistant District Attorney Richard Neely asked Smith why, after all the years of deception, he had suddenly found the need to unburden himself.

Smith claimed that while he was on the run, after abducting Ozbun, he visited the cemetery where Victoria Zielinski was buried, and had a revelation.

"For the first time in my life I recognized that the devil I had been looking at in the mirror for forty-three years was me," Smith told the court. "It was at that time I realized that my life had reached a point at which I had a choice of doing one of two things. I could kill myself, or I could return to San Diego and face what I was."

Neely saw Smith's confession as self-serving—an attempt at a reduced sentence for the California indictment.

The judge was not persuaded by Smith's sudden burst of honesty. He sentenced Smith to life imprisonment without the possibility of parole.

As a result of new legislation a year later, Smith would be made eligible for parole as early as 1982.

Smith informed the Board of Prison Terms just before a parole hearing in 1987 that he had married the mother of a former cellmate—and he was helping his wife run a travel agency. A position, he claimed, he would assume full-time if released.

A prison evaluation made that year, obtained by *The Los Angeles Times*, concluded that Edgar Smith "has gained significant maturity, insight and self-awareness. At this time, there do not appear to be any *psychiatric reasons* for a parole date not to be granted."

But the following year, Smith's psychiatric evaluation had a more critical conclusion. The report stated that Edgar Smith still had "conflicts which could lead to recurrences of his violent behavior toward women."

All subsequent parole hearings ruled *against* Smith's release.

"Edgar is a master at manipulating the system," said former wife, Paige Hiemier, who divorced Smith following his 1976 California trial and conviction. "He manipulated his way out of Death Row in New Jersey. He conned William Buckley. And now he is doing in California what he has always done. Edgar is working the system, until the odds are in his favor for parole. But people need to recognize that his last victim is very lucky to be alive today. The next woman he goes after may not be so fortunate."

Unanswered Questions

The evidence against Edgar Smith in 1957 was circumstantial.

The blood evidence was inconclusive.

The time of death was imprecise.

There was no discernable motive for premeditated murder.

If the victim was struck by a rock, or if her head struck a rock due to a fall, was impossible to positively determine.

With what they had, police and prosecutors could put Edgar Smith at the scene, but could not *prove* him guilty of murder.

For that, they needed a confession.

And they got one, or something that passed for one. A statement made to Prosecutor Fred Galda, after a night without sleep, which was never signed by the suspect, and was admitted into evidence by Judge O'Dea.

And that statement was enough to persuade a jury to convict Smith of first-degree murder, carrying a sentence of death.

That, and his continued denial.

If Smith had admitted from the start that he had been with the girl at the sandpit, that he had made unwelcome physical advances which had resulted in a struggle and an exchange of blows, and he had, *without intention,* harmed her fatally, he would have been charged with *second-degree* murder at most.

Instead, Smith waited nearly fifteen years, isolated on *death row,* for an outcome that could well have been available to him in 1957.

One can only speculate that Edgar Smith felt confident he

could see the conviction overturned, and gain his freedom, much earlier.

Judge Morris Pashman had said, before releasing Smith on time served, "I do not necessarily agree that the crime had to be more than a *second-degree* murder."

Pashman had gone on to say he did not believe there had been any intent or premeditation involved, and Edgar Smith had been charged with first-degree murder *simply because he had stated he had left the girl alive and with another man.*

"I truly believe," Pashman had concluded, "that you, and you alone, Mr. Smith, brought on the first-degree murder charge and that *you alone*, and *you alone as it were,* were responsible for the ultimate jury verdict of death."

Denying the crime had raised the stakes—and ultimately raised Edgar Smith's sentence from one of fifteen to twenty-five years with the chance of parole—to one of death by electrocution.

After receiving the letter from William Buckley, I was able in time to find more details about the events in California that had sent Smith back to prison for life.

But there were a number of additional questions I would have liked to have answered.

In 2000, with the help of a lawyer friend in California, I discovered where Edgar Smith was incarcerated.

At the time, I had recently relocated from New York City to Columbia, South Carolina.

While I was working on what would be my first published novel, I wrote a letter to Edgar Smith.

Smith's reply was gracious, and apologetic.

For reasons I could fully appreciate, Smith wrote that he could not honor my request for a face-to-face interview.

1st Photos of Viet Mass Slaying

WEATHER
Some flurries and
colder today.
High in the upper 30s.
Details on Page 1-C.

THE PLAIN DEALER

OHIO'S LARGEST NEWSPAPER

128TH YEAR—NO. 324 ★ ★ ★ ★ ★   CLEVELAND, THURSDAY, NOVEMBER 20, 1969   96 PAGES   10 CENTS

FINAL
Stocks & Races
Dow-Jones off 5.51

Exclusive

This photograph will shock Americans as it shocked the editors and the staff of The Plain Dealer. It was taken by a young Cleveland area man while serving as a photographer with the U.S. Army in South Vietnam.

It was taken during the attack by American soldiers on the South Vietnamese village My Lai, an attack which has made world headlines in recent days with disclosures of mass killings allegedly at the hands of American soldiers.

This photograph and others are two special photos as they are the first to be published anywhere of the killings.

This particular picture shows a clump of bodies of South Vietnamese civilians which includes women and children. Why they were killed raises one of the most momentous questions of the war in Vietnam.

Cameraman Saw GIs Slay 100 Villagers

A clump of bodies on a road in South Vietnam.

"All the News
That's Fit to Print"

The New York Times

LATE CITY EDITION
Weather: Partly cloudy, chance of showers today, tonight, tomorrow. Temp. range: today 80-66; Saturday 64-60. Temp.-Hum. Index yesterday 76. Full U.S. report on Page 71.

SECTION ONE

VOL. CXX...No.41,412   NEW YORK, SUNDAY, JUNE 13, 1971   NQLI   50 CENTS

Tricia Nixon Takes Vows In Garden at White House

Vietnam Archive: Pentagon Study Traces 3 Decades of Growing U. S. Involvement

U.S. URGES INDIANS AND PAKISTANIS TO USE RESTRAINT

CITY TO DISCLOSE BUDGETARY TRIMS FOR DEPARTMENTS

NIXON CRITICIZED AS MAYORS MEET

Vast Review of War Took a Year

The Weather

The Washington Post

THURSDAY, AUGUST 16, 1973

FINAL

Nixon Denies Role in Cover-up, Admits Abuses by Subordinates

U.S. to Appeal Court Order On Milk Data

Says Tapes' Release Would Be 'Crippling'

Pocket Veto In Recess Ruled Illegal

"All the News That's Fit to Print"

The New York Times

LATE CITY EDITION

Weather: Continued mostly cloudy, cool today, tonight and tomorrow. Temperature range: today 56-65. Tuesday 50-63. Details on Page 81.

VOL. CXXIV...No. 42,830

NEW YORK, WEDNESDAY, APRIL 30, 1975

20 CENTS

MINH SURRENDERS, VIETCONG IN SAIGON;
1,000 AMERICANS AND 5,500 VIETNAMESE
EVACUATED BY COPTER TO U.S. CARRIERS

U.S., GREECE AGREE TO END HOME PORT FOR THE 6TH FLEET

Air Base at Americans at Athens Is Also Closed, but Some Facilities Remain

FORD UNITY PLEA

President Says That Troops Leave Posts Departure 'Closes a Chapter' for U.S.

END OF DEFENSE

Troops Leave Posts in Capital and Turn in Their Weapons

A commando from an American helicopter helping evacuees on the top of a building in Saigon for flight to a U.S. carrier.

Abram Offers Bills To Curtail Abuses Of Nursing Homes

CAMBODIA ORDERS FOREIGNERS OUT

74 Saigon Planes Fly 2,000 to Thailand

"All the News That's Fit to Print"

The New York Times

LATE CITY EDITION

Weather: Partly cloudy today and tonight. Fair, pleasant tomorrow. Temp. range: today 61-78. Thursday 64-85. Highest Temp.-Mon. Details on Page 95.

VOL. CXXIII...No. 42,588

NEW YORK, FRIDAY, AUGUST 9, 1974

15 CENTS

NIXON RESIGNS
HE URGES A TIME OF 'HEALING';
FORD WILL TAKE OFFICE TODAY

'Sacrifice' Is Praised; Kissinger to Remain

By ANTHONY RIPLEY

SPECULATION RIFE ON VICE PRESIDENT

Vice President Ford meeting with newsmen last night

President Nixon on TV as he announced his resignation

The 37th President Is First to Quit Post

By JOHN HERBERS

March 17, 1995

Dear Mr. Abramo:

Edgar Smith attempted to kill a woman in California four or five years after his release. During the trial, he volunteered the information that he had in fact killed Victoria Zalinsky. He is still in jail somewhere in California. I'm sorry, but the Firing Line segments with Edgar Smith are no longer available. There is a repository at the Yale University Library but you would have to make your own arrangements if you wish to view it. With all good wishes,

Yours cordially,

Wm. F. Buckley Jr.

Following the 1976 conviction in California, William F. Buckley Jr. openly admitted he had been "taken in" by Smith regarding the Victoria Zielinski case, and added that Smith "should never be released from custody."

Joseph Abramo
1600 Park Circle #602
Columbia, SC 29201

March 25, 2000

Mr. Edgar H. Smith
California Men's Colony
P.O. Box 8101
San Luis Obispo, CA 92409-8101

Dear Mr. Smith:

Writing this letter is one of the most difficult tasks I have ever taken on; simply because in doing so I risk the possibility that you may not respond and how greatly disappointed I would be if that were the case.

I have been interested in your story since reading <u>Brief Against Death</u> some years ago. I found the book quite accidentally at a yard sale. It took me a while to find a copy of <u>Getting Out</u> at the New York Public Library. After reading your second book I found myself not so interested in your innocence or guilt as I was about what your story said about our legal system. How pleading guilty to a crime you said you didn't commit could result in your release from prison where pleading innocent had continually failed.

Hoping to follow up your history subsequent to your release from prison in New Jersey I ran into brick walls. Finally I decided to write to William F. Buckley. He was able to tell me of your trouble in California. With the help of a friend in the legal profession I was finally able to locate you at the California Men's Colony.

I am interested in documenting your story. And in doing so, to go beyond what I can simply extract from your two books and court records. Toward this goal I was hoping that you would be willing to correspond with me and possibly meet with me sometime. I will reserve any specific questions I have for after I hear whether or not you might be inclined to communicate.

As I said at the start, sending this request has opened up the possibility of rejection. As a writer I am no stranger to rejection but never find it easy to accept. I have no way of persuading you to cooperate, particularly since I myself have no idea of what you could possibly gain by doing so. However I pride myself in being fair, open minded and objective as a writer and a human being. If you cared to talk about your past, your present and your hopes for the future I would be all ears.

I pray you are well, physically and spiritually. I hope you will grant me audience.

Sincerely,

Joseph L. Abramo

Edgar H. Smith
B-82784   Room 6160 X
Post Office Box 8101
San Luis Obispo, California
93409-8101

April 4, 2000

Mr. Joseph Abramo
1600 Park Circle #602
Columbia SC 29201-4104

Dear Mr. Abramo:

I have received your letter of March 25th. You come across as genuinely interested and sincere, and I appreciate that. However, for reasons ranging from personal to legal, though primarily the former, I find it necessary to decline your request for an interview, whether in writing or in person. I have had a number of unhappy experiences with the media in particular and with writers in general. One reporter for a New Jersey newspaper related to the district attorney a conversation which had been, by agreement, off the record; another New Jersey reporter used heavily edited quotes to make her point; and a third reporter, a stringer for the *Los Angeles Times*, repeatedly denied an interview with me, simply went ahead and invented the story he wished to write, complete with bogus quotations.

Again, Mr. Abramo, I do appreciate your interest, and I regret being unable to help you.

Sincerely,

EDGAR H. SMITH

CC: CURTIS L. CLARK
     LAW OFFICES
     6906 PORTOLA ROAD
     ATASCADERO CA 93422

Ghosts

Always bear in mind
that your own resolution to succeed
is more important than any one thing.
—Abraham Lincoln

It always seems impossible until it's done.
—Nelson Mandela

Justice never sleeps.
—Tadahiko Nagao

Perseverance, secret of all triumphs.
—Victor Hugo

The dead cannot cry out for justice.
It is a duty of the living to do so for them.
—Lois McMaster Bujold

Y2K

Throughout 1999, there were predictions and fears regarding what was called the *Y2K Bug*.

Also known as the *Millennium Bug*, it was a problem in the coding of computerized systems that was projected to create havoc in computers and computer networks around the world at the beginning of the new century—which prompted a year of international alarm, panicked preparations, and programming corrections.

In the United States, business and government technology teams worked feverishly with a goal of checking systems and fixing software before the end of December 1999. Although some industries were well on the way to solving the Y2K problem, most experts feared that the federal government, and state and local governments, were lagging behind. A Y2K preparedness survey, commissioned in late 1998 by a New York computer industry consulting firm, indicated that among thirteen economic sectors studied in the United States, government was the least prepared for Y2K.

In October 1998, in an effort to encourage companies to share *all* critical information about Y2K, President Clinton signed the *Year 2000 Information and Readiness Disclosure Act.*

The law was designed to encourage American companies to share Y2K data by offering them *limited liability* protection for sharing information about products, methods, and best practices.

The average American did not comprehend the technical aspects of the danger—but were made aware that a serious threat was predicted.

And although the threat was ultimately found to be largely exaggerated—it was nevertheless a contributor to nearly an entire year of national anxiety.

After receiving a letter from Edgar Smith in April, 2000, I decided I had likely discovered all I was going to learn about the night of March 4, 1957 in Bergen County, New Jersey.

Smith had been incarcerated in California for nearly twenty-four years, nine years longer than he had been imprisoned in New Jersey.

I wanted to write about the case, but I needed to put it on hold.

In September, 2000, I received word from St. Martin's Press that my private eye novel, *Catching Water in a Net,* had been selected for publication—and all of my energies were then focused on editing and rewrites.

Meanwhile, the presidential election on November 6—and its aftermath—were creating serious concerns about the efficacy of our electoral system.

Catching Water in a Net was released on October 1, 2001.

A month later, I attended the Anthony Boucher Memorial World Mystery Convention, better known as *Bouchercon,* held that year in Washington D.C.

The traditionally celebratory atmosphere of the annual gathering of crime writers and fans was dampened by the events of September 11.

The 9/11 attacks, just fifty-one days earlier, frightened even those whose occupation was dreaming up frightening fiction.

I did come away from the convention with professional advice.

I was counselled by my new writing colleagues that my publisher would be expecting a follow-up to the first book, featuring the same lead protagonist.

I was advised that if I was interested in another publishing contract, I would be wise to meet that expectation.

I worked on a second Jake Diamond mystery, *Clutching at Straws,* with little distraction—and sent it off to New York.

It was accepted in 2002, and scheduled for an April 2003 release.

I began working on a third mystery in the series.

Edgar Smith was far from my mind.

Then, on January 30, 2003, I first learned of Gerald Mason.

I was living in Columbia, South Carolina, working on the third novel, when I took a short break to glance through a daily newspaper, *The State.*

Front page news was the arrest of a man at his home—only a few miles from where I sat.

Gerald Mason was just two days shy of his sixty-ninth birthday—and he was wanted for crimes committed more than forty-five years earlier.

Columbia

The investigation into the shooting deaths of Officers Richard Phillips and Milton Curtis in El Segundo, California in 1957, had hit a dead-end by 1960.

In September, 2002, a phone call to the El Segundo Police Department, from a woman claiming she had new information about the murders, became the first promising lead in more than four decades.

The woman said her uncle had bragged about being responsible for the killing of two El Segundo police officers.

The case file, which had been gathering dust for more than forty years, was located and pulled out of storage.

The *uncle* lead did not pan out, but the cold case was reopened by an entirely new generation of investigators.

Homicide Detectives Kevin Lowe and Dan Macelderry inherited the coldest case on the books.

The only *hard* evidence was a thumb print from the stolen 1949 Ford driven by the perpetrator, a print which had been created by combining two partial prints.

A handwriting sample from the man who purchased the murder weapon in Shreveport not long before the murders.

And the belief that one of the gunshots, fired at the fleeing automobile by Officer Phillips as he lay dying, *may* have struck the driver.

In 1957, due to the primitive methods of forensic investigation, and the lack of national databases, none of these *clues* had led to a guilty suspect.

Now, in late 2002, the fingerprint was digitally imaged using technology unthought of in 1957.

And, after the events of 9/11, there was finally a nationwide database of fingerprints for comparison.

A digital copy of the print was entered into the FBI system.

In a matter of minutes, Gerald F. Mason was identified.

In April 1956, Mason had been arrested, fingerprinted, tried, and then sentenced to three years in prison for house-breaking and larceny.

The sentence was reduced to eight months and Mason was released in 1957, shortly before the murder weapon had been purchased in Louisiana.

Investigators then dug through boxes of evidence collected over the years to see if any other evidence could be connected to Mason.

A forensic document examiner compared the handwriting of the George D. Wilson who checked into the Shreveport YMCA in 1957 to the handwriting of Gerald F. Mason from a South Carolina eye examination report.

The two were considered identical.

Lowe and Macelderry travelled to Columbia.

Gerald Mason was stunned when Detectives Lowe and Macelderry, and El Segundo Police Lieutenant Craig Cleary, arrived at his door on January 29, 2003.

Lowe described Mason's reaction.

"He just kept saying, *I don't understand. I don't understand why you are here.*"

"He never denied it, he never reacted," reported Cleary, who took Mason into custody. "He just stared off and shook his head."

But, if Gerald Mason was *stunned*—his family, friends, and neighbors were *shocked.*

A Model Citizen

Before making the cross-country trip to South Carolina, Lowe and Macelderry had collected all of the information available on their suspect.

Gerald Mason had no record of criminal activity after his arrest and conviction for breaking, entering, and theft in 1956.

Mason married in 1960. He and his wife raised two daughters.

He owned and operated several service stations before retiring in the 1990s.

Long-time friends said it was hard to understand how a man who lived a quiet, law-abiding life for more than four decades could be charged with killing two California police officers in 1957.

The people who knew Gerald Mason for years struggled to comprehend the arrest of their good friend. They described Mason as a simple, helpful, and outgoing family man.

For more than 30 years, Dayton Sisson, 83, lived next door to Mason in Cayce, about 10 minutes from downtown Columbia. Sisson and Mason shared a driveway and years of their lives in the quiet neighborhood.

The two helped one another cut down tall pine trees that threatened to snap and crash onto their homes during storms. They played golf and helped each other build garages. Mason, the handyman, was always the supervisor.

"If it had not been for Gerald, I would not have a garage like this," said Sisson. "I really hope it's not true."

Mason's brother, Don, said the arrest was a case of mistaken identity. "Jerry," his brother insisted, "is not capable of killing anyone."

C.M. Carter, who lived a couple of doors down from Sisson, also knew Mason for about 30 years. But he recalls nothing about his old neighbor that gave any indication Mason might have had a criminal past.

"I keep thinking back," Carter said. "He didn't even have a temper, and *everybody* has a temper. And nobody had ever heard him mention California."

Carter said if there was any inkling Gerald Mason committed a crime, he is sure the two would have discussed it. They had plenty of time to talk during their many rounds of golf, dirt bike rides, or trips to nearby Lake Murray.

"The whole thing is so mind-boggling," Carter said.

Carter and Sisson had no doubt they really *knew* their neighbor, Gerald Mason, and both said *he was and always would be a friend*.

Mason's neighbors at the retirement community where he lived described him the same way.

"He was a handyman, who helped fix sprinklers and water lawns," said Oscar Peeler, 85, who lived across the street from Mason. "Jerry was the best neighbor I ever had."

But, regardless of the general disbelief among those who knew Mason for decades—the thumb print and the handwriting were enough to convince Lowe, Macelderry, and Cleary they had finally found the man who had cold-heartedly killed two of their own.

That, and the bullet shaped scar on Gerald Mason's back.

What Goes Around

In February, 2003, Gerald Mason returned to California for the first time since 1957.

This time to face trial for murder.

On March 24, 2003, in Los Angeles Superior Court, Gerald Mason plead guilty to the killing of Officers Phillips and Curtis.

And voiced remorse for his acts.

"It is impossible to express to so many people how sorry I am," he stated in court. "I do not understand why I did this. It does not fit in my life. It is not the person I know. I detest these crimes."

Mason's apology was not enough for the families of the victims.

And, in court, children of the slain officers, who had been toddlers when their fathers were killed, let Mason know what they felt.

"Your cowardly act shattered our lives forever. You caused our mother to become a widow with three babies to raise alone," said Carolyn Phillips. "There is no way to describe our pain. No way to describe the emptiness and anguish we have felt all of our lives without Dad. We cannot and *will not* forgive you."

Keith Curtis, who noted his sister had died the previous year without seeing her father's killer brought to justice, said, "Gerald Mason, your family may be shocked—but my family has been devastated."

As in the case of Edgar Smith, a plea bargain was arranged between the District Attorney and the Defense.

The assault and robbery, rape, and grand theft auto charges would be dropped, and Gerald Mason would be allowed to serve his prison sentence in South Carolina, if he would openly plead guilty to the 1957 killings.

In 1972, the death penalty was found unconstitutional by the Supreme Court of California. The ruling in *People v. Anderson* spared the lives of more than 100 death row inmates, including Sirhan Sirhan and Charles Manson.

It also saved Gerald Mason from a date with the executioner.

Mason was sentenced to two terms of life imprisonment—to be served consecutively—with a minimum incarceration of seven years.

When asked how he came to be in California with a weapon at the time of the murders, Mason said, "I didn't have a family life. I didn't have any place to go after I was released from jail, and things were not going well for me. So, I took off for California. I bought the gun in Shreveport with the intention of using it simply as a deterrent since I was hitchhiking."

When asked why he attacked the teenagers and raped a 15-year-old girl, Mason said he *really didn't remember.* As far as why he murdered two police officers in cold blood, he simply stated, "I thought, *if I don't get them, they're going to get me.* So, when the one officer turned away from me, I shot both of the officers, got back into the car and drove away."

For law enforcement, Mason's arrest and conviction were a victory, and a testimony to the perseverance of the Los Angeles County investigators, some of whom were not yet born when Mason perpetrated the crimes.

To what extent it helped the families of Officers Phillips and Curtis is impossible to say. The events of July 22, 1957 changed their lives forever.

However, there seemed to be some consolation.

The widow of Milton Curtis said, "I'm not his victim anymore. My son is not his victim anymore. I'm so grateful, and I had to wait this long. It's worth the wait."

In a 2003 interview, Jerri Mason Whittaker, Gerald Mason's daughter, stated, "There really are no words to describe the range of emotions we have gone through. Even so, I could not have had a better father."

The trial and conviction of Gerald Mason had very little effect on those not directly affected.

Americans had much more serious apprehensions.

On March 20, 2003, five days before Gerald Mason was sentenced to life imprisonment, the United States unilaterally invaded Iraq.

Operation Iraqi Freedom began with a *shock and awe* campaign of aerial bombardment.

Bombs were dropped on a farming community outside of Baghdad where intelligence incorrectly believed Saddam Hussein was in hiding.

The decision to invade Iraq would lead to fear, uncertainty, and volatile conflict in public opinion not demonstrated since Vietnam.

National anxiety that far outweighed concern about the fate of Gerald Mason or Edgar Smith.

The Y2K threat prompts preparation checklists. Florida electoral votes determine the outcome of the 2000 presidential election after a recount and Supreme Court ruling.

The United States begins bombing of Baghdad and the Iraq invasion in March 2003.

Police sketch of suspect in the killing of El Segundo officers Phillips and Curtis from witness description, 1957, alongside a mug shot of Gerald Mason from his 1956 arrest in South Carolina which was obtained after a fingerprint match in 2002.

Mason in California court, March 2003, where he pled guilty to the 1957 murders. He was sentenced to consecutive life imprisonment terms and allowed to serve his time in South Carolina, where his wife, children, and grandchildren lived and could visit regularly.

American Dreams/American Fears

The American Dream no longer supplies the world
with its images, its dreams, its fantasies.
It supplies the world with its nightmares now.
The Kennedy assassination, Watergate, Vietnam.
—J.G. Ballard

Of all the things you choose in life, you don't get to
choose your nightmares. They pick you.
—John Irving

Courage is knowing what not to fear.
—Plato

I do not fear Satan half so much as
I fear those who fear him.
—Saint Teresa of Avila

The American Dream

In 1934, Americans and others around the world were in the midst of the *Great Depression.*

Millions were starving, hoping their leaders could rescue them.

Leaders like Franklin Delano Roosevelt and Adolph Hitler.

In the homeland, gangsters were romanticized by some and hunted by others.

Civil wars, military coups, and totalitarianism were rampant in Central and Eastern Europe.

On February 6, the French far-right movement attempted a coup d'état against the Third Republic.

Later in February, civil war in Austria created the Austrofascist Federal State.

In May, Clyde Barrow and Bonnie Parker were ambushed and killed in Louisiana.

On June thirtieth, the *Night of the Long Knives,* Adolph Hitler ordered the assassination of at least one-hundred people who he *feared* would threaten his rise to power.

In July, John Dillinger was shot to death by FBI agents in Chicago.

In August, Adolph Hitler became *Führer,* the supreme leader of Germany, following the death of President Paul von Hindenburg—instigating a course of events that would redefine *inhumanity.*

And discussion at the dinner table, for those fortunate

enough to sit at supper, was dominated by talk of Babe Ruth's retirement from the national pastime and Al Capone's imprisonment at the newly opened Alcatraz Federal Penitentiary.

On September 19, Bruno Hauptmann was arrested for the Lindberg baby kidnapping.

On November 1, Winston Churchill warned Britain that Germany was re-arming *secretly, illegally and rapidly.*

It was, in many ways, the worst of times.

But Americans were resilient. Innocent. Still hopeful.

We had won the *Great War,* outlasted the Spanish Flu, given women the right to vote, survived prohibition—we would, together, as a nation, persevere.

Fears of Nazis and Communists, child abductions, serial killers, mass murder, political assassinations, and government trickery were still things of the future.

Americans had their families, baseball, the *New Deal,* Glenn Miller, The Three Stooges, Shirley Temple.

In 1934, American parents still clung to the dream that their children born that year had the opportunity to be anything they wished to be.

Including the parents of Charles Manson, Gerald Mason, and Edgar Smith.

Dreams Unfulfilled

Gerald Fiten Mason was born in Columbia, South Carolina on January 31, 1934.

Eight days later, on February 8, 1934, Edgar Herbert Smith Jr. was born in Hasbrouck Heights, New Jersey.

Two American boys with their entire lives before them.

On March 4, 1957, twenty-three-year-old Edgar Smith lived in a newly purchased trailer home with his young bride and their ten-week-old daughter when he borrowed a friend's car to search for heating fuel.

Before returning home, Smith killed fifteen-year-old Victoria Zielinski and left her battered body at the bottom of a lonely sandpit in Mahwah, New Jersey.

Four months and eighteen days later, on July 22, 1957, twenty-three-year-old Gerald Mason, recently released from a South Carolina jail for home invasion and burglary, found himself in El Segundo. With no solid prospects for the future, he had decided to try his luck at a new start in California.

That evening, Mason raped a fifteen-year-old girl, and later killed two police officers when he was stopped for a traffic violation.

Two young men whose American dream would never materialize.

Three innocent victims who would no longer dream.

Five families whose dreams became nightmares.

It would be nearly twenty years before Victoria's family would finally be *certain* about who had taken her life.

It would be nearly forty-six years before the families of Officers Richard Phillips and Milton Curtis would see their murderer found and brought to justice.

For these families—and for a generation of Americans who witnessed nuclear proliferation, the *Red Scare*, Birmingham, Dallas, Mỹ Lai, Memphis, Chicago, Kent State, Watergate, Gacy and Bundy and Dahmer, Jonestown, Waco, Oklahoma City, Columbine, 9/11, and the relentless conflicts in the Middle East—life would never be the same.

It had become more and more difficult to deny fear.

To alleviate the general sense of homeland insecurity.

And the United States of American has become less and less united.

Gerald Mason's life ended in a South Carolina prison on January 22, 2017, nine days before his 83rd birthday—after serving fourteen years.

Edgar Smith passed away two-months later, on March 20, 2017, in a California prison, less than six weeks after his 83rd birthday. He had spent fifty-five of his final sixty years of life behind bars.

Two old men with nothing more to fear.

Fear Itself Revisited

Fear is an extremely strong emotion.

It is in many cases an understandable emotion—though often a crippling one.

Fear for the safety of our families, fear of failure, fear of what we do not understand, fear of ill health, old age, death.

And there are less defensible or less rational fears. Phobias.

Fear of spiders, snakes, needles, heights, crowds, enclosed spaces, flying, the dark, and of *others* who do not look or speak or worship the way we do.

Fear can influence behavior. Cause people to act inappropriately, badly, even criminally.

And fear can be used to coerce and control people.

Nazi leader Hermann Göring explained how people can be made fearful and to support a war they would otherwise oppose.

"The people don't want war, but they can always be brought to the bidding of the leaders. This is easy. All you have to do is tell them they are being attacked, and denounce the pacifists for lack of patriotism and for exposing the country to danger. It works the same in every country."

Former U.S. National Security Advisor Zbigniew Brzezinski argued that the use of the term 'war on terror' was intended to generate a *culture of fear* deliberately because it *obscures reason, intensifies emotions and makes it easier for demagogic politicians to mobilize the public on behalf of the policies they want to pursue.*

Much like the 'war on crime', the call for 'law and order'.

This is fearmongering.

The encouraging of phobias.

The spreading of frightening and exaggerated rumors of an impending danger to purposely arouse fear in order to manipulate the public.

Fear of Communists, fear of Muslims, fear of immigrants, fear of people of color looking to take our jobs or take over our suburban neighborhoods.

Fear is the enemy of reason.

It breeds irrational, reactionary behavior by individuals and frequently by large segments of populations.

Reactions to fear that lead to the rise of Nazism, Stalinism, McCarthyism, Terrorism, MAGA and Trumpism.

Frightened people will follow those who promise safety and security and, as a result, fear is exploited to gain power.

And those who employ fear tactics to obtain power are, illogically, most often reacting to their own private fears.

The world, as he saw it, terrified Adolph Hitler.

Josef Stalin was a man afraid of any and all opposition.

"Power does not corrupt," said John Steinbeck. *"Fear corrupts—perhaps the fear of a loss of power."*

Or perhaps, the fearmongers attempt to ease their own trepidations by seeing to it that everyone around them is *more* frightened than they are.

Those who feel threatened will do the unthinkable.

Somehow, Martin Luther King Jr. threatened James Earl Ray.

Something fearful motivated Timothy McVeigh in Oklahoma City.

Something frightened Dylan Klebold and Eric Harris at Columbine.

The men who hijacked the planes on September 11, 2001, were surely schooled to *fear* the *infidel*, and to believe they were acting in self-defense.

Over the past seventy years, from hiding under school desks to the terror of 9/11 to the assault on the United States Capitol in early 2021, Americans have come to be increasingly frightened—despite Franklin Delano Roosevelt's admonition.

And with fear comes mistrust.

A protectiveness and a *take care of my own* philosophy that excludes all outsiders.

And with fear comes divisiveness.

Conflicts between those of different races, ethnicity, political ideology, and religion.

War and civil war.

As Marian Anderson said, *Fear is a disease that eats away at logic and makes man inhuman.*

In a moment, fear can end lives and change lives forever.

It is difficult, if not impossible, to understand why human beings inflict violence and destruction upon their fellow human beings.

In 1957, Edgar Smith and Gerald Mason ended the lives of three fellow human beings.

Robbed each of their future.

Took them from their families.

Forever.

Whether or not we or, for that matter, the perpetrators themselves, can ever adequately comprehend what led to the abhorrent and inexcusable act of murder—it is not unreasonable to consider *fear* as a contributing factor.

Fear experienced by the killers themselves.

Particularly in cases of unpremeditated murder.

It is more than likely that on March 4, 1957, Edgar Smith did not leave his trailer with the intention of taking a life.

It is reasonable to imagine that Smith offered a ride to a

young girl he knew from town, that he made inappropriate advances, he was rejected, she may have violently resisted, and that he struck back and seriously injured the girl.

And then, as frightened as Victoria Zielinski surely must have been, it was Smith's fear that took over. Fear of Victoria.

Fear of the damage Victoria could do to *him*, the threat she posed to *his* marriage and perhaps *his freedom*, if she exposed him as a vicious attacker, or worse, an attempted rapist.

And, in a moment when all other rational resolutions eluded him, Edgar Smith decided there was only one way to insure Victoria's silence.

On July 21, 1957, Gerald Mason likely had robbery on his mind—but could not have predicted, or even imagined, that his unpardonable actions at the Lover's Lane would lead to the murder of two police officers.

But, when he was stopped by Phillips and Curtis for a traffic violation, his fear kicked in.

Fear of being arrested and found guilty of armed robbery, car theft, and sexual assault.

Gerald Mason could likely have driven off with no more than a citation—the criminal acts perpetrated earlier that evening had not yet been reported.

However, fear led to panic—and Mason decided there was only one way to escape.

Fear is the enemy of reason.

And, as Shakespeare said in *Antony and Cleopatra*, "*In time we hate that which we often fear.*"

This is the fear that Franklin Roosevelt called *fear itself.*

Since the end of World War II, this kind of fear has become more and more salient across our nation.

Has created divisions not experienced since the Civil War.

Has shaped a homeland insecurity.

This is the fear we must conquer to preserve our democracy and our freedom.

References, Resources, and Notes

A Troubled Peace

Fear Itself

Franklin Delano Roosevelt was inaugurated thirty-second President of the United States on March 4, 1933.

The only thing we have to fear is fear itself came from President Roosevelt's *First Inaugural Address.*

Samuel Rosenman, Editor. *The Public Papers of Franklin D. Roosevelt, Volume Two: The Year of Crisis, 1933,* New York: Random House, 1938. 11–16.

The Hook

Edgar Smith. *Brief Against Death.* Alfred A. Knopf, 1968.

The State. Columbia, South Carolina. January 30, 2003.

Exits and Entrances

President Truman's address to the joint session of the Congress outlining what came to be known as the *Truman Doctrine* was delivered on March 12, 1947. (*The Avalon Project.* Documents in Law, History, and Democracy.)

Executive Order 9835, Prescribing Procedures for the Administration of an Employees Loyalty Program in the Executive Branch of the Government, March 21, 1947. (Teaching American History, Ashbrook Center.)

National Security Act of 1947. Public Law 253, 80th Congress; Chapter 343, 1st Session; S. 758. July 26, 1947.

For those interested in the events in the Indian subcontinent and in Palestine following the British Empire withdrawals from these areas in 1947 and 1948, *Freedom at Midnight* (1975) and *O Jerusalem* (1972) both by Larry Collins and Dominique Lapierre are highly recommended.

Roswell, Rockwell, Rock and Roll

1956 Presidential General Election results. (United States Election Atlas.)

Shlaim, Avi. *The Protocol of Sèvres, 1956: Anatomy of a War Plot.*

International Affairs, 73:3, 1997.

Billboard Top 100 Charts, 1940-2016.

Berlitz, Charles and Moore, William. *The Roswell Incident.* Grosset & Dunlap, 1980.

Eisenhower, Dwight David. *Speech at the Philadelphia Convention Hall.* November 1, 1956.

Halberstam, David. *The Fifties.* Villard Books, 1993.

January

Duck and Cover. Government Nuclear Civil Defense film, 1951.

Eisenhower, Dwight David. *Second Inaugural Address,* January 21, 1957.
(The American Presidency Project.)

Greenberg, Michael M. *The Mad Bomber of New York.* Union Square Press, 2011.

Shaffer, Tamar. *Murder Gone Cold: The Mystery of the Grimes Sisters.*
Ghost Research Society, 2006.

Taylor, Troy. *The Two Lost Girls.* Whitechapel Productions, 2015.

The Island

Eisenhower, Dwight David. *Special Message to Congress,* January 5, 1957.

Hahn, Peter L. *Securing the Middle East: The Eisenhower Doctrine of 1957. Presidential Studies Quarterly* 36.1: 38-47, 2006.

Details of the crash of Northeast Flight 823 on February 1, 1957 were gathered from *New York Times* reporting in the days following the event, *The Daily News* Archives, New York City Department of Corrections History, and *Atlas Obscura.*

The Boy in the Box

Stout, David. *The Boy in the Box: The Unsolved Case of America's Unknown Child,* Lyons Press, 2008.

Blood and Sand

Victoria

There is sadly little biographical information available about Victoria Zielinski, the victim, independent of that associated with accounts of the crime itself.

Her background and physical description here are very general and are taken from various newspaper articles from March, 1957.

Details on Victoria's visit to the Nixon home—time of arrival and departure, route taken, the clothing she wore—were well documented in trial testimony. As were the attempts by her family to locate Victoria on the evening of her disappearance and the following morning.

The initial descriptions of the scene are from Captain Wickham's original investigative report, and from trial testimony.

(*Police Department Investigative Report No. 9180.* Township of Mahwah.)

Bergen

Details about police activity at the scene on March 5 and March 6, 1957, were constructed from police investigative reports, newspaper coverage, and the trial testimony.

The initial interview of Joe Gilroy by Bergen County First Assistant Prosecutor Fred Galda, and Gilroy's accounts of March fourth and the following day, come from police records and later trial testimony.

In this instance, as in others throughout this book, interviews and testimony have been abridged to eliminate repetition and keep the narrative moving.

Eddie

Biographical information about Edgar Smith appears in his book, *Brief Against Death*, Alfred A. Knopf, 1968.

Famous First Words

The initial interview of Edgar Smith by Fred Galda, beginning close to midnight March 5, 1957, and continuing into the early hours of March 6, is in the public record.

A Night Without Sleep

Trips to try to locate Smith's pants, the areas where he said he had been sick, and the place he said he had discarded his shoes were described by detectives in subsequent trial testimony.

Prosecutor Guy Calissi's and Assistant Prosecutor Fred Galda's questioning of Edgar Smith at the Mahwah Municipal Building is in the public record.

Interaction between Smith and Detectives DeMarco, DeLisle, and Spahr are recounted in police reports and by Smith himself in *Brief Against Death*.

A Note About *Brief Against Death*

I was first introduced to the Edgar Smith murder case through Smith's own book, *Brief Against Death*, published by Alfred A. Knopf in 1968, in Smith's eleventh year on Death Row.

Smith editorializes a great deal throughout the book, describing numerous examples of what *he* perceived as prejudicial practices by police detectives, prosecutors, and the trial judge—and blunders by his defense attorneys.

Arguments Smith would later use in motions to appeal his conviction.

Reading the book led me, as it did many others including

William F. Buckley Jr., to question Smith's guilt. Of course, this is exactly what Smith's book was meant to do and it succeeded in eventually reopening the case through appeals to federal courts.

As a result of research done over the past fifteen years, I have collected what I consider more *reliable*—or at least more *official*—records of the interviews and the trial testimony presented here and have used Smith's accounts from *Brief Against Death* only when I found they were consistent with police reports and trial records.

The Night Before

Prosecutor Galda's interview of Edgar Smith in the late afternoon of March 6, 1957, which was entered into evidence as Smith's *statement* and a *concession of guilt,* was transcribed by a stenographer and is in the public record.

The Sandpit

The continuation of Galda's interview of Edgar Smith on March 6, 1957 is, again, from the transcribed record. I have abridged the document from its more than forty pages down to what I felt were its salient details.

My intention, again, was to keep the narrative moving at a respectable pace, to avoid repetition present in the complete statement itself—and to also avoid the repetition of details later offered in trial testimony.

Arraignment and Indictment

Smith's appearance before Magistrate Frank Young is in the public record.

The copy of the Grand Jury indictment is in the public record.

Selser

Smith's account of the events of March 4 and 5, 1957, as stated to his attorney and later presented to Guy Calissi for consideration, is in the public record.

References to world events—summarized from historical records—have been included to remind readers of the changing sociological, political, and cultural climate in America during various time periods coinciding with critical stages in the two complex murder cases.

Information was collected from a number of sources which included *Wikipedia, The People History,* various world almanacs, and personal recollection.

Trial and Error

Testimony in the Edgar Smith murder trial was given over the course of nine days in 1957 in a Bergen County courtroom—from opening statements on the thirteenth of May, through the reading of the verdict on the twenty-seventh of May.

Hundreds of pages were transcribed and are in the court records and public records.

As in previous sections, I have abridged the trial proceedings and testimony to avoid repetition.

I attempted to offer the reader enough of the critical testimony and evidence to perhaps form a personal opinion as to the innocence or guilt of Edgar Smith in the murder of Victoria Zielinski based exclusively on the trial record—as would be expected of a jury.

Calissi

Headlines from before, during, and after the Zielinski murder trial come from newspaper archives.

Gilroy

Small Boy Down a Well, Manorville Saves Benny Hooper. Time Magazine, May 27, 1957.

Hommell

The introduction of Donnie Hommell by the Defense in cross-examination as a possible suspect became one of the most controversial and contentious aspects of the trial—particularly later in the trial when Defense Attorney Selser called Edgar Smith to the witness stand.

In his cross-examination Selser questioned Hommell about persons who may have been able to support or contradict *his* account of his movements on the night of the murder. Few if any of those persons were ever called to testify at the 1957 trial—or at subsequent appeals hearings.

June

Face the Nation interview with Nikita Khrushchev, June 2, 1957. CBS Archives. (Full transcript available through *Credo*, University of Massachusetts.)

El Segundo

Details of the events related to the robbery and rape in Hawthorn, the murder of Officers Phillips and Curtis in El Segundo, and the subsequent discovery of evidence, were collected from numerous sources.

—Newspaper reports from the times of the incidents.

—Recorded interviews with the *Lover's Lane* victims, families of the slain officers, and police investigators.

—Aired television documentaries covering the case including *Forensic Files* and *48 Hours*.

A New Decade

Inauguration Day

Kennedy, John Fitzgerald. *First Inaugural Address*, January 20, 1961.

Buckley and Lichtenstein

For more about William F. Buckley Jr. see *William F. Buckley Jr., Patron Saint of the Conservatives*, John B. Judis. Simon & Shuster, 1988.

1968

King, Martin Luther Jr., *I've Been to the Mountaintop*, Memphis, April 3, 1968.

Thirteen Years

An Unlikely Ally

McCarthy and His Enemies, William F. Buckley Jr. and L. Brent Bozell, Henry Regnery Company, 1954.

Firing Line, a.k.a. *Firing Line with William F. Buckley Jr.*, was a public affairs television program syndicated by WOR-TV in New York, which premiered on April 4, 1966 and ran for 240 episodes before moving to PBS in 1971.

The program ran for 1,504 episodes, and more than thirty-three years, making it the longest running public affairs program in television history when the final episode aired on December 26, 1999.

Young Americans for Freedom (YAF) is an ideologically conservative youth activism organization—founded in 1960 as a
coalition between traditional conservatives and libertarians on
American college campuses. It is a 501(c)(3) non-profit organization and the chapter affiliate of Young America's Foundation.
The purposes of YAF are to advocate for public policies consistent with the *Sharon Statement*, which was adopted at a
meeting in the home of William F. Buckley Jr. in Sharon, Connecticut on September 11, 1960.

The Young Americans for Freedom, William F. Buckley Jr., *National Review,* September 24, 1960.

The Approaching End of Edgar H. Smith Jr., William F. Buckley, Jr., *Esquire Magazine,* November, 1965.

Certiorari

Sutton, Jeffrey S. and Jones, Brittany. *The Certiorari Process
and State Court Decisions, Harvard Law Review,* May, 2018.

Judiciary Act of 1925, 43 Stat. 936. February 13, 1925.
Federal Judicial Center.

Supreme Court Case Selections Act (Pub.L. 100–352, 102 Stat.
662), June 27, 1988.

Note: Although not in effect at the time of Smith's case, the
Case Selections Act was adopted to limit the types of appeals to
the Supreme Court that would tend to overload the docket of
the High Court and/or delay the sentencing of a lower court,
particularly in capital crime cases.

Note: Following the Oklahoma City Bombing, the United States
Congress passed the *Antiterrorism and Effective Death Penalty*

Act (AEDPA), signed into law by President Bill Clinton in 1996, which further limited the power of the Supreme Court to delay capital convictions involving terrorism or otherwise.
However, AEDPA in effect limited the power of federal judges to grant relief in *all* habeas corpus cases. Many consider AEDPA unconstitutional.

The Waiting

Edgar Smith Letter to Judge George Barlow, *Getting Out,* Edgar Smith, Coward, McCann & Geoghegan, 1972.

What is and What Should Never Be

Summer of '69

Vietnam Casualty Statistics by Year and Month, 1966-1971. American War Library.

Bauer, Patricia. *Tate Murders: American Crime,* Encyclopædia Britannica.

Turning Seventy

Billboard, Number One Albums of 1970.

Edgar Smith Letter to Bill Buckley, *Getting Out*, Edgar Smith, Coward, McCann & Geoghegan, 1972.

Leap of Faith

Kreitner, Richard. *April 28, 1970: President Richard Nixon Approves a U.S. Invasion of Cambodia, The Nation,* April 28, 2015.

My God! They're Killing Us: Newsweek's 1970 Coverage of the Kent State Shooting. May 4, 2015.

Unacceptable Terms

Smith, Edgar. *Letter to William F. Buckley,* Spring 1970.

Smith, Edgar. *Getting Out,* Coward, McCann & Geoghegan, 1972.

Non vult contendere. Latin. The defendant in a criminal case *will not contest* the charge. A plea legally equivalent to that of guilty. *The Law Dictionary.*

Greenwald v. Wisconsin, United States Supreme Court, Ruling 390 U.S. 519, April 1, 1968.

From Barlow to Gibbons

Writ of Mandamus. An order by a court to a *lesser* court or government official to perform an act required by law, which has been refused or neglected.

A type of court order that may be sought as a remedy if a governmental agency, public authority, or corporation serving government fails or refuses to do its public or statutory duty. (*Legal Dictionary*)

Hearing at Last

Transcripts of Habeas Corpus Hearing, Federal Courthouse, Newark, New Jersey, January, 1971.

Hurry Up and Wait

Letter from Edgar Smith to William F. Buckley. August, 1971.

The Approaching End

Let the Games Begin

Proposed Plea Procedure. Submitted to Edgar Smith's attorneys by the New Jersey Attorney General—representing procedures agreed to by the defense attorneys and the Bergen County prosecutor. (Public Record)

Letter from Edgar Smith to William F. Buckley, October 24, 1971.

Delay of Game/End Game

Psychological Report on Edgar Smith.
Dr. Ralph Brancale. November, 1971.

Transcripts of Edgar Smith Plea Hearing. November 30, 1971 to December 6, 1971. Bergen County Courthouse, Hackensack, New Jersey.

Freedom Is Just Another Word

Getting Out

Smith, Edgar, *Getting Out,* Coward, McCann & Geoghegan, 1972.

Firing Line

Firing Line with William F. Buckley Jr., The Story of Edgar Smith, Part One, Episode S0029, December, 1971.

Firing Line with William F. Buckley Jr., The Story of Edgar Smith, Part Two, Episode S0030, December, 1971.

The Fickle Finger of Fame

The Trentonian, December 8, 1971.

Asbury Park Evening Press, December 12, 1971.

Lies and Truth

Lies

Photos of Viet Mass Slayings, *The Plain Dealer,* Cleveland, Ohio, November 20, 1969.

Syphilis Victims in U.S. Study Went Untreated for 40 Years. The New York Times, 1972.

Vietnam Archive: Pentagon Study Traces 3 Decades of Growing U.S. Involvement. The New York Times, June 13, 1971.

The Pentagon Papers: The Secret History of the Vietnam War, Bantam Books, 1971.

Nixon Denies Role in Cover-Up, *The Washington Post,* August, 1973.

Nixon Resigns, *The New York Times,* August 9, 1974.

Letter from William F. Buckley to J.L. Abramo, March 17, 1995.

Truth

Celebrity Convict's Myth Exposed, The Los Angeles Times, July 5, 1989.

Edgar Smith Admits '57 Jersey Slaying, The New York Times,
March 30, 1977.

Letter from J.L. Abramo to Edgar Smith,
March 25, 2000.

Letter from Edgar Smith to J.L. Abramo,
April 4, 2000.

Ghosts

Y2K Bug, *Encyclopaedia Britannica*, May 2009.

The State, Columbia, South Carolina, January 30, 2003.

Neighbors Wonder How Friend Could Be in Jail on 45-year-old Murder Charge, Associated Press, February 10, 2003.

Man Sentenced to Life in Two 1957 Police Murders,
Los Angeles Times, March 25, 2003.

The Ghosts of El Segundo, CBS News Forty-Eight Hours, 2004.

ACKNOWLEDGMENTS

Many thanks to all of the news organizations—in New Jersey, New York, South Carolina, and California—that provided me access to more than four decades of reporting on both the Zielinski and the Phillips/Curtis murder cases as well as newspaper articles regarding Edgar Smith and Gerald Mason.

Thanks to the State of New Jersey, Bergen County, the State of California, Los Angeles County, and San Diego County for making available police reports and trial transcripts with regard to Edgar Smith's arrest and murder trial in 1957, Smith's hearing in 1971, Smith's kidnapping trial in 1976, the murders of Officer Phillips and Officer Curtis in 1957, and the trial of Gerald Mason in 2003.

Thanks to the New York Public Library for helping to locate a rare copy of *Getting Out* by Edgar Smith.

Thanks to Stanford University and the Hoover Institute for providing transcripts of both of Edgar Smith's appearances with William F. Buckley on *Firing Line*.

Thanks to all those who encouraged me by agreeing that unrelated criminal cases involving two men who were both born in 1934, both committed murder in 1957, and both died in prisons in 2017 was—coincidentally or not—a subject worthy of exploration.

The question of whether the murders contributed to the unrest of the times, or whether the general unrest of the times motivated the criminals, or both, is left to the reader to consider.

Finally, thanks to my daughter—Isis Alexandra—for continually showing me what courage is.

J.L. ABRAMO was born and raised in the seaside paradise of Brooklyn, New York on Raymond Chandler's fifty-ninth birthday.

A long-time journalist, educator and theatre artist—Abramo earned a Bachelor of Arts degree in Sociology and Education from The City College of New York and a Master of Arts Degree in Social Psychology from The University of Cincinnati. At Cincinnati, Abramo led the published research study *Status Threat and Group Dogmatism* (*Human Relations,* 31 (8): 745-752).

Abramo is the author of *Catching Water in a Net,* winner of the St. Martin's Press/Private Eye Writers of America Award for Best First Private Eye Novel; the subsequent Jake Diamond Novels *Clutching at Straws, Counting to Infinity, Circling the Runway* (Shamus Award Winner) and *Crossing the Chicken*;

ABOUT THE AUTHOR

Chasing Charlie Chan, a prequel to the Jake Diamond series; the 61st Precinct novels *Gravesend* and *Coney Island Avenue; Brooklyn Justice;* and the generational novel *American History.*

Homeland Insecurity is Abramo's first book-length work of non-fiction.

For more about the author please visit:

JLAbramo.com

On the following pages are a few
more great titles from the
Down & Out Books publishing family.

For a complete list of books and to
sign up for our newsletter,
go to DownAndOutBooks.com.

Bad Guy Lawyer
Chuck Marten

Down & Out Books
March 2022
978-1-64396-249-8

The only time Guy McCann stops talking is when he's downing scotch. Guy was a hot-shot attorney for the West Coast mafia until he got cold feet and split town, earning a target on his head. Now he's lying low in Las Vegas, giving back-room legal advice to second-rate crooks while pining over his old girlfriend Blair, a working girl with a razor wit and zero inhibitions.

When Blair is committed to a psychiatric ward, Guy is drawn back to the dangerous underworld of Los Angeles. Next thing he knows, Blair has escaped from the hospital and Guy's former mafia associates are on her trail, with Guy caught in the cross-fire.

Groovy Gumshoes
Private Eyes in the Psychedelic Sixties
Edited by Michael Bracken

Down & Out Books
April 2022
978-1-64396-252-8

From old-school private eyes with their flat-tops, off-the-rack suits, and well-worn brogues to the new breed of private eyes with their shoulder-length hair, bell-bottoms, and hemp sandals, the shamuses in Groovy Gumshoes take readers on a rollicking romp through the Sixties.

With stories by Jack Bates, C.W. Blackwell, Michael Bracken, N.M. Cedeño, Hugh Lessig, Steve Liskow, Adam Meyer, Tom Milani, Neil S. Plakcy, Stephen D. Rogers, Mark Thielman, Grant Tracey, Mark Troy, Andrew Welsh-Huggins, and Robb White.

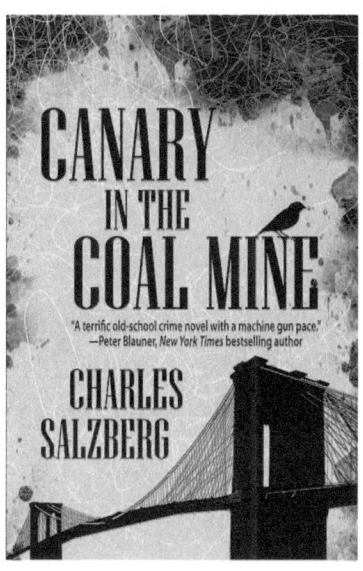

Canary in the Coal Mine
Charles Salzberg

Down & Out Books
April 2022
978-1-64396-251-1

Pete Fortunato, a NYC PI who suffers from anger management issues and insomnia, is hired by a beautiful woman to find her husband.

When he finds him shot dead in the apartment of her young boyfriend, this is the beginning of a nightmare as he's chased by the Albanian mob sending him half-way across the country in an attempt to find missing money which can save his life.

The Damned Lovely
Adam Frost

Down & Out Books
May 2022
978-1-64396-253-5

"She wasn't pretty but she was ours…" Sandwiched between seedy businesses in the scorching east LA suburb of Glendale, the Damned Lovely dive bar is as scarred as its regulars: ex-cops, misfits and loners. And for Sam Goss, it's a refuge from the promising life he's walked away from, a place to write and a hole to hide in.

But when a beautiful and mysterious new patron to the bar turns up murdered as the third victim of a serial killer terrorizing the local streets, Sam can't stop himself from getting involved. Despite their fleeting interaction, or perhaps because of it, something about her ghost won't let go…

www.ingramcontent.com/pod-product-compliance
Lightning Source LLC
Chambersburg PA
CBHW020526110726
47899CB00004B/1267